BODILY

HARM

A gripping crime thriller full of twists

CHARLIE
GALLAGHER

Published 2017 by Joffe Books, London.

www.joffebooks.com

© Charlie Gallagher

ISBN-13: 978-1-912106-66-0

For my girls

Author's Note

I am inspired by what I do and see in my day job as a front-line police detective, though my books are entirely fictional. I am aware that the police officers in my novels are not always shown positively. They are human and they make mistakes. This is sometimes the case in real life too, but the vast majority of officers are honest and do a good job in trying circumstances. From what I see on a daily basis, the men and women who wear the uniform are among the very finest, and I am proud to be part of one of the best police forces in the world.

Charlie Gallagher

Chapter 1

The town of Langthorne had once been a popular holiday destination, and a highly desirable place to live. The old part of the town was made up of large Victorian townhouses, many of which had been converted into flats that continued to demand high prices despite the general economic malaise. The town's coastal location meant that its economy had relied on holiday visitors until cheap foreign holidays killed the tourist trade. Langthorne, like many similar towns, now suffered high unemployment and social decline. With the sudden demand for council housing for people not in work, the government had commissioned new-build areas to put them in, or, as many people quipped, 'Let's put all the scum together.' Epping Hill Estate (known to the locals as Effingell), on the edge of Langthorne, was a prime example of such a "solution."

Langthorne High Street was typical of any seaside town at the beginning of winter. With the sun down, the temperature had plunged and people pulled their coats closer as they stood in the early evening air, scented by chip shops and diesel fumes. Two sixth-formers, Jamie Horan and Sophie Hayward, stepped out of the chippie carrying overflowing cones. Sophie threw a chip at her friend and it bounced off his shoulder. She pointed a thumb at an elderly gent, indicating that he was the culprit. Jamie pretended to walk after him before turning round and laughing. Linking arms, they headed down the High Street with a solitary seagull limping in their wake.

Sophie heard Lady Gaga playing in her schoolbag and stopped to retrieve her phone. She tucked her long brown hair behind her ear and answered the call. 'Hey, Mum, I'm just on my way to the bus stop. No, Mum, I told you I was going to get the bus. Jamie's walking me there, he's here right now.' Sophie rolled her eyes. 'Yes, Mum! I'm coming straight home. Yes . . . I know it's getting dark. Fine then, I will, yep, okay . . . okay, Mum.' She ended the call, her smile returning as she looked at Jamie.

He playfully bumped shoulders with Sophie. 'Your mum's worried about you.'

'Of course she is. She knows I'm with you!'

'Cheeky mare!' Jamie laughed and threw a chip at her.

'She always worries when it gets dark. She thinks that everyone who's out after dark is a crazy random.'

'Yeah, I heard. She's not far wrong you know, Soph, this *is* Langthorne.'

They arrived at the bus stop, pushing and shoulder barging each other, slapping hands that tried to snatch at quickly cooling chips. They had stayed on in town after school and wandered round the shops. Catching a later bus would allow them to avoid the teenage school crowd, all vying for the back seat to the sound of a million different ringtones, all shouting. The double-decker bus was already at the stop and they dumped their chip wrappers in a nearby bin, flashed their passes at the driver and hurried up to the top deck. Sophie squealed as she ran to the back and threw herself onto the long seat. 'Back seat, yay!'

Jamie followed more slowly. He put in a white headphone bud and sat down beside Sophie. She beamed at him again and turned to the window, wiping the condensation with her sleeve and peering out into the gloomy night.

* * *

Neither of them noticed the hooded figure follow them onto the bus and up to the top deck. Keeping his head down under his hood, he peered around from under his thick eyebrows to check that he was alone, save for the two kids he had seen walk over from the chip shop. He had heard much of their conversation, seen the girl playfully punch the boy. But more to the point, he had seen the phone. He had sized up the lad and seen the white iPod headphones hanging round his neck. It was only two stops until the bus reached the Epping Hill Estate. He had about eight minutes.

The bus pulled away. No one else had come upstairs. The man sat close enough to listen to the young couple chatting. The lad had produced a copy of *Autotrader* magazine. He was going to do his driving test soon and he might get a Golf. The boy bragged about his parents footing the bill for 'a decent one, just a couple of years old, they said.'

The man felt for the knife in his jacket pocket, the rusty blade folded into the handle. It would be more than sufficient to get the job done, whether he used it or not. The girl's incessant giggling cut through him — so natural, so carefree. His thoughts turned black. *I'll fucking change that.*

Four minutes from his stop, the man rose to his feet, rocking against the metal pole when the bus slowed for a corner. He felt in his pocket for the small bag of heroin wraps. Still there. He had checked it time and time again. With one hand on the knife in his pocket, he moved towards the kids at the back. They were absorbed in their conversation. The girl's head was bent over the magazine, looking at a picture of a 2012 Volkswagen Golf. The man was standing right over them when they finally looked up.

'Stay calm, kids. Just give me your fucking stuff and neither of you gets cut,' he said quietly. He whipped the knife out of his pocket, the rust crunching as he fingered it open.

The boy's smile fell away. The girl gave a small gasp. Her wide eyes followed the blade as he moved it back and forth in front of their faces. Moving the knife was a good tactic. It should give them something to focus on other than his face, but it wasn't working. The boy was looking at him, not the knife. He wasn't showing the shock and fear the man had expected.

'You got something to say, kid? You wanna get fucking hurt, you little cunt?' The man's voice was louder now. His hood fell back as he spat out the word 'cunt.' The kid was supposed to flinch but he hadn't moved. 'You can start with your iPod there, fella, then your wallet and your phone.' He turned his attention and the knife blade to the girl. 'And you! You can give me your phone and your cash.'

* * *

Jamie's mind raced as he took in the figure standing in front of him. He was well built and had an ugly scar running along his right cheek, finishing up just under his ear. Faded tattoos on his neck crept down under a grubby T-shirt. His flushed, sweaty skin shone in the artificial bus lighting.

Without thinking, Jamie brought a fist up under the man's chin and rose to his feet. He was not particularly big for his age, but for several years he had been attending his dad's self-defence classes and by now was pretty proficient. The blow forced the man to take a step backwards. Jamie whipped off his jacket and stepped forward and wrapped it round the hand that held the knife. He followed this with a sharp elbow to the face, using his momentum as he stepped into the man, who lost his footing as surprise and the movement of the bus conspired against him. Jamie knew he had to stay on the attack and he fell onto him, punching again and again. He put his knee on the jacket, and the knife clattered to the floor.

Then a sharp pain made him gasp and straighten up. He twisted round and felt down the side of his body. His fingers came into contact with a needle. The metal tip was bent where it had been driven in. Jamie had no time to react. His vision blurred as a blow smashed into his nose. The man pushed him backwards and he crashed to the floor. The man stood up and kicked him. Jamie curled himself up to ward off the impact. Sophie let out a scream that reverberated through the bus. Jamie could only watch, helpless, as the man stepped over him, raised his arm and slashed at her. Sophie didn't scream again.

* * *

The bus driver heard the scream. He was well used to kids mucking about up top, but this sounded serious. He slammed on the brakes and the three top-deck passengers were thrown forward.

He began to mount the stairs. He looked up and saw a figure appear at the top. They stared at each other. The bus driver opened his mouth, but before he could speak, the man swung his boot. He hit the floor, and then the driver heard the bus doors hiss open, and his assailant flipped up his hood and disappeared into the night.

Chapter 2

Detective Sergeant George Elms had been trying to get to sleep for an hour. He'd just drifted off when the sound of his mobile phone echoed round the room. He fumbled for the lamp switch.

'H . . . hello?'

'Hello. I'm hoping this is George Elms? I've been given your number. I'm told you are the on-call DS for tonight.'

'I'm the what?'

'The on-call DS?'

'Ah, yes, of course. Sorry. You woke me up.' George propped himself up on his elbow.

'Oh, Sorry. It's John Adcock, I'm the patrol sergeant. I was hoping you would still be up and that I wouldn't be disturbing you.'

'Doesn't matter,' George lied. 'Luckily I'm in the spare room so you haven't woken the wife up too.'

'Well, we've all ended up there a few times, George,' was the eventual reply.

'Oh no, it's not that. I mean, she's pregnant and she gets up a lot in the night. I've got an early start so I kip in here so she doesn't disturb me...' George was aware that he had trailed off to a rambling stop.

'I see.'

'So is it just advice you're after, or are you turning me out of my spare bed?'

'I'm afraid we're beyond advice by now. We're gonna need you to come take a look.'

George was forced to sneak back into his bedroom to get his clothes. He thought he had successfully negotiated the wardrobe in silence, using the light from his mobile phone screen, when Sarah's voice made him jump.

'And I was worried about waking *you* up!'

Instinctively, George turned his light source towards the sound, blinding his wife with an image of their daughter.

'Sorry, hon. I've been called in.'

Sarah put an arm across her eyes to block out the light. 'I didn't think you were putting on a shirt and tie to get a glass of water.'

'I'll tip a glass of water over you in a minute! I've no idea when or if I'll be back . . .'

'Of course you don't. When do you ever?'

'See you when I'm older!' George left the room.

* * *

It was close to midnight when George arrived at the crime scene on the edge of the Epping Hill Estate. He clutched a coffee, hurriedly purchased from a nearby service station, trying to glean a little warmth from the cup. A double-decker bus with the interior lighting still on was skewed across the road, as if it had come to a stop in a hurry. Three patrol cars, each with their blue lights flashing, were at the scene, blocking the road to oncoming traffic. Other patrol cars were positioned further down the road to ensure the area remained sterile. Four uniformed police officers wearing high-visibility clothing were rubbing their hands and glancing longingly back at their heated vehicles.

George parked his own Renault Laguna a short distance from the bus. The patrol sergeant walked towards him and indicated George's coffee. 'Ah, I was just about to send a PC to get the coffees in. We were waiting in case you wanted one.'

George smiled. 'I could go for another latte, thanks.'

'White coffee it is. John Adcock. We spoke on the phone.'

'Of course. What do we have, John?'

The stocky sergeant took a breath. 'Three victims in all. The incident started upstairs from what we can tell. A man with a knife had a go at robbing two kids from one of the local schools. It didn't go too well.'

'Kids?' George took a sip of his coffee.

'Both seventeen. The lad's pretty shaken up but he's given us a sketchy account. Says that they were sat in the back seat and some bloke in a hood suddenly went up to them. The man pulled a knife and demanded their phone, wallets et cetera. Seems the lad put up some resistance and there was a scuffle. He reckons he got a few hits in before the man stabbed him with a needle. It was left sticking out of his side.'

'Dirty needle, I suppose?'

'Quite possibly. The boy's got a nervous few blood tests ahead of him, waiting to see just how dirty. The man then pulls his knife on the girl.' The sergeant paused. 'She received a nasty slash across the face and throat. It's made a bit of a mess. The paramedic reckons it must have been a blunt blade so there was a lot of blood. Both her and the lad are at the hospital. It's not a deep cut, just an ugly one that bled a lot. The bus driver was knocked out, the girl called us, it took the call-taker a little while to make sense of what she was saying by all accounts. I spoke to the driver briefly while he was getting patched up. Seems he heard a scream, pulled over to see what was going on and got a boot in the face.'

George watched two officers talking in low tones behind the sergeant. 'So the driver's in hospital too?'

'Yeah, Langthorne General. They're keeping him in for observation for the head injury, but he's also got a suspected broken collarbone from the fall.'

'He'll still be there then. I think I'll pop in on him when I'm done here. CSI not here yet?'

'They've been contacted. They had already been called out to another job the other side of the county so they warned us it'll be a long wait. We'll be holding the scene all night anyway, so they may well wait and hand it over to the early turn.'

George looked over to the bus, its lights and reflective livery standing out in the gloom. Beyond it was a park that bordered the Epping Hill Estate.

'I'll put another call in to CSI. I want them out sooner rather than later. Can you call up and make Control aware that we'll need a search team here at first light?'

'Yep, I'll do that straight away.'

'And, John, you might want to request a bigger resource here. We're going to need to extend this cordon to cover the whole park, both sides of the bus.'

Sergeant Adcock stared. 'The whole park?'

'Yeah, this bloke must have made off across the park and he may well have dropped something, stood on something or licked something, so we'll need it kept sterile until the search team have done their bit.'

'I'll have to see what I can get here.'

'Understood.' George started walking towards the bus. Then he turned and said, 'Oh, and John, how long was it between the incident and the police being called?'

'A few minutes from what we can tell. Just long enough for our offender to get far enough away to give us a cat in hell's chance of finding him.'

George sniffed. He paused at the open bus doors before stepping on, avoiding the middle of the gangway and trying not to touch any of the handrails. He trotted up the stairs. Adcock had said the kids had been attacked on the back seat, but there were drops of blood all along the aisle. Sterile bandage wrappers fluttered in a draught from an open window. George used a tissue to push it shut. He noticed a well-defined footprint where some blood had pooled. No doubt the print came from a paramedic's boot, but you never knew. Maybe they'd get lucky for once. A yellow plastic number two stood like a miniature sandwich board, the sort used by CSI to indicate something significant. George counted five others, each of them telling part of the story but he would need the gaps filling in.

The night seemed to have turned colder by the time George stepped off the bus, and he was grateful for the coffee Sergeant Adcock handed to him.

'Thanks, John.'

'No problem. Anything on there that takes your interest?'

'Nothing obvious. CSI might get something. Do we know if the man was wearing gloves?'

'Both the boy and the driver were pretty sure that he wasn't.'

George nodded. 'Unfortunately that might not help us on a public bus. There'll be a million different prints on there, but you never know.' He took a cautious sip of his coffee. He'd been caught out enough times by heat erupting like lava from under the plastic lid.

'Any chance of you getting back to the wife at a reasonable hour then, George?' Adcock smiled widely.

'Much as I like our spare room, I'm afraid it's the hospital to chat with our driver and then I'll need to head to the nick to make a start on this. I'll have to get the report done. Management always want something to read with their toast when they arrive in the morning.'

'Not much you can say, is there?'

George rubbed at his chin. 'You did the right thing getting me out. You would have been under the microscope if you hadn't. I assume the kids are still at Langthorne General too?' Adcock nodded. 'Then I'll get some of their details from the officer that's with them and put together some sort of investigation plan.'

Adcock was still smiling. 'And there's me thinking that you just came for a quick gawp and then went back to bed till sun-up.'

George smiled back and checked his watch. 'At least it makes it worth being hauled out of bed. I'm used to it now. Ever since I was assigned to Effingell, it's a rare evening when I'm not called out.'

'You're *assigned* to Effingell?'

'I am. Anything above minor that happens on this patch comes to me and my team.'

John laughed. 'Well! Who did *you* piss off?'

George pulled his collar closer round his neck. 'I have no idea, John. No idea at all.'

* * *

George wasn't surprised to see the staff at Langthorne General's A&E department still rushed off their feet in the early hours of a midweek morning. Stuffy warm air enveloped him, thanks to the industrial-strength heating, on full blast in an attempt to limit the losses on the elderly wards and ensure no one else was able to sleep.

George guessed the driver, Tony Mitchum, was in his mid-forties. He was in good shape for a man of that age, despite the sling round his left arm.

'Dangerous job, driving a bus,' George said.

Tony was sitting up in bed surrounded by a flimsy curtain. On one side was a crying child and on the other a man was coughing incessantly.

'Well, that'll teach me to stop. I've been driving for twenty years and I should know by now. First rule of our job, don't stop until you get somewhere busy and then call the police.'

'You live and learn. I'm Detective Sergeant George Elms. I'm sorry you got caught up in this. This man — did you get much of a look at him?' George looked around for somewhere to support his notebook. He was forced to stand, and settled on jabbing the edge of it into his midriff so that he could scribble notes.

'Not really. I got a brief glimpse when he got on. He was a typical Epping Hill type, so I usually avoid eye contact.'

'The CCTV's usually pretty good on the buses. Hopefully we'll get a decent look at him on there.'

'You'll have a hard job. That bus is down to have the CCTV system sorted out — it's on the blink. They still send us out in it though. What did they say . . ?' Tony looked at the ceiling, '. . . that's right, it has no impact on public safety. Ironic, eh?'

George gave a thin smile. 'This guy, did he pay with the right money?'

'Um . . . yeah, he did. I was running low on change so I remember. I was happy that I got a couple of kids with passes and a man with the right money. Why's that?'

'It means that he's ridden the route before. We might not have CCTV from this journey, but he'll have been captured at some point. So, they got on at the same stop, the kids and the man?'

'They did, yeah. In the town centre.'

'And, let me guess, the kids got on first?'

'They did.'

'And you haven't seen this man on this route before? It would probably have been at the same sort of time. I suspect he knew it was a quiet bus.'

'I haven't, but this isn't my usual route. I'm covering. I normally do the East Yellow Run.'

George smiled at the driver, and then at the nurse who had pulled the curtain back and had been quietly waiting for him to finish his interview. 'Well, I'll leave you in the capable hands of the staff here. No doubt I will speak to you again, Tony.' He turned to the nurse. 'Sorry to get in your way. Look after this man. He's had a rough night.'

'That's what we're here for,' was the nurse's curt reply.

Chapter 3

George Elms' eyes were heavy as he walked into the meeting room of Langthorne House Police Station. The tension was almost tangible. It was four minutes past ten and George was arriving for a meeting that had been hurriedly called with no explanation as to why. He found a spare seat. George saw officers he knew from other stations around the county. This worried him immensely.

The meeting had been called by Chief Superintendent Graham Huntington, Lennokshire Constabulary's Temporary Area Commander for the southern region. Most of those present had never met the man, but those who had, described him as an angry, demanding man who had bullied and clawed his way up through the ranks.

George could hear hushed theories being discussed about the reason for the meeting, when the door opened, and silence fell. The officers stood up as the chief superintendent entered the room. Huntington paused for a second and nodded, then marched to a desk at the front of the room, positioned below a large projector screen. He turned to face the officers and rested a hand on the high-backed leather chair that had been brought in for him. His secretary, and note-taker for the meeting, Jean, took up position at the end of the desk, sitting sideways to the group. Huntington stood in silence. He took his time to give the room permission to sit down.

'Thank you, parade.'

The officers sat down.

Huntingdon turned to the secretary. 'Jean, are the inspectors not joining us?'

'Er, no, sir. You asked . . . I mean, they have been told to meet at ten this morning, sir. You were planning on speaking to them separate . . .' Jean trailed off.

Huntington smiled. It didn't reach his eyes. 'I think I'll speak to everyone at once.'

Jean scurried to the back of the room and slammed the door in her haste. Huntington gave another mirthless smile.

'I expect you're all wondering why I asked you to come in this morning.'

George almost snorted at the word, "asked."

'We have suffered an incident overnight that was not out of the ordinary and in the grand scheme might not even look like a major incident. But it is the final straw. A young, bright and decent schoolgirl was slashed in the face by a would-be robber. Her male friend was stabbed by a dirty needle and a bus driver ended up with a fracture when he tried to help. Early signs suggest this is yet another overspill from the residents of the Epping Hill Estate. Now, I'd like to think of this as a meeting of minds, an opportunity, if you will, to do something that we so rarely get to do, namely, to pool our collective intelligence and expertise in response to a common problem.'

The door at the rear swung open and Jean stepped aside to allow the six inspectors to enter. They nodded at the commander, as if to say that this was not a major inconvenience at all, and that they hadn't each been in the middle of something much more enjoyable.

Huntington began again. 'Thank you. I was just beginning to explain why I have asked you all to attend. You will all be aware of the incident that occurred overnight. Now, as I was saying, this meeting is purely to allow us the opportunity to get together and do what we rarely get the time to do. There is much expertise and experience in this room — a think tank, you might say — and I believe we can utilise this to solve Lennokshire Police's biggest problem.' Huntington turned to face the screen behind him. He waved a remote control and a colour-coded map appeared on the screen. He turned back to his audience. 'Epping Hill Estate.'

Jean rose and switched the lights off. Epping Hill was coloured dark blue, the outlying areas light blue, and the ring road surrounding the estate was highlighted in yellow, as were the three major roads in and out of the area.

'Okay, a quick show of hands, anyone who has not dealt with a job in Epping Hill Estate.' A single hand rose at the back of the room, belonging to one of a group of inspectors who had remained standing at the back of the room. Huntington strained to look at him. 'You haven't?'

'I've not had the pleasure yet, sir. I'm a transferee, sir, from the Met. Haven't been with you long.'

Huntington smiled. 'Even so, that should've been plenty of time.' Muted laughter went around the room.

'The Epping Hill Estate,' continued Huntingdon, 'is a blight on what is an otherwise calm, law-abiding and pleasant area of the county. That estate accounts for sixty-three per cent of all the crime in our area. In *my* area. It is awash with druggies, thieves and other bottom-feeding scumbags that make the ordinary people of this town afraid to drive past it, let alone through the place. Last week alone, seventeen violent crimes were committed by residents of the Epping Hill Estate. And they don't limit their activities to the estate either. Hell, they can beat the shit out of each other, for all I care, but they carry out robberies, aggravated burglaries and assaults on people in other parts of the area. It cannot continue. I want action, people, and I want ideas.'

Huntington looked around the room. The officers looked back, silent.

George's pocket vibrated. Glad of the distraction, he pulled out his phone and slid his thumb over the screen. The text message was from his wife, Sarah. *It's got to be contractions this time! This could be it!* x

He couldn't keep the smile from spreading across his face, his exhaustion suddenly slipping away as he surged with adrenalin. He had to get out of there, he shot up a hand.

'Yes?'

'Sir, I have to go.'

'What?'

'Sir, yes. I'm sorry, but I think . . . well, I think my wife is in labour.'

Huntington took some time to respond. 'Well, of all the excuses . . .'

George nodded and hurried out of the room. As he left, a female officer was suggesting possible solutions to the Epping Hill problem. George was glad to be leaving the room before Huntington answered, and put the female officer down. His sexist views were well known. Female officers, according to Huntingdon, should spend their days filing documents and making coffee, while the men did the real police work.

In the corridor, George called his wife.

Sarah answered immediately.

'It's real then, this time?' George asked.

'I'm not sure. I mean, it feels real. There's a good couple of hours between the contractions, if that's what they are. But it's not the same as when I had Charley. My mum's here, and she said that's what happened with her. She was in labour for almost three days with me, so I don't think there's any real urgency just yet.'

'You speak for yourself. I just want to be there with you. I should be home already but there's been some meeting I got roped into. I can be home in about half an hour.' George checked his watch, his hand shaking a little. He was out of practice when it came to working through the night. His top button hung undone, his thin-knotted tie seemed to be tightening. He tugged at it, feeling throttled.

'Just come home and get some rest. You're definitely going to need it if this isn't another drill. I'm going to wait a while and see what happens.'

'Okay, yeah. You've given me the perfect opportunity to slip away. Is it painful?'

'Not really. Not yet.'

'Hang on in there, hun, and I'll see you soon.'

George could see the backs of seated officers in the meeting through a glass slit in one of the doors. He took his opportunity and walked away.

* * *

When the meeting finally dragged to its weary end, the officers filed out in silence. Huntington was perfectly satisfied with the inconclusive result. He would have been seen by those on high to be taking action, and that was all he cared about. He was about to leave when he noticed that one of the inspectors was lingering at the back of the room, evidently waiting to speak to him. Huntington did his best to ignore him.

'Sir?'

Huntington recognised the inspector who had spoken up earlier in the meeting — the transferee from the Met. He pretended not to hear.

'Sir?' the inspector said again.

'Did you forget something, Met Police?'

'I wanted to talk to you about your Epping Hill problem.'

Huntington sat down and leaned back in the chair, looking up at the man. He exhaled. 'Well, for a start, old son, there's a problem with what you just said. It is not *my* Epping Hill problem at all. It is *our* problem. Welcome to the force.'

'Oh, it's not something I could bring up in the meeting, sir. It's a bit . . . outside the box.'

Huntington leant forward and rested his hands together on the table. 'And what is this idea that will solve all of Lennokshire's problems? I ask you to bear in mind that I plan to have a coffee upstairs in five minutes.'

The inspector smiled. 'That's perfect, sir. I'd rather not talk about it in here anyway. Perhaps I can get you a coffee in town?'

Huntington laughed. 'Do you know how many officers on this station would like to take me out for a private cup of coffee to discuss police matters?'

'Based on what I've heard, sir, none.' The inspector turned and walked towards the door. There, he stopped and turned to face Huntingdon. 'If you had bothered to ask, I might have told you that for the last two years in London I ran one of the most successful and hard-hitting pilots ever seen in the force. It was aimed at wiping out the source of all the trouble which, as we both know, is drugs. It was succeeding until a change of management forced us to stop. If you have the balls to do it, I believe I can help you eliminate your Epping Hill problem in a matter of months.'

Huntington raised an eyebrow. 'You talk a good game, Inspector. You city boys always do.'

'You're a temporary area commander, right?'

'Well, I don't really see—'

'I know what it's like. You jump through all the hoops and say all the right things, but at the end of the day if there are people above you that think you're not the right man, then there's nothing you can do about it. Epping Hill is their excuse, isn't it? I've no doubt there are people above you that would rather you *didn't* pass the board, and while Epping Hill remains a problem for which you have no solution, they will get their way. You'll never pass that board, sir, with respect. You'll just continue to work twice as hard as those that sit on it.'

'Well, I don't know how it works in the city, but . . .' Huntington tailed off.

'Costa do a nice coffee, sir. I'm Detective Inspector Craig Jacobs, by the way.'

Huntington ran a hand through his hair. 'Well, good for you.'

Chapter 4

'Coffee, guv?' Jacobs asked.

Huntington glanced disdainfully around Costa Coffee. A scrawny lad was noisily scooping up empty cups and plates from the early-morning rush.

Jacobs indicated a table in the corner and went to get the drinks.

'Come here a lot, do you?' Huntington said when Jacobs returned.

'It's decent coffee.' Jacobs sat down and watched Huntington push at the head of froth on his drink.

'Well, it wants to be at three quid a cup.'

'Some things are worth paying for, sir.'

'So this is an investment, is it?'

Jacobs looked puzzled. 'Investment?'

'In your career. You bring me over here and spend three quid on a cup of coffee, and I'm impressed. Then we all live happier, more successful lives.'

'Ah, I'm with you. You think this is about me giving you some sort of sales pitch that will raise my profile. Well, let me tell you right from the start, I'm not here because of my career. In fact, I don't care if you run this thing without involving me at all, just as long as you consider running it.'

Huntington leant back in his chair. 'Well, it's not often I *do* get a fancy cup of coffee, so you've got the time it takes for me to drink this at the least.'

'Places like the Epping Hill Estate,' Jacobs began, 'are a problem that every police force in the country has to face, and the key to solving that problem is intel.'

'Well, you've cracked it, son! You brought me out of my office and all the way over here to tell me that I need to gather intelligence? Jesus.' Huntington shook his head.

'No, sir. I'm not nearly finished.' Jacobs took a breath. 'I had a similar problem when I was in the Met. We had an area that was a virtual no-go, run by the criminals who lived there, as well as some particularly nasty ones from outside. I got together a team of people and injected them into the area undercover. They did all the intel stuff you would expect. They talked to the right people, watched what was going on, found out who was who—'

'We've tried setting up intel operations in Epping Hill several times. It's always the same problem — it's a closed community. You walk a group of people into the area who start asking questions and appear to have a penchant for doughnuts and the good people of Effingell will string them up as gavvers soon as you can say "assistance required." These people are scum — unemployable down-and-outs, the dregs of society — but they are not completely thick'

'You're right.' Jacobs paused. 'The reason we are so conspicuous is because we have to play by the rules. We have to follow the guidelines that say who we can and can't watch and when we can do it, who we can and can't communicate with and how we do it. We stick out a mile in their environment.'

'And you have another way?'

'Yes. The idea came about after a large undercover operation was carried out across London. It was a resounding success . . . to start with. The intelligence we had was fantastic and we made nine arrests, all of them top dogs. The supply line was cut. We seized houses, fancy cars and a pile of drug money. It was absolutely beautiful. Then we took the job to court. The defence solicitors looked at the evidence and knew their clients were screwed, so they went for the human rights angle, the only chance they had. They pulled the legislation apart and eventually they managed to get just about every shred of evidence gathered using undercover officers dismissed. The Crown offered no evidence at all on six of the defendants, in case it was proven unlawful and the officers themselves prosecuted. One got an eighty pound fine for cannabis possession and another got six months' suspended, and this was only because he'd knocked his wife about. It was a total disaster. What hurt the most was that we had to give everything back to them. But we learnt some valuable lessons.'

'Go on.'

'We went back, but with just five people this time. We mocked them up as a group of travellers — caravans, the lot, and they parked up right in the middle of the patch. Even the local police didn't know they were on the same side. Then we spread the word that these fuckers were not to be messed with. Travellers always seem to get a certain respect from lowlife, but we started a lot of stories about this group. The local response officers even had a few slides made of a daily briefing dedicated to the travellers, giving warning markers of ultra-violent men who were not to be underestimated. We created identities with fake criminal records for GBH, attempted murder, arson with intent — you name it. We faked intel reports linking them to just about every type of violent crime there is.'

Huntington waved his hand. 'I get the point. Undercover with a twist. It's not groundbreaking, though.'

'You're right. But undercover police officers had failed previously because they couldn't *act* like the people around them. We made sure that our people had free rein to do just that.'

'Meaning?'

'The people on the Epping Hill Estate use violence and reputation to work out a pecking order. The traveller family didn't just have a similar backstory, they represented competition.'

For the first time, Jacobs had Huntingdon's full attention.

'Competition?'

'That's right. If you want to find out who the alpha male is in a pack of animals, you storm straight in there acting like it's you, and the alpha is the one who comes looking for a fight.'

Huntington was silent for a while. 'You want to put a group of police officers into the Epping Hill Estate with the intention of becoming competition for the drug dealers? And you want them to achieve this by using violence? And you wonder why the Met wouldn't take this on? I think you've wasted enough of my time, Inspector.' Huntington stood up to leave.

'They wouldn't be police officers, sir.' Jacobs looked his area commander in the eye. 'You'd take them on as a civilian group, call them "neighbourhood liaison" or something for the books. They don't have the restrictions the police have because they never present any evidence at court. They simply get the information.'

'So you want us to sanction the creation of a group of people who would use violence to get information for us?'

'Any assaults or crimes of any type that are reported to us will be fully investigated and the persons involved will be prosecuted to the full extent of the law. And if they are police employees, the IPCC and any other appropriate body will be informed.'

'You think that no one would ever report, don't you?'

Jacobs smiled. 'Based on my experience, and yours too no doubt, I *know* that no one will make any reports. I took the liberty of looking at the Epping Hill history. Almost all the crimes are related to drugs in some way. It's a closed society and it polices itself. The trouble is, the offending spills out of the estate. The good people of Langthorne get burgled or robbed by residents of the estate who need to fund their habits. We can never beat the drugs problem completely, but we can push it away, force them to go further afield to get their hit. That way they don't reflect in your figures.'

Huntington stood up and pulled on his suit jacket. 'I need to be getting back.'

Jacobs watched him leave. He knew he wouldn't get an enthusiastic green light on the spot. In fact, this was just the response he'd expected. The man had heard something quite outside of his comfort zone. He would think about the proposal, Jacobs was sure of that, and it would probably take some time. Jacobs got up and returned to the counter. He might as well take another overpriced coffee back with him.

Chapter 5

'Foxtrot Yankee Six Three Zero from Control.'

Foxtrot Yankee Six Three Zero was still attempting to open his deli-bought sandwiches, which appeared to have been wrapped for a game of pass-the-parcel. After three layers police constable Ed Kavski was finally seeing something edible. He sighed and pressed the radio "talk" button on the dash.

'Yankee Six Three Zero go ahead.' He looked at his colleague, Ben Parkin, who was fighting with his own sandwich parcel, licking a finger that had pierced through to the bread.

'Foxtrot Yankee Six Three Zero, what is your current status?'

Ed had already made the Control Centre fully aware of his schedule for the day. He pushed the button on his car radio and said, 'We're on taskings today, Control, plain clothed.'

'Foxtrot Yankee Six Three Zero, that's all received. We've currently got a call in Luton Road, Chatham. A male has taken his two-year-old daughter from the mother and has her confined in a bedroom. Do you receive so far?'

'So far.'

'The local patrol don't have a Taser officer in this area today and you're booked on with one. Would you be able to attend and assist? Firearms are making their way but they have a long ETA.'

Ed looked at the thick-cut white bread of his sandwich. It was going to be tasty. Then, with an exaggerated sigh, he scrunched up the multiple layers and dumped the untidy package on the back seat. He checked his watch.

'Yeah, Control, we'll go in the first instance and see if we're needed. Can you keep Firearms rolling please, as we'll need to get back to our tasking as soon as possible?'

'That's all received Foxtrot Yankee Six Three Zero and very much appreciated. I'll show you making your way.'

The unmarked Audi A5 bumped down from the kerb and onto the road. Ed flicked a switch, and the grills flashed blue and the siren began to wail as they picked up speed and made their way to the nearby town of Chatham.

* * *

Michael Hunt was not a bad man really. He was a petty criminal and general pain in the police's backside, but not nasty. He was well known to the police, mainly for a number of incidents involving his girlfriend, Zoey, and for petty violence when he had a bellyful of beer inside him. Lately, he had been quiet and had not visited a police custody suite for several months, in what was possibly a personal best. This quiet spell was now coming to an end.

Hunt's long-suffering girlfriend stood with a small team of police officers on the pavement outside her flat, shouting words of abuse that were extreme even by the standards of this deprived area. She was five feet tall. Once healthily plump, she had become increasingly skinny as the relationship with her domineering boyfriend progressed. But with the police around her, she had suddenly found her voice. She screamed up at the window of Flat Three, 19 Luton Road.

'Where's my fucking babby? You touch even a hair on her head and I'll rip yer fucking bollocks off, Michael, you cunt!'

Sergeant Paul Donovan arrived at the scene as two police officers were trying to restrain the hysterical woman. 'Get her out of here,' he barked.

'He's got my kid, you cunt!'

The sergeant pointed up at the window and said flatly, 'And aren't you just a happy reminder that a little un is always better off with her mother.'

'Fuck you!'

Sergeant Donovan walked towards the entrance as a couple of PCs shoved Zoey into the back of a police car.

Michael Hunt had started the day with a supervised meeting regarding a dispute between him and his former girlfriend over child contact. It took place in a council building where basic childcare services were provided for those who needed them. It was also where Social Services facilitated meetings between feuding couples about access to their children. Michael had taken his two-year-old daughter, Lilly-May, to the toilet, where he had sat her in the sink and squeezed out through a single window. Then he reached back inside, grabbed the giggling toddler and made his way out into the crisp winter morning. He had been gone forty minutes, driving away in his mate's battered old Ford Orion, before anyone had raised the alarm.

That was six hours ago. Michael had completed part one of his plan with a surprising amount of cunning, before realising that he had not got as far as considering part two. As was generally the case with Michael, drink provided a handy solution, and soon his anger was beginning to get the better of him.

* * *

The local beat officers had brought in a negotiator, who was attempting to talk to Michael and appeal to his common sense. His responses were slurred. Common sense had long since gone out the window.

Keith, the negotiator, had joined the force and then found that he had no stomach for confrontation. Seeing this, his superiors gave him roles that made use of his 'softer skills.' Now, Keith was on the phone to Michael, listening to him slur about how much he loved "his" Lilly.

'No one doubts that for a second, Michael.' Out of the corner of his eye, Keith saw a dark blue Audi A5 pull up.

'I'd ne . . . never hurt her, yous know that. Not unless *yous* make me.'

'We're here to help, Michael. I give you my word. We all want the same thing.'

Keith rubbed at his mouth, watching as two men stepped out of the Audi. The driver was a thick-set man whose muscular torso strained against his black polo shirt. A long tattoo trailed up the length of the man's right arm and under his sleeve. He strode to the rear of the car, opened the boot and pulled out a bright yellow box, resting it on the boot rim.

'You know I'd never hurt little Lill. Her mum, though, you bring her up here and do me a swap and I'll do her some proper fucking harm. She ain't seen nothing yet, you get what I'm saying?'

'Now, Michael, we were discussing how we can help you. We've got plenty of time. You want Lilly-May to be safe and we want that too, so let's talk about how we come up and get her.' The man by the car took out a yellow Taser from the box. He removed his sunglasses and threw them into the boot. He strode towards the front door of the property, followed closely by his colleague.

Keith was aware that a Taser officer had been called for. This made sense in a siege situation. He had been involved in numerous jobs like this one, and it was normal for the Taser officer to introduce himself to the negotiator, to get an idea of how the target was behaving. So Keith was a little surprised to see the men walk past him towards the building.

* * *

Ed Kavski pushed the heavy communal front door and waited for his colleague Ben. The door shut in the face of Sergeant Donovan, who had followed them to the building.

'Eh, excuse me! Hold on,' he called out.

Ed looked back over the stair rail and looked at the sergeant scuttling up after them, red-faced and flustered.

'Sergeant Donovan, ground commander for our little situation here,' he panted.

Ed continued to climb the stairs, two at a time. On the third and last set of stairs, he turned to Ben. 'Do you wanna have a chat with our ground commander here?'

Ben nodded and turned to the sergeant. 'Hello, Sarge. We're hoping to get in there to talk to him . . .'

Ed reached the top of the stairs.

* * *

Outside, Keith was still trying to get Michael to surrender. 'So, you see, Michael, if you'll let me come up there and accompany young Lilly-May down the stairs with you, me holding one hand, you the other, then we can bring this to a close. You won't be manhandled or even handcuffed in front of your daughter, you have my word.' He waited for a response.

'But I don't trust you fucking lot, do I. I mean what essssactly does the word of a gavver mean? Fuck all, Kevin, fuck *all*!'

'Keith. It's Keith.'

Michael laughed again. 'Well, I like Kevin, Kevin. Didn't you say I was in charge, *Kevin*? So say your name, *Kevin*! Say your fucking name!'

* * *

Ed pushed the top and bottom of the door. It flexed from the middle, which indicated that the door had a single lock halfway up. He stepped back and kicked it, just below the keyhole. There was little resistance —the wood splintered and cracked and the door fell inwards at an angle, as the top hinge came away with a crunch. To the left of the door was a tiny kitchen. The living room and Michael Hunt were on the right.

Michael was talking into the phone. 'Say your name is fucking Kevin!' Then his amused expression gave way to one of terror as a large man stood over him, raised the Taser and pulled the trigger.

'Michael, this isn't a game. Let's get back to how we can bring this to a peaceful resolution, for everyone's sake. What do you say, Michael?' Keith's voice came through the phone just as twelve thousand volts of electricity passed through Michael's body.

In among a pile of stolen toys sat Lilly-May, giggling as her dad's legs shot out straight, his body went rigid, and he slid to the floor.

Chapter 6

4.30 a.m., the next morning. Graham Huntington slipped out of bed and left the house. He was wearing his gym clothes and carried his immaculately pressed uniform in a briefcase. In the past, he had used this period to do a decent run or session on the bike, but recently had found himself spending less time on the gym floor and longer in the post-workout steam room. It was his time for quiet contemplation. After the gym session he would drive his electric blue BMW sports car to the station and be in his reserved parking space by 6.30 a.m. All this for a shift that began at eight.

Today, however, Huntington's routine had been disrupted.

The night before, his wife had asked him if he would take the cat to the vet in the morning. Apparently it was due in for an operation, although this was the first he'd heard of it. He lost the argument, and was outside the vet at 7.15, ready for the vet's to open at 7.30. His irritation increased as the cat reached out a claw through the bars of its carrier and scratched the black leather seat. A student vet appeared to open up the surgery at 7.19 a.m., and Huntington leapt out of the car and thrust the cat at her.

Pet disposed of, he sped off in the direction of the station. He made good progress until he saw a marked police car in the distance, pulled across the slip road to the motorway that would take him speedily to where he needed to be.

Huntington beat the steering wheel in frustration.

* * *

PC Playmont was manning the roadblock, and he stepped away from his marked car as the little sports car approached. The driver's window was already down and an angry face looked up at him.

'Why is the road closed?'

'There's been an accident up on the motorway. This junction is closed. I'm going to have to ask you to keep moving, sir, as you're causing an obstruction on the roundabout here.' PC Playmont knew that it was a serious accident. People were fighting for their lives out on the tarmac while the world expressed its annoyance at the inconvenience.

The man in the sports car turned round in his seat and looked back. The traffic was having no difficulty navigating past him. He faced the officer again. 'I'm not causing any obstruction. I need to get to Langthorne nick as soon as possible.' Now PC Playmont could see part of the man's police uniform, with his rank neatly embroidered on his shoulder.

Playmont wasn't impressed. 'Yeah, understood, sir. If you carry on round and take the next exit you'll find yourself heading towards Hythe. Stay on that road, which takes you right through and down to the sea. Once you get to the bottom of the winding hill and come to some crossroads just take a left and you should then be able to follow the road back into Langthorne and you'll know where you are.'

Huntington produced a tepid smile. 'I'm pretty sure that if you ran a check on my registration, you would find that I can be let through.'

Playmont stifled a swear word. 'You can be let through? Are you aware of the serious incident on the motorway, *sir*?'

'My radio hasn't informed me of anything major.'

The officer bent down closer to the window of the low-slung sports car. 'There's been a fatal accident involving a nicked car and a Vauxhall Corsa carrying three teenagers to Thorpe Park. We're hoping at this time that it doesn't become a triple fatal. Now, I hear what you're saying and out of respect for rank I will let you through right now if you so order me, but I will need to record your force number on this scene log here, and the reason for driving up onto the motorway and manoeuvring your personal vehicle through the ambulance staff working on the casualties. I have your force number, sir, as it's written on your shoulder there, and I will record your reason as *needs to get to work on time*. Is that okay?'

Huntington gave the officer a cold stare, and grated into first gear. 'What was your name again?'

'PC Betts, sir. You drive safe now. All the emergency services are currently tied up, you see.'

As Huntington's BMW pulled back into the traffic and drove away, another officer returned from the motorway services with two coffees. He looked at Playmont from under the rim of his hat, which was slightly too large and worn far too low. 'What was that about?'

'What was what about?' Playmont repeated, watching the sports car disappear.

'You just said my name.' PC Betts placed the coffees on top of the patrol car and began fishing in his pockets for sachets of sugar.

Playmont smiled. 'No I didn't.'

* * *

8.06 a.m. It was some time since Huntington could recall being late for work. He strode through the foyer of Lennokshire's largest police station with a face like thunder.

His expression didn't scare Chief Superintendent Helen Webb. 'Where the hell have you been?'

'Sorry, Helen. I had something to do first thing and then a section of the motorway was closed—'

'I need to speak to you in my office, now.'

Helen Webb was ten years younger than Huntington and already senior to him. It hadn't taken her long to get there either. Two reasons why Huntington disliked the woman. Added to this was the fact that she *was* a woman. She was generally well respected, and was a major reason why his career had stalled. She was also bossy when the pressure was on, and Huntington was not a man who enjoyed being told what to do.

'What, about being late?' A flush crept over Huntington's cheeks.

'Don't be ridiculous, Graham. Get yourself a cup of coffee. I need to round up George Elms and I'll be right with you.'

Huntington was striding towards Helen's office, coffee in hand, when he heard Jean calling out behind him.

His PA was slightly out of breath as she approached him. 'You're on your way to Helen Webb's office, then?'

He stopped. 'Yes, yes, I am, Jean. What's this about?'

'I don't know. She's been looking for you all morning and wouldn't say why. I did a bit of digging and all I know is that the attempted robbery still seems to be at the front of everyone's mind and—'

'The school kids on the bus?'

'Yes.'

'What's the issue with that?' Graham stopped suddenly. 'Jesus, no one's died have they?'

Jean shook her head emphatically. 'Well, thank fuck for that. That would be all I need right now.' Huntington strode on. Jean dropped her notebook, apologised, picked it up and hurried along in his wake.

'So do we have a suspect, then?'

'I don't think so. Certainly no one's in for it, and I don't think there's a name.'

'That'll be it then. A full day since the incident and no one in the bin for it, that's enough to give Ma'am Webb the hump.'

Jean looked embarrassed. 'No, sir, I don't think that's the case. The girl . . . You see, her auntie is the mayor. There's been a lot of media interest.'

Jean looked confused as Huntington suddenly burst into a smile. 'So it is true!'

'You knew, sir?'

'You think I call meetings of all the area's supervisors for every seventeen-year-old roughed up on a public bus? I got wind that she was connected, I didn't know it was the mayor though. Helen Webb can have the hump all she likes, my response has been immaculate.'

* * *

The only personal touches in Helen Webb's office were some pictures of her husband and twin two-year-old daughters. They were arranged facing out towards the person sitting opposite her.

Huntington was rarely fazed when summoned to Helen's office, but usually miffed. Today was unusual - he was almost looking forward to it. As Helen entered the room, he puffed himself up, he was ready.

'I see you managed to get yourself a coffee.'

'I did.' Huntington picked up the cup he'd placed on Helen's desk. He hoped she hadn't noticed the watery ring it had left.

'I've seen Jean hanging around outside. I'll go and ask her to get us a fresh one.' She stopped at the door and looked at the table. 'I'll get some coasters too.'

'Hello, sir.' George Elms clearly hadn't expected to see the temporary area commander filling the only seat on the visitor side of the desk.

'George!' Huntington had met George a couple of times before. He was aware that he had a reputation as a decent detective. Huntington's greeting was more enthusiastic than usual.

'No baby, then?'

'Oh, well no. We've had a few false alarms actually. Sorry about the timing, sir, I already need to tick the little one off when it does finally arrive.'

'Ah no need, George. Now, tell me, what the hell are we doing here?'

'I think it must be about this job from the other night. The mayor's niece was the victim.'

'The mayor? I see. Any idea on suspects?'

'No. Seems lady luck had a night off. The bus's CCTV is knackered, and there was no one else on the bus, besides the driver. He got a look at him, but not a good one, so we have a fairly general description.'

Huntington sighed and rubbed his chin. 'So, I assume we're just waiting for forensics? What about CCTV from the bus stop?'

'Forensics have dusted and there are prints, but they're not going to be much use. It's a public bus. We're still waiting on the CCTV review for the bus station — the driver did say that they all got on at the same stop. They also found a wrap of what we assume is heroin. It was on the top deck but towards the front. We'll test it to see what it is and if it has any DNA, but as far as evidence for this incident goes, it's pretty useless.'

Helen returned as George was speaking. 'So, George here has brought you up to date on the Sophie Hayward robbery?'

'So it seems,' said Huntington.

Helen sat down. 'Right, I want to know what we are doing about it.' Helen's voice rose when she was stressed.

Huntington, who been sitting back with an ankle over a knee and lazily trying to catch a glimpse of bra through a gap in Helen's blouse, quickly placed both feet on the floor.

'And for fuck's sake, George, go and get yourself a chair,' she said.

Huntington was immediately on the defensive. 'You know what I have been doing. I have kept you up to date on every single operation, project and exercise carried out on that area. Just yesterday morning I led a meeting where every sergeant and inspector in the area was set the challenge of assisting with finally crushing the scourge that is Epping Hill.' He slapped his hand on the desk.

Helen stared at the hand. 'Nothing's worked in there, Graham. You're not here so I can question you about what you have and haven't done. I know you've done a lot of work there, but it's all been tried before and I've seen Jean's notes from this meeting – it's just more of the same. We've had community days, they were a disaster, flooding the place with uniform hasn't worked either, the criminals just move. Epping Hill has always been a shit hole, but a contained shit hole. Now the scum from that estate are preying on good, decent people, including seventeen-year-old girls on their way home from school. It's just not on, Graham.'

George had returned with a wheeled chair. He had sat down next to the area commander and now rolled backwards, as if in retreat.

'How do we even know this robbery was carried out by someone from Epping Hill? For all we know, it was someone who knows her from school and lives in a well-to-do area. They have bad people as well, you know.' Huntington crossed his arms.

'George?' Helen barked at the sergeant, who was fiddling with his tie.

'Oh, well, ma'am, sir, the main thing is the bus route. It was on Templar Road, which as you know has a park either side. It's a good place for a robbery if you are from Epping Hill, as the park borders the estate. The dog picked up a track from the bus, something moved across the park and through the small woodland bit and out into the estate. Unfortunately it lost anything specific after that as there was a fair amount of foot traffic. Also, the description — a white male, stocky, shaved head and tattoos. Your typical Epping Hill resident, in other words. Like I mentioned, there was a bag of wraps found, probably heroin. It might not have been dropped during the incident, but we're working on the assumption it was—'

'There you are. Epping Hill strikes a-fucking-gain.' Helen rarely swore. Huntington should have known that now was not the time to argue.

'That doesn't mean they're from Epping Hill. It just means they made off into the estate and from there—'

'Oh, come on, Superintendent, it's a pretty obvious deduction, don't you think?' The ensuing tense silence was broken by a tap at the door.

'Come in!' Helen and Huntington shouted together. Jean came in with a tray of three mugs, looking flustered.

'Sorry for the wait, ma'am, these coffees take a little while to do their thing.' She gave a nervous laugh as she placed the tray on the desk. No one responded. 'Will there be anything else?' she asked.

'Thank you, Jean, no.' Helen gave Jean a warm smile. It dropped away as she turned to the two men. 'I want a full incident room set up for this robbery.'

'I had a word with George this morning while we were waiting for you to get in,' Helen said. 'George and his team are leading the investigation on the ground. I want you to make sure he has all the resources he needs and, of course, to oversee the investigation. I will be handling the press, which in itself is becoming a full-time job. George pulled a double on the night the robbery came in so he's

39

set a few balls rolling and is taking a little time off this afternoon.'

'I assume the press are picking up on the mayor link?'

'That's one aspect, yes.'

Huntington could well imagine. A white British teenage schoolgirl with a pretty face gets attacked and the whole world is in shock. An Eastern European prostitute of the same age has two fingers cut off in a drug dispute, and a paragraph might squeeze into the middle pages of the local paper.

Helen sighed. 'Unfortunately, the timing could not have been worse.'

Huntington waited while Helen tapped at her computer, moved the mouse an inch and looked up at George, who had scuttled yet further back on his chair. 'George, you have bits to tie up before you go home, I'm sure?' She held his gaze.

'I do, yes, I do. Sir, I'll hang around and give you an update before I shoot off, yeah?'

'Yes, if you would.'

George got up and left.

Helen clicked her mouse again. She huffed, slid open a drawer and put on a pair of fashionable glasses. She continued to click away, her brow furrowed. Then she spun the monitor around so Huntington could see. She got up and stood behind him.

The screen pixelated and froze, then the video began to run. Huntington narrowed his eyes. The grainy image of a police car appeared in the middle of a dark screen. The camera then swung to a group of people standing under yellow blobs that were possibly streetlights. He couldn't make out how many people there were. They all wore dark clothing and had their hoods up, making identification impossible. The police car came to a stop and the doors could be seen opening and closing. Young, male voices came through the tinny speakers close to the camera. '*Here they fucking come, boi*,' and '*Fucking mugs, mate. Think they can just come in here.*' Two officers approached the group. The quality of the video was too poor to identify them, but Huntingdon could tell they were male, at least. One sounded middle-aged and the other a little younger.

'*All right, lads,*' said the older officer, '*What you doing hanging about here at this time of night?*'

'*What you say to me, you fucking mug?*' said a hooded youth.

'*Oi!*' The younger police voice lacked conviction. '*Oi! Now we didn't come over here swearing at you like that, did we?*'

'*You didn't have to fucking come over here at all, did ya, Po?*'

'*I see a group of kids hanging about on the street corner at one in the morning and I got every right to be coming over and asking what you're up to. Do your parents know you're out?*'

'*Ha! Our parents, mug? Fucking Po. We is just out here being, innit, a human being, you get me!*' The others laughed. '*Listen to me, yeah, leave this place of sin, yeah. There ain't no need for you here, yeah. Ya too fucking late or I swear down you will find yourself all fucked up.*'

Huntington felt his anger rising. He would show him what it was to be fucked up! He would show him a place of fucking sin. The images on the screen seemed to have frozen, but Huntingdon saw it was a standoff, which the middle-aged man ended.

'*Come on, Steve. Let's leave these gents to their evening.*'

'*Yeah, bye, Steve!*'

There was a short pause and then the officers turned and headed back to their patrol car and drove away. The last few seconds of footage showed the gang of hoodies cheering and whooping. One of them brandished what looked like a handgun. He pointed the weapon at the camera in a shooting stance before stuffing it back under his top.

Helen pressed the escape key. A YouTube header came on the screen, with a list of videos under a banner reading, "up next." The video was titled, "Epping Hill belongs to us."

'Graham, this video was uploaded in the last twenty-four hours. It's one minute and twelve seconds long. It can do indescribable damage. A local journalist has already seen it and has mentioned it in today's paper, making a link between the police's total lack of control over Epping Hill and the incident with Sophie. The timing couldn't be any worse.'

'It's just one video. We could cite hundreds of positive outcomes from Epping Hill over the last year, six months even. The amount of criminals that have been convicted, we could add up all the fines paid, it would be an impressive total—'

'No, Graham,' Helen interrupted. 'We have been approached by a national newspaper for a response to this, and from what we understand they are looking to run it as a major story. I mean, you can just see how this could be reported. Graham, that video tells the whole world that Lennokshire Police are running scared of the very people we should be clamping down on.'

'Major story?'

'The press have somehow managed to get hold of quite horrific pictures of Sophie's injuries. The mayor only needs to sanction the release of those pictures and they've got a significant story. Add this video to the mix and we've got a real problem. At least one of the nationals has given us warning that they could lead with this story anytime.'

'Lead?'

'Yes. Possibly on the front page.'

Huntington ran his fingers through his hair. He struggled to find suitable words. 'I assume you want me to prepare an official response?'

'No, Graham. The media guys are doing that, along with the chief.'

'The chief!' Graham felt his chest tighten further.

'Yes. Of course he must be alerted, Graham. Can you imagine if we hadn't told him and then he read about it in his morning paper? He's fully aware of the job, of the actions that have been taken and of the Epping Hill project as a whole.' Huntington's head slumped forward, and Helen's tone softened. 'What we would like from you now is a response. Not to the media, but to the people of Epping Hill, Graham. This is your baby and everyone knows it. You need to start making a difference in there, and fast.'

Huntington inhaled deeply in an effort to swallow the words he really wanted to say, and muttered, 'I will.'

Huntington walked away from the meeting with his Blackberry to his ear. 'Jacobs? It's Graham Huntington here. Listen, I was thinking I could do with another one of those overpriced coffees.'

Chapter 7

Peto Court, Epping Hill. George Elms disliked this block of flats almost as much as the residents disliked living in them. This place was hell, where the inhabitants brought out the worst in each other.

George paused for a second, peering at the solid metal security door that would allow him access to the long, featureless corridors. A light drizzle did nothing for the sombre, brick exterior of the block with its evenly spaced windows. Some didn't even have the regulation dirty net curtains, being covered instead with crudely cut pieces of chipboard or beach towels.

The decay continued inside. The council had been in the process of "refurbishing" the corridors but the process had stalled at the stage where all the paint had been stripped from the walls and most of the floors ripped up, with neither being replaced. The update itself had been prompted by a problem with leaking waste water, but the damp patches and sewage smell lingered.

He opened his notebook and reminded himself of the flat number and the notes he had hurriedly scrawled twenty minutes earlier. *Peto, Flat 22, gf Liz and 2 y/o girl* he read and hesitated at the bottom of the urine-soaked stairwell. This was what was known as a "just" job.

'Oh, George,' Helen Webb had said, 'Could you just . . . ? On your way home. It shouldn't take long.'

He hoped that was true. His foot sent an empty cider can rolling down the stairs, the noise amplified by the emptiness of the halls and the solid concrete steps. He walked along a corridor on the second floor. George hesitated at number 20, which had the '0' missing. He moved on to the next one. The door of Flat 22 looked flimsy, and the letterbox rattled with every knock. There was a muddy footprint on the door and a bit fell off it as George knocked again.

Elizabeth Wallis was twenty years old and much prettier than her surroundings. George had been given some background. It seemed she had once been full of potential, with loving parents who had wanted her to have a decent education. Then she had met a "bad boy," and all too quickly she'd got pregnant and was lost to his way of life.

Lizzie stood in the doorway, clutching her child. She wore a grubby, stained, white vest top and jersey shorts which were slightly too tight. Her hair was scraped back in a straggly ponytail.

She avoided eye contact. 'You looking for Chris?'

George smiled. 'I'm not, no. Is it Elizabeth?' He knew they could always tell a copper, uniform or not.

'Lizzie.' She looked a little worried.

'Lizzie, thank you. Do you mind if I come in?'

Lizzie stepped aside, gripping her child. George squeezed past. He entered a small bedsit, made even smaller by the double bed that dominated the room. There was a tiny kitchen area at one end. It was tidy, though.

'Lizzie, did you want to sit down?'

Lizzie sat on a small sofa under the window and pulled her daughter onto her lap. Outside, the drizzle had stopped and the sky had begun to clear a little. The window suddenly glowed as the sun emerged from behind a cloud.

'Alright, Katie?' Lizzie hugged her daughter and smiled nervously at George. He sat down on the edge of the bed.

'Lizzie, there's no easy way to say this. I am here to talk to you, but it's about Chris.'

Lizzie stopped rubbing Katie's back. He could see in her eyes that she had guessed that he was not here to deliver good news.

'Chris was involved in a car accident in the early hours of this morning. Lizzie, I'm very sorry, but Chris died at the scene. The paramedics did everything they could but his injuries were just too serious.'

Lizzie's expression registered nothing. The news didn't seem to have sunk in. 'What car? Chris doesn't drive. He doesn't have a car.'

'He was in someone else's car. He was the only one in it. We're not sure where he was going or where he'd been. We're still sort of piecing it together, really. Listen, Lizzie, can I give someone a call and get them round here? Or maybe drop you round at a friend's place? You shouldn't be on your own.'

Lizzie nodded. 'Yeah, I'm supposed to be going to Jackie's anyway — Chris's mum. She'll be waiting in for me. We were gonna go to the park.' Lizzie broke into a sort of smile which quickly disappeared. 'She won't know, will she?' There was panic in her voice.

'I don't think she could know yet, no. I'll drop you round there and I'll talk to her, all right?' George didn't relish the thought of delivering the bad news twice, but he knew that Lizzie couldn't be left on her own.

'I'll let you sort out what you need and get ready.' George rose to his feet and went towards the door. He was surprised to find her standing right behind him, barefoot, but apparently ready to leave.

'Lizzie?' he said softly.

'Yeah?'

'It's quite chilly out there. Do you want to put something on, maybe get a jacket for young Katie there?'

Lizzie stared at George for a couple of seconds, and then backed away and sat down on the bed. She placed Katie next to her and lifted her hands to her face. She began to weep, silently.

'I'll put the kettle on,' George said.

Lizzie nodded. For the first time in seven years, George had a cup of coffee in Peto Court.

Chapter 8

'So here we are again.' DI Craig Jacobs smiled broadly as a coffee was placed in front of him. 'And you're buying!'

'Don't get too excited about it, pal. Remember, I'm just looking at options at the moment and you *might* be one of them.'

Jacobs was not downhearted. He knew that he had the area commander hooked.

'So, I assume you have questions for me, now that you've had time to think?'

'Yeah, I have some questions. I have to say, when you said this was a bit out of the box I had no idea it would involve sending in a bunch of civilian workers to bully their way into the ranks of the drug dealers.' Huntington peered around nervously. It was ten thirty and Costa was quiet. A teenage staff member was busy nearby, struggling to operate a mop bucket.

'I'll be honest with you, sir, the man who implemented this in the city was a brave guy. He did insist on some restrictions and criteria, but even so, it does take some balls.'

'Restrictions? Criteria? What did he insist on specifically?'

Jacobs poured sugar into his cup, and leaned back. 'Well, first we sat down and talked about personnel. We agreed there should be five or six people, which is enough for safety but not so many that the place was swamped. We handpicked the team, and I have to say we made a good job of it. They were perfect — two lads and a girl from Firearms, one from the tactical team and a couple of civvies. One was the safety trainer and the other was an ex copper and a driver trainer.'

'I thought you said they were all civvies?'

'They were. At least they were by the time they started. They were all transferred on to civilian contracts and given a career break from the police. That way their pensions weren't affected and they went back to being coppers when the career break ended. Initially this was signed for six months while the scheme was being piloted, but you can extend career breaks for as long as you want, as I'm sure you know.'

'Of course,' Huntington waved his hand. 'So what happened to this team when it all stopped?'

'Most of them were similar to me, sir. We were at the coalface as it were, and we could see the impact we were having. We went into the area hard. We prepared the ground by making a name for them out on the street, so there was really very little actual work needed to get a foothold. The street dealers folded pretty quickly, they told us how to get to the suppliers, who was doing what, and even offered to distribute for us.'

'And did they?'

'Well, sir . . . yes, they did. It was necessary. Like I said, you have to do things ordinary coppers wouldn't, and what better way than taking part? No one suspected a thing, not at any point.'

Huntington exhaled, and looked across to where the lad had now knocked over the mop bucket and was trying to dry the floor with kitchen towels. 'It doesn't rest easy with me. I mean, the intel guys have done some buying of gear in the past, but there's always an arrest out of it, an instant result. I assume with this there is a period of time where we would be dealing drugs to the scum of Epping Hill while we wait for the main suppliers to rear their heads? And where would we get the drugs from in the first place?'

Jacobs ignored the question. 'The beauty of this job is that it gives you back control of the estate. In the past you've bought from a dealer who's got a few wraps of something naughty in his pocket. He gets nicked, and before he's even in custody someone's taken his place. If you want to make a difference, and I mean a *real* difference, you've got to look at getting to the people that are bringing the stuff in and giving it to these idiots. Six months, sir. Run it as a pilot operation for six months, but I promise you we will have made a massive difference within four.'

'And the drugs? You didn't answer my question,' Huntington persisted.

'The drugs we get from the competition. Like I say, we go in there and make a bit of a noise. The uniform boys out on the street have already given us a reputation, so we'll be in business very quickly.'

'In business?'

Jacobs smiled. 'Sorry, bad choice of words.'

'So we would need to select the team from the force here?'

'Well, yes. The success of the pilot depends on the personnel in your team. However, I happen to know that some, if not all, of the members of the city team would transfer down here if they felt they might be able to see a pilot through.'

Huntington dabbed at his lips with a serviette. 'Transfer them in?'

'It would make sense. I could have a word. That way we get a team who've done something like this before. They can avoid repeating previous mistakes and really hit the ground running. It also takes away the problem of uniform officers recognising colleagues and blowing the operation, and it's easier for your books because you can just transfer them straight in as civvies.'

Huntington nodded 'I would need to meet them. They would have to understand that there are rules, and that they're not in the city now. I'd need to be satisfied before I give them the green light.'

'Of course. I'll arrange a meeting with Ed Kavski. He ran the team the last time around and he would be a key acquisition — he's ex-military and he's a good man.'

Huntington looked at Jacobs. 'I'm not sure this job needs a *good* man.'

Chapter 9

'Taxi for you?' The taxi driver poked his head out of his window, looking at a figure sheltering in a shabby telephone box. A fine drizzle fell on Epping Hill.

'Well, if it isn't Effingell's finest taxi service!'

'How you doing, friend?' The taxi driver watched the man slide to the middle of the rear bench.

'Can't complain, you know how it is. Where's the accent from, man?'

'Iran my friend, my home once.' The taxi driver sighed.

'And now look at you. Sat on the outskirts of Effingell.'

'Yes indeed, sir. Now, where can I take you today?'

The man leant forward, closer to the mirror. 'Well now, I'm not entirely sure about that. I was hoping you might know. Didn't someone tell you what my destination should be?'

'Someone told me?'

'That's right. Someone might have mentioned that you work for *me*?' The last part of the sentence was almost whispered. The driver looked in the mirror. The man was leaning back into the rear seat. The taxi driver suddenly remembered a conversation with one of the Polish drivers, who had told him a story about picking someone up who didn't know where they were going. He told him that he was expected to know the destination. All the drivers had done it. It was like a trial run, where the passenger worked out if he liked you or not. He said that those the passenger liked got more work — different to the normal cabbying, but it paid well. Those he didn't like weren't treated so well. He'd heard of them getting assaulted, more than once, until they got the message and stopped working the taxis.

The car slowed while the driver hesitated. 'So I work for you, too?' His throat felt dry and tight.

'Well, you don't have to. This is a free country.'

'Okay, well, I know where to take you then, sir. And I have something for you. I keep it in the back, tucked down the seat.'

The man turned and tugged at his seat. The driver looked back to check if any cars were following. He'd heard stories from the other drivers, those that had been there far longer than his two months. They talked about undercover cops with baseball caps driving bashed-up old Vauxhall Novas or Citroën Saxos, a cigarette on the go and a young girl in the passenger seat. You would pass them by and go about your business, not realising that they were checking your plate, watching your fares or preparing to pounce.

'Good work.' The man had found what he was looking for and sat down again. He was handling a brown padded envelope, gently moving his hands up and down it, feeling every bulge. He looked out of the window.

'And the rain has stopped. Ain't that just the way. So, Iranian, you said?'

'Yes.'

'How long you been over here then?'

'Eight months.' He kept his answers short. He wasn't looking for a conversation.

'Eight months in Effingell.' The passenger sniffed and looked out of the window.

'No, I come here two months ago. I went to Gravesend for a while. They put us in a communal house, but now I have a house with just me and my family.'

'Big family?'

'With my wife, and I have three children.'

'Three fucking children! Three fucking children and you gotta feed them all, clothe the little fuckers and get them their fucking iPhones on a taxi driver's money. I tell you, I got speaking to an Indian fella, he was saying that they come here for a better way of life for their children, to be a little better off, like.'

The driver made listening noises and prayed for the traffic lights to change. They were nearly there.

'So the Indian fella's kids, they ain't seen nothing like some of the shit we get over here. But now they get to see it all, maybe have a quick go on someone's fucking X-Box, or realise that the way you get fanny over here is to have the latest gear, you understand? And now all they want is what every other fucker's got. Do you see my point? We're fucking spoilt, see, we get what we want, and especially the kids.' The man was leaning forward again.

'I think I see.'

'No, you don't. Way I see it, you come 'ere for a better life and it ain't for me to say whether you're right or wrong, but you do come 'ere, and you bring your family and you *are* richer. You get a house to keep yourself dry and warm and some cash to put food on the table and in Iran, maybe that's a rich man's life, but here, you're nothing. And that means that your family, when they get old enough to understand, they're gonna see you as nothing too.'

The brakes squeaked as the taxi pulled up in Newington Crescent, level with a row of garages. You could leave it by foot, along a small alleyway that ran along the back of the garages and out into terraced streets. Just like he had been told.

'This is the place then, sir.'

The man in the back looked around. 'So it is.'

He undid the top two buttons of his jacket, pulled it open and slipped the parcel into the inside pocket. He took his time to do it up, and then his right hand touched a pocket on the outside of his jacket. He shuffled along to directly behind the driver's seat. The driver tensed and reached for the door handle, watching the mirror. The man pushed the back door open and straightened his coat before bending and knocking on the window. The driver opened it halfway.

'I understand this is your first fare, so you won't know how it all works.' The man placed an unlit cigarette in his mouth. 'You want one?'

'No, thank you.'

The man thrust a ten-pound note through the window, which dropped onto his lap.

'That's the fare. You keep the change now. I enjoyed the chat. I hope you listened to me, though. Where you are now, it's all about the money and there's plenty out there to be earned. I always need people like you, people that know when they're on to a good thing and can keep their mouths shut, you understand?'

The driver nodded.

'Sure you do. There's no risk for you. If the police ever stop your car and find anything, it's just a parcel tucked down the back seat, nothing to do with you. You just tell the fuckers that you drive a cab, you ain't got no control on people sitting in the back and stuffing envelopes down there now, have you? Trust me, it's been done a hundred times and the driver is always the one that walks. Most of the people you see out driving taxis are doing their bit for me, it's no skin off their nose, see.'

The driver nodded again.

'Later, when your shift's done, you'll have a look down the back seat. You'll see that one of your passengers will have left an envelope for you, you understand? This is your first time, friend, so the package is sweet this time round. You won't always make that, but keep your nose clean, your head down and get the job done and you'll earn a week's wage in a fucking heartbeat. That okay with you?'

'Yes, sure. I understand. Thank you.'

The man pulled up his coat collar and lowered himself to the driver's level. The cigarette bobbed in his lips as he spoke. 'You'd be a mug to fuck up this sort of opportunity. Just think of that family of yours, you understand? The only job of a father and a husband is to put food on the table, right? And keep his family safe.'

The man stood up, thrust both hands into his jacket pockets and strode off. The driver exhaled and watched him walk away. The driver checked himself in the mirror and wiped the sweat from his forehead with his sleeve. He exhaled again and stepped out of the car. He checked that the crescent was empty, then opened the back door and leaned in to thrust his hands down the seat, as the man had done before him. Sure enough, his fingertips touched paper. He pulled the parcel out. He looked around again, seeing no one, but still he reached through the car to place the parcel on the front passenger seat. He moved quickly back to the driver's seat, pulled the door shut and picked up the parcel. Giving a last check all around him, he opened it up. He reached in and pulled the contents out into the light. Twenty pound notes, crisp and new looking. He counted them in hundreds, more money than he had ever seen passing from one hand to the other.

Suddenly there was a thump on the window. A large figure loomed and leered through the glass. It pointed a long finger and thumped again. The driver jumped back. The figure shouted through the glass, and yanked the door open. A sudden draught of air picked up the bank notes and sent them flying off the driver's lap.

'Fucking idiot!'

The driver was knocked sideways by a blow to the side of his head. More of the notes fell off his lap and into the foot-well. The door slammed shut again. The car shook as someone got in the back, and then there was silence.

The driver lifted a hand to the side of his throbbing face. 'Just take it. I don't want trouble,' he said. His voice quivered. He didn't want to turn and see who was in the back. He knew from home that if you looked at them and they thought you might know who they were, it was worse, you might give them no choice.

'I gave you clear instructions, didn't I?'

'You come back?'

'Of course I did. And you failed my test. I told you, didn't I? I said to wait for your shift to end, that any packages down the back of the seat should be left there. You get stopped now, how you gonna explain five hundred quid in wads of twenties? Then the gavvers, see, they look at who you've had in your cab, they link you to me and all of a sudden I'm in a whole world of shit. But that ain't gonna happen. Have I made myself clear?'

The driver nodded.

'Now come on, you nodded the last time, which in this country means yes. Clearly you hadn't taken it all on board. You know it means yes, right?'

'Yes, I do, I know, and yes, I understand you, sir.'

'You understand me. Good. What's your name?'

'Soheil. Soheil Afshar.'

'Well, okay then, Soheil. We got off to a bad start, or at least you got off to a fucking stinker, but you still got potential, all right? Now then, I can't make it any clearer. You follow my instructions to the letter in future, Soheil, because despite my chipper outlook, I am a fucking horrible piece of shit and I will not hesitate in making an example of you *and* your family to get my message across. So, is it clear now?'

Soheil nodded.

'That means yes in your culture, right?'

'Yes, I understand.'

'Well, that's good. I only wish all of them spoke English as well as you do.'

The rear door opened and the figure was once again standing at the roadside lifting a cigarette to his lips. He tapped on the driver's window and Soheil lowered it, all the way this time. 'You'll hear from me, and no doubt *about* me. My name is Smith. You remember that.'

Soheil nodded. He watched Smith walk away. He bent, gathered up the money and stuffed it back in the envelope and down his jumper. He would head straight back home before continuing with his day's work. The last thing he wanted now was for the police to pull him over and ask questions about the bundles of cash, his bruised cheek, and the man called Smith.

Chapter 10

'Not a big fan of the quiet life, are we, PC Kavski?' Inspector Andrea Watts stood glaring at the PC who had been summoned to her office.

Ed Kavski smiled. 'What would be the fun in that?'

'Ah yes, *fun*. That just about sums up your attitude towards your job, the police as a whole and your own safety. I don't really give too much of a shit about your safety, and why should I when you clearly don't care about it yourself?'

Ed raised an eyebrow. Andrea had to be under a lot of pressure for her to swear. It sounded odd in her Australian twang, softened by the twenty years that had passed since her move.

'But the way you go about things, someone else is going to get seriously hurt. Michael Hunt could very well—'

'Michael Hunt is an idiot who was playing games with your negotiator.'

'Michael Hunt could very well have been dangling that child out of the window for all you knew!' Andrea flopped heavily into her seat. She expelled a long sigh, and Ed had a feeling he might be over the worst.

Sure enough, she came back softer. 'You just don't think, Ed. You go in, all guns blazing, with no regard whatsoever for the rules of engagement.'

'With respect, ma'am, that job was at a stalemate and I got it done. Within five minutes of our arrival, our man was in custody.'

'But Ed, you have to understand that the outcome is not the most important thing with police processes. We have to be able to show that we followed procedure, that we went by the book the whole way through and cannot be criticised, even if it all turns to rat shit. And Ed, *you* are the only one that didn't act according to those procedures. I simply do not understand why you refuse to follow orders.'

Andrea was leaning forward. One elbow rested on the table while the other hand was busy unclipping her tie and undoing her top button. She looked every bit like someone who had been facing questions from above as to why she couldn't control her staff and what she was going to do about it.

'Ed, you leave me no choice. Your Taser ticket is immediately revoked and you need to hand it in to me now. I'm also putting you back in uniform, and you'll be working with a response team until the investigations into this incident, as well as last week's, have been completed.'

'Last week?' Ed looked puzzled.

'Last week, Ed, when you Tasered a sleeping man.'

'Ah, yeah. Well, as a matter of fact, that man was very much awake.'

'Even if that was the case there can be no denying that he was naked and lying in bed.'

'He was, true, but I weren't gonna fuck about letting him get up and dressed before I gave him the warning. I was authorised to Taser the bloke.'

'Yes, if necessary, in order to control him, not in order to prevent him sitting up and asking who the hell had just burst into his bedroom!'

Ed crossed his arms. 'Expert in unarmed combat is the intel we got given.'

Andrea waved a hand. 'Forget it. Save it all for the professional standards people, because they're going to want to speak to you about it. The superintendent might want to talk to you as well — he's still batting off questions from the press about today's incident.'

'And in the meantime you're busting me back to section. How long is that for?'

'Yes, I am, and I had to fight to make that happen. Some very influential people were looking at either suspending you completely or sticking you behind a desk for the foreseeable future. But make no bones about it, Ed, if you step even slightly out of line, you *will* be back in the station sat behind a desk, auditing crime reports ten hours a day.'

Ed wiped his mouth, considered a reply but changed his mind. He was glad to be excused before he said something he would regret. He stepped out of her office and looked around at the clerks and civilians who were indeed involved in computer work for ten hours a day. He uttered a silent thanks to Andrea. He knew that she would fight for him. She had already, on a couple of occasions in the short time he had worked for her. But he knew eventually even she would give up on him.

Ed took the lift to the ground floor where he stopped as his phone vibrated in his jeans pocket.

'Well, this is a blast from the past!' Ed smiled.

'Yeah, what's it been, three whole months?' Inspector Craig Jacobs sounded chipper.

'Hang on, mate, stay there.' Ed hurried outside and walked until he was satisfied that he was out of earshot.

'Inspector,' he said. 'Has it really only been three months? Feels like an age since I was doing a proper job.'

'How are you, Ed?'

'Shit, mate. And you?'

'Similar I suppose. What's your problem? Let me guess, they don't appreciate you up in the north of the county?'

Ed cast a look back at the building. 'They don't seem to appreciate my methods, put it that way.'

'I'm having the same experience mate, I'm almost thinking we made a mistake leaving the big city. You getting a hard time?'

'Well, I'm getting the results but I can't seem to keep myself out of trouble. Seems they don't have the same sort of attitude to getting the job done as we had in London, you know? It's got to the point where I think we might not be compatible.'

'Well now, that's music to my ears, Ed, because if you were having a good time up there on the periphery, I would have had a battle on my hands. This way you get to come quietly.'

'You what? Where am I coming quietly?'

'To work for me.'

Ed made sure he was facing away from the station. 'We're on already?'

'I don't hang about. We can have another crack at what we didn't finish in our previous life. I won't go into detail now, but I'll sort out a meeting in the next couple of days.'

'Really? Next few days?'

'Yes, mate, could be as soon as tomorrow. Keep your phone with you and I'll be in touch.'

Jacobs ended the call.

Ed grinned. All of his frustration was immediately gone. He reckoned he would be back doing what he did best in a very short time.

Chapter 11

Smith sat in a haze of cigarette smoke. The large flat screen showing MTV was the only light source in the room. He sighed as his mobile phone trilled. The number was withheld.

'Yeah?' Smith's eyes narrowed against the smoke of his cigarette.

'Smith, it's Marlowe.'

'Marlowe! Long time since you felt the need to call me. What's the story?' The sofa creaked as Smith settled back into a more comfortable position.

'Listen, Smith, I just called to tell you what I know. I ain't stirring no shit and I ain't saying nothing about nothing, this is just what I see.'

Smith picked up the remote and muted the TV. He swept his dark fringe from his eyes. 'What you got, friend?'

'It's just that we've got this new guy driving with us and I hear that he's driving for you too.'

'The raghead?'

'Soheil.'

'That's the fella.' Smith heard movement from upstairs. His girlfriend flushed the toilet.

'Yeah, well, I was working the other day. I went past the cop shop in Langthorne and I see Soheil.'

'What, he got himself nicked?'

'That's the thing, he weren't nicked, at least it didn't look like it. They let him out the front for a start and some lad, a copper, he walked him out and shook his hand right there in the street. When have you ever been walked out the front and shook hands with the filth? Something's not right there. I wanted you to know.'

Smith lit another cigarette. 'You think he was talking to them?'

'No doubt of it. Just no way of knowing what he was saying.'

'He was on his own?'

'I couldn't see anyone else with him. Like I said, I ain't looking at causing no shit for anyone. I just thought you'd want to know. We've all got a lot riding on this, and if he's in there talking we might all be fucked, you know?'

'I appreciate it, you did good. Do the others know about this?'

'I spoke to Tim today but that's all. I wanted a second opinion like. He said I should give you a bell.'

'Okay, cheers for the call, Marlowe. I'll sort it.'

Smith put the phone down on the arm of the sofa.

A voice called from upstairs. 'Who was that, hon?'

'Christ,' muttered Smith. 'Work!'

The stairs creaked. Smith's girlfriend wore one of his old shirts and nothing else. Her hair was tousled. 'You all right?'

'I said, it's just work!' he said without looking up, and she backed out of the room. Smith waited for her to leave and picked up his phone.

'Smudge, wassup?' The voice was blurry with sleep.

'Tone, you free this evening?'

'Can be, mate.'

'Come to mine, whenever.'

'Okay, what you got?'

Smith dragged on his cigarette. 'I could do with your assistance, mate. I need to deliver a message.'

Tone gave a knowing laugh. 'Just let me eat, man, and I'm with yer.'

Chapter 12

'How's the boy?' George Elms asked his wife, Sarah.

She moved to sit on the bed besides him. She'd just pulled the curtains wide open, causing George to blink at the sudden sunlight.

'The boy? Look, I thought we'd discussed this.'

George rolled over and chuckled. 'I told you, if it's a girl you can stick it back in. I mean, what use is a girl?'

Sarah gave her husband's bare back a light slap. 'I'm going to tell her what you said about her when she gets here.'

'I'll tell her now.' George moved across to his wife and rested his ear against her bump. He pretended to listen. 'I'm not sure he's up,' he said, looking up at Sarah.

'Maybe *she's* having a lie-in.'

George manoeuvred himself so he was looking down at Sarah's stomach. He lifted the maternity T-shirt. 'Right, you in there, if you're a girl then I suggest you stay right where you are, got it?' He looked up at Sarah. 'Anything?'

'What do you mean, "anything?" She's been moving around a lot this morning actually.'

'Any movement now, though, any sign that *he* might have got the message?'

Sarah placed her hands either side of the bump, 'I think I just felt a thumbs-up.'

'That'll do me.' George jumped out of bed, spun to face Sarah, and put his hands on his hips. 'You fancy seeing if we can shake him up a little, maybe prompt him to surface?'

Sarah looked him up and down. 'To be honest with you, George, I'm really rather looking forward to getting this young fella out now, before I consider putting anything else in.'

'You have such a lovely way with words.' George looked thoughtful. 'I guess I should have a shower. I assume you have plans for me today, hence the wake up?'

With a grunt, Sarah put her feet on the floor. 'I do indeed. Your mission, should you choose to accept it, is to pick up your daughter from school at three. Can't remember the last time you did that. She'll be ever so excited to see her dad waiting for her.'

George smiled. 'Now *that* I can manage.' He turned towards the door to the en-suite bathroom.

'And then there's food shopping . . .' Sarah called out. George stopped in his tracks.

'Ah, there's the catch. You know I'm no good at Tesco.'

'Charley knows what we need. She'll be there to help you.'

'Charley? Our six-year-old daughter knows what we need? She'll help *me*?'

'Exactly. So you don't need to worry.'

George nodded and stepped into the bathroom. As he turned on the shower, he called back, 'You know you just called him "fella," right?'

* * *

George was still grinning as he took in his reflection. He had started the shower running, and the mirror was already starting to steam up. He had left his watch on the windowsill, the afternoon was half gone. He stepped into the shower just as he heard his wife calling out. He couldn't make out what she wanted and he lifted his face to the warmth. She would shout it louder if it was important.

'George!' He still didn't reply. The shower suddenly stopped. There was a switch on the wall on the outside that cut the power to the shower. George tugged the curtain back, white suds ran down his face and forced his eyes shut. He spat soap with his reply, 'Sorry, dear, did you say something?'

'Yes, *dear*, I was about to ask if you were going into work this evening, or if we might be able to spend it together as a family for once. Maybe this time *you* can be the one that rushes me to the hospital for a false alarm. And you need to hurry up if you're getting Charley.'

George brushed suds from his face. 'I see, and to hurry me up, you delay me even further by turning off the shower?'

'That's correct.'

'Okay, and I don't have to be back at work until tomorrow morning, as I put in a double. Is that to your satisfaction, milady?'

'It'll do.' Sarah smiled. She switched the shower back on and George squealed. The water came back cold.

* * *

Charley's face lit up when she saw her dad's Laguna parked up close to the school gates. George stepped out of the car and acknowledged a community support officer monitoring the gates, who recognised him despite his casual wear. Charley broke into a run, her blue gingham school dress flapping. George caught her up and spun her round.

'How's my little Char-Char?'

'Why are you here?' Charley said into his ear.

'You know I'm your dad, right?'

Charley grinned. 'You're silly.'

'We both know that, Little Lady. Listen, Mummy's sending us shopping this afternoon, but I reckon we could just go get some ice cream and pic 'n' mix and then pretend you forgot — what do you think?'

Charley giggled. 'Noooo! Mummy told me what we need and she said I had to make sure you behaved.'

'Well, good luck with that.' He opened the car passenger door and held it for her, pretending to doff his cap. 'Your Highness.' But as he closed the door, George's smile faded. He had met the stare of a man standing on the other side of the road, leaning against a tall fence. Something passed between them, and then the man pushed off the fence and strode away.

George thought quickly, then pulled open the passenger door and leaned in. 'Charley, I gotta go and speak to someone. I'll be two minutes.' He walked over to the community support officer.

'I need to borrow your radio.'

The officer unclipped the radio hanging from her belt. 'Thanks. Listen, I think I've just seen someone who really shouldn't be here. Can I ask you to stand with my daughter — she's in the car. I'll just call it in and then I'll be back.'

The officer nodded and George set off. The man was now almost a hundred metres ahead. His hands were thrust deep in the pockets of his oversized duffle-coat. He had pulled up his scarf, covering his mouth. George jogged after him. The man glanced back and broke into a run.

The man clearly knew the area, for he made for an alleyway that led to the school playing fields and woodland beyond. George knew it too. It was a good place to disappear.

By the time George emerged from the alleyway the man was halfway across the field, but George had gained on him. At the entrance to the woods, the man looked back over his shoulder and saw George closing in on him. He stopped running and held his hands up.

'Will! Interesting to find you here.'

Will was panting. 'I was just walking past . . . I live near, you know that. I was walking home.'

'Walking home via the primary school?' George put the radio up to his mouth and pressed the button to speak. 'Sergeant Elms to Control.' Both men stared at it, waiting for a response.

'*Last caller, go ahead.*' The operator sounded surprised. The radio would have shown them an ID assigned to a police community support officer at a primary school, so they must have been wondering why this call came from an off-duty detective sergeant.

'Control, this is Sergeant Elms. I am on a PCSO's radio and I've stopped a male. Received so far?'

Will wrung his hands and shifted from one foot to another. 'I can't go back! I can't go back there. They're gonna kill me in there, they said so!'

George recalled the interview at Langthorne House. Will, a forty-two-year-old man with a pot belly and scraggly hair, had spent most of the time in pieces.

'*So far,*' replied Control.

'I have a male, William Forley, apprehended in the field at St Mary's Primary School. Can you run him through please and confirm details? I believe he's on licence. He should have a prison recall tagged to any breach of his conditions. I'll also need a local unit to my location, please.'

The wind was strong in the open field, snatching the voices away. George turned his ear to the radio to hear the response. There was a beep to confirm that a reply was coming and then a blow struck the side of his head. It brought him down onto one knee. As he turned to look at his attacker, a fist connected with the bridge of his nose. Will got in a couple more shots before George was able to raise a forearm and push him away. He got to his feet, but Will came at him again, punching him in the midriff and causing George to bend forward, winded. Will aimed a final hit into the side of George's head, and broke into a run, heading for the woods.

George picked himself up, and propelled by rage, broke into a sprint, soon catching up with the fleeing man. Will made it to a gap in the fence where a worn path led into a woodland trail. George shoved Will hard, sending him crashing into the fence post. He sank to the ground. George loomed over him.

'What the fuck are you doing?' George landed a punch in Will's face using the hand gripping the solid radio, adding to the force of the blow. 'You want to fight me now?'

He hit Will again, and met no resistance. Will was beyond fighting back. George held his fist in the air and fought against the desire to smash Will's stupid fucking kiddie-fiddling face. His face throbbed where the blows were already starting to swell. Over the radio Control was demanding a welfare check on him. He kicked Will hard in the stomach.

'Control, this is DS Elms, I'm all in order here. The male decided he fancied a fight. He is now detained and has been nicked for assaulting a police officer. Is there an ETA on that other unit, please? I don't have any cuffs with me.'

'They've just arrived, Sarge.'

George peered out across the field and made out two uniform officers jogging towards him. He held up his hand in greeting.

'They're gonna kill me if I go back,' Will whined. 'Every day. They beat me every day.'

George looked down at him. 'And yet you couldn't stop yourself, could you? You're a danger to every one of those kids, because you just can't help yourself, can you?' He turned to face the uniform officers.

'All right, Sarge?' George recognised the female officer, PC Jones. She'd once smashed a door for him when he'd headed up a search team. She brushed past him and rolled Will onto his stomach, with his face pushed into the frozen mud. She wrenched his arms up behind him and put on the cuffs.

The male officer, whose name tag read PC Carpenter, looked at George. 'You okay, Sarge?'

George looked down. His shoes were scuffed and sodden, his jeans were muddy at the knees, and his polo shirt had come untucked. It had been ripped at the neck. His head and ribs felt tender to the touch and his temple throbbed. 'I'm okay, yeah.'

'Right, you'll need to make a statement. Do you want to do it at the nick or I can do it at your home?'

George checked his watch. 'I need to get my daughter home. I left her with a PCSO.'

'She's fine. It was the PCSO who pointed out where you'd gone. They were playing a game of I Spy.'

George was relieved. 'I'll take some statement forms with me and write it up. You can just pop in and nab it a bit later, if that's okay?'

The officer nodded. He and his colleague hauled Will to his feet. George's cheek had already swelled so that he could see it out of the corner of his eye. One of his eyes was half shut and the front of his shirt was sopping wet. He shivered.

'Have you said the words?' PC Jones asked.

'No, he's all yours.'

'Will, you're nicked, mate, for assaulting a police officer — and you're in breach of your licence, aren't you?' She paused but Will did not respond. 'You do not have to say anything, but it may harm your defence if you do not mention something which you later rely on in court.

Anything you do say may be given in evidence. Do you understand?'

'I can't go back there. I'll kill myself if I go back there.' Will's voice was barely audible, and the two officers made no reply. They took him under the shoulders and walked him back across the field.

George returned to his car, where the shock on his daughter's face was clear. He looked in the rear-view mirror. His face was tender and red, his eye already turning black. 'Right then,' he said. 'Let's go home and see your mother.'

Chapter 13

'Well, you really do look like shit.' Superintendent Helen Webb paused at the door to her office.

George rose to his feet, and managed a smile. 'Thank you, ma'am.'

'On a normal day, I would say that you ought to be at home, but this isn't a normal day, is it?'

'I've had very few of those since I was assigned Epping Hill, ma'am.'

'Quite.' Helen went to her seat and picked up her phone.

'Jean, could we possibly have a couple of coffees in here, please? Thank you.' She looked at George. 'Coffee okay?'

'Fine.'

Helen replaced the receiver. 'In relation to William Forley, he was put before the next available court and was sent back to prison for breaching his licence. Apparently they were able to get statements from a few other parents who had seen him there at least twice. We can be sure he was building up to offending again. Who knows, perhaps he was planning something much worse.'

'How long does he go back for?'

'The rest of his sentence is three years. He should serve the lot, too — they won't put him out on licence again. It was a good result, George. You did well.'

'It's not long enough though, is it?'

'Perhaps not. But we aren't responsible for that side of things, are we?' Helen changed the subject. 'Right, you know what happened last night?'

'The assault? I don't know the details.'

'Soheil Afshar, our victim, is a thirty-two-year-old Iranian male. He was found outside Premier Taxis in the Epping Hill Estate at about four o'clock this morning.'

'Iranian? Hate crime?'

'We don't know at this stage, we haven't been able to speak to him.'

'That taxi service is twenty-four hour, right?' George said.

'Yes, it is, and there wasn't much business at that time of night, as you can imagine. Three taxi drivers were on and all were inside the office. Add to that one operator and we've got four witnesses.'

'I know that rank well. It's got a waiting room and a counter downstairs and the drivers' room upstairs. All are glass-fronted and the visibility out onto the road is very good.'

Helen nodded. 'And everyone automatically looks out when a car pulls up, especially at that time in the morning.'

'A car?' George asked.

'The operator said that a car pulled up and our Mr Afshar was pushed out of the back, but that's all we have.'

'Type of car?'

'Nothing.'

There was a knock on the door and Jean entered, carrying a tray with two coffees, a sugar bowl and a small plate of chocolate digestives. 'We had some left over in the tea fund,' she said.

Helen smiled. 'Thank you, Jean.'

'And none of the drivers saw anything?'

'So they said.'

'We got their details though, right?'

'Yes, of course.' Helen leaned towards him. 'Are you thinking of giving them another go?'

'Well, yes,' George replied, 'but I say nick all four of them for the assault. Unless someone can tell me different, this man was found outside the building they were sitting in. If they won't give us any details, maybe we should put them in a position where it's in their interest to talk.'

'They knew him, too.'

'The victim?'

'Yes, he works there. He's a taxi driver.'

George stirred his coffee. 'Really? Well, there you are then, all the more reason to bring them in. Was he on the clock at the time?'

'No, he finished at six o'clock. Oh, and he also works here.'

'Here?'

'He's an interpreter. He's only been used a couple of times but the last one was just a couple of days ago. He was in the custody area assisting an Iraqi male. Seems he speaks several of the Middle Eastern languages fluently and his English is excellent.'

'An interpreter? So he's topping up his money here — good money too, I understand. You think there's a link to him being here and then turning up as our victim?'

'I really don't know. We won't learn anything until we get to talk to him.'

'Not necessarily, ma'am. If we go scoop up our four witnesses and put some pressure on them, we might be able to find out a little bit more at least.'

Helen picked up her phone. 'Jean, could you arrange for the patrol sergeant to come up here, please. Yes, a matter of urgency. Thank you. Oh, no, don't worry. We won't be needing an extra coffee.'

George smiled. 'She's thorough.'

'She's terrified is what she is. Spends all day at Graham's beck and call. Who wouldn't be?'

'Well, you, for one.'

Helen gave a ghost of a smile. 'Well, that is very true, George.'

'How bad are the injuries?'

Helen's smile faded away. 'Well, when he was first found there was talk of them being life-threatening, but we believe he's out of those particular woods now.'

'That bad?'

'He looked it. He was in and out of consciousness and the paramedics said they suspected internal bleeding, head and body, but it's mostly a lot of bruising. He has taken quite a beating and the head bleeds a lot, as you will know.' Helen took a long sip of her coffee.

'Are you okay, ma'am?'

Helen shook her head. 'Epping Hill, George. Tell me, do you think there's more we could be doing with that place?'

'That is a big question. It's basically down to town planning, council decisions, political pressures, housing demands, job losses. We can't be responsible for those things, ma'am. All we can do is react to what goes on there, and we're as good as we can be at that. No one helps out, and there are never any witnesses.'

'React? You think we should be more proactive?'

'I think it's the only way we're going to have an impact.'

'You have some ideas?'

'Some.'

'No one knows the Epping Hill Estate better than you, George. Have you run your ideas past Graham?' George took a gulp of his coffee. 'You can be as candid with me as you like, George. This is off the record. I know that Graham can be . . . difficult.'

'I haven't, ma'am. I mean, I wouldn't waste my time.'

Helen nodded. 'You need to brief your team. I want them to be the ones interviewing those four. Once you've done that, come back and speak to me about some of your ideas for ridding us of the Epping Hill problem.'

George swallowed the dregs of his coffee and stood up. 'I'll see what I can do.'

'Keep me updated with the results of those interviews, won't you?'

'I will.'

'And, George . . .' George stopped as he was walking out. 'I know you're stretched, so try and get your team to take on the Soheil assault. Your personal priority remains the bus attack. I need regular updates to pass up the line — the media is still all over us.'

'Understood. I'm due to speak to the girl today in hospital before she goes into surgery. I've got some enquiries to do at the bus station and other bits and bobs, so hopefully I'll have a positive update for you later.'

'I'm sure you will.' Helen picked up a biscuit.

Chapter 14

The man known to the Effingell underworld as "Smith," pulled the door shut and stepped into the shadows. His breath floated away in the dim glow from the street lights. The cold nipped at his ears and he silently cursed himself for forgetting his hat. He tugged at the elastic hairband holding back his stubby ponytail. Smith left the shadows, satisfied that no one was watching. He walked down a stone path and crunched onto gravel, sticking close to tall garden fences, out of the light.

Smith's careful walk took him to the rear of a house located two up from a corner plot. He stood still, watching and listening for any movement, and checked his watch. Five twenty, as usual. Smith liked his journeys to coincide with the evening rush hour. That way his car would be lost in the traffic, just another commuter sitting in a dark, metal box with steamed-up windows.

The garage door was chipped and peeling, revealing rusty metal. It had slipped off its rungs on one side and he had to lift it up to open it. He squeezed up the side of the Volkswagen Passat. The engine came to life first time, and Smith carefully backed out of the garage, then edged along the bumpy, potholed road as he manoeuvred round the outside of the car park. He noted movement at the back entrance to Pussycats — a massage parlour with a long list of unadvertised extras. A hooded figure stepped into the brightly lit interior and was gone. Smith switched the headlights on and drove the short distance to a main thoroughfare, where he joined the rest of the traffic. He was moving in the general direction of Coldred Industrial Estate.

Coldred Industrial Estate was a relatively new addition to the area and could hardly have been built at a worse time. The recent global slump had touched just about every business, but had whipped the mat right out from under the manufacturing and transport companies, both of which were a significant part of Coldred's revenue. Numerous units now stood vacant, deathly quiet under a full moon.

Smith drove his Passat into the grounds of one of the larger units. A sign reading 'WATT HAULAGE' in tall yellow letters still clung to the grey metal front. Smith turned his lights off and drove past the unit, round to the back, where he stopped and turned off the engine. The air outside felt even colder after the warmth of the car, and he wrapped his arms across his chest, his breath visible in the moon's white light. Smith watched and waited. He got back in the car, pulling the door shut and starting the engine for a blast of heat.

Suddenly he could see headlights. It looked like two large vehicles, one a 4x4, the other a pickup. They were approaching fast, much faster than expected and there were not normally two of them. Something was wrong, but he had no time to react. The cars came round the side of the unit and split up, one sped round the back of his car while the other swerved to the right before turning and accelerating, heading straight for the passenger side of Smith's stationary Volkswagen.

'Ah, fuck!' Smith got into first gear, but in his panic he slipped the clutch, stalling the car. The 4x4 smashed into the passenger door. Smith was thrown first towards the impact then the other way, as the side airbags exploded. There was a sudden pain in his right shoulder. The passenger door bent in towards him. The car shook as the 4x4 moved slowly backwards with a shriek of metal. It skidded to a stop fifteen metres away, its engine revving. Regaining his senses, Smith fiddled with the keys in the ignition, until finally the engine turned over and the car fired. Then there were more bright lights, but this time on the offside. He turned his head in their direction. The lights were high, and closing in quickly. The vehicle veered at the last second, so the impact was centred on the door directly behind him. The car spun, rear first, as the pickup powered through. Metal ground against metal and the steering wheel airbag inflated. Smith was whiplashed at an angle, colliding with the dash. The gear stick dug up into his chest, and his face was burnt by the charge in the airbag.

Shaken and disorientated, Smith sat up. He put a hand to his forehead and it came away covered in blood. His head throbbed and he struggled for air. He realised he'd been winded. His right shoulder screamed in agony every time he tried to move, and the arm hung, limp. Smith peered out through the car's smashed windows, but the night was dark and silent once again.

The driver's door was jammed shut and Smith had to kick his way out. His legs were unsteady and he hauled himself to his feet with his left arm. He bent double and retched. Then he heard a car approaching again, this time more slowly. He stared into the headlights and stood still, waiting.

Two car doors opened. The headlights dipped to scorched rings. He could make out a black BMW.

'Lawrence,' a voice said.

He'd spent a great deal of time and effort hiding his real name. He recognised the voice, though.

'Mr Baurman. I remember when we used to just shake hands when we met.' Smith spat blood.

'You're a fucking idiot, Lawrence. You have not made me happy.' Baurman lit a cigarette and revealed an untidy beard.

'I guessed I might have pissed someone off.' Smith tapped his own pockets for his cigarettes, and Baurman offered him the packet, his fashionably battered brown leather jacket creaking as he stretched forward. Smith took a cigarette and accepted a light.

'The Iraqi,' said Baurman, 'tell me your thought process behind that.'

Smith exhaled smoke. 'Afshar? He's Iranian,' he replied, immediately regretting his correction.

'I see. How many times have we met in person, Lawrence?'

'Twice maybe?'

'Twice. And you think I have come out to see you in the freezing cold, just to argue about his fucking *nationality*?' Smith had always made considerable effort to avoid upsetting Baurman. His temper was legendary and Smith, who abided by few rules, knew that you shouldn't cross this man.

'No, I don't suppose you did.'

'Your thought process?' Baurman said again.

'I had a phone call. I get told that he's seen coming out of the cop shop. He's new to the business, see. I thought he might've made a bad decision and told them what he knew, so I made a statement to the rest of them that that wasn't fucking acceptable. It was a show of strength.'

'A show of strength?'

'Yes.'

'Well, it certainly was a show, but for whose benefit? I have my sources in Epping Hill, and they tell me the police have been at the taxi rank. It is currently cordoned off while forensic officers in white *fucking* paper suits get out

82

their fine tooth-combs. This could become a murder charge, and what then? More police resources sniffing around *my* business asking questions of *my* drivers and potentially nicking them for what *you* did. Have you any idea what a man will say who is facing a murder charge?' Smith was silent. 'They will say *anything*, Lawrence. They might even tell the truth. Far from warning these men off from talking about you, and more importantly about *me*, you have put them in a position where they just might have to.'

Smith didn't move. He had become more accustomed to the dark and could now make out Baurman and the two men who flanked him. They were both middle-aged and impeccably dressed, with no discernible necks. Their bald heads appeared to sit directly on top of their broad shoulders. Baurman, on the other hand, wore an untidy beard which merged with his untidy hair. He habitually wore jeans with short-sleeve shirts, and tonight a leather jacket hung open, covering a wiry, muscular frame.

'I'm sorry, yeah. You know, I just thought—'

'You didn't think at all, Lawrence, did you? You've become a liability, and I'm not willing to clear up the mess you've made. I will be looking for a replacement with immediate effect, someone who can work Epping Hill with a little more,' Baurman paused, 'common sense.'

Smith took a step towards Baurman. 'But you can't . . .' One of the henchmen stepped in front of his boss. A door opened at the back of the BMW and a third heavy got out.

'The message should be clear to you by now, Lawrence.' Suddenly the sound of an engine could be heard. Baurman stopped speaking, and all the gathered men turned and looked at a small car driving towards them from behind the unit. It pulled up a short distance away, a Vauxhall Corsa that had been converted into a sort of van. It said "Hunter Securities" on one side. A young man stepped out.

'What's going on here?'

Baurman looked at Smith. 'You see what happens when you're around, Lawrence? It all gets fucked up and people get hurt unnecessarily.' He turned away and nodded to the third heavy. 'Clean this up.'

Baurman sat down in the back seat of the BMW. Smith watched the heavy bring out a black object from underneath his jacket. The young security guard had lifted his radio to his mouth, but he had no time to speak. He stumbled backwards as two shots ripped through him, into the side of the Corsa, where he slumped to the ground, his eyes wide open.

The heavy walked to the rear of the BMW and opened the boot. He stood part concealed behind the lifted boot, his hands busy, then emerged holding two flaming bottles, and walked across to the pickup and the 4x4. He brought both bottles down hard on their bonnets, one after the other. Sheets of flame instantly consumed the metal. Smith looked on helplessly as the heavy calmly walked back to the rear of the BMW, a few seconds and he was holding a third flaming bottle. He made straight for Smith.

'Fuck! No!' shouted Smith. Pain shot up his right leg and through his body, and his right arm flopped as he ran. He turned back just in time to see his Passat engulfed in flames before losing his balance and crashing to the cold ground. The heavy then brought out a fourth flaming bottle. He walked over to the Corsa and shoved the dead security guard into the open driver's door with his free arm, before bringing the bottle down on the bonnet. He removed his blood-stained jacket and threw it into the inferno.

The BMW's engine gunned and the car turned, sweeping the yard and briefly illuminating Smith and the four burning cars before powering away into the night.

Chapter 15

The custody area was busy at Langthorne and four more prisoners, brought in for serious assault, did nothing to ease the workload. George Elms sat watching the chaos unfold and writing up a custody record, doing his best to keep out of the way. He wanted to speak to the custody sergeant, but he'd seen the tension on Andrew Musto's face. He knew the sergeant could be prickly, so decided to wait.

The superintendent apparently had no such qualms, and she bustled past George. 'Andrew!'

The custody sergeant turned away from his screen, irritation written all over his face. 'Ma'am?'

'Where are we with the four?'

'Ma'am—'

'How about you let me update the superintendent, Andy?' George steered Helen Webb back into the custody office.

'Is he a little stretched down here?'

'Who?'

'Musto. He seems agitated.'

George chuckled, 'I think anyone who works down here gets a little *agitated*. All I can say is, they're welcome to it.'

'So what did we get?' Helen asked.

George bit his bottom lip and shook his head. 'Not much.'

'We thought it might be a long shot.'

This surprised him a little. She had taken the bad news rather well. 'We did. It would have been better if they'd been nicked at the scene and brought straight in. Someone either got to them, or they had enough time to get their stories straight. None of them wanted legal advice and all four of them answered everything with *no comment*. They know we can't pin anything on them. It's all purely circumstantial.'

'Okay, so what else have we got?' Helen said.

'The victim. I phoned earlier, and he's being kept in a coma while they assess him for internal bleeding, but we should be able to talk to him in the next couple of days. Shame, really. I'm up the hospital in an hour or so to see Sophie, and I was hoping to do both at the same time.'

'Our bus victim?'

'The very same.'

'That's good. I would appreciate a phone call to let me know what happens with her. Have you read the first account she gave?'

'I have, yeah. I'm confident we can get some more detail now she's had a bit of recovery time.'

'Okay, just give me a brief update, whatever it is.'

'No problem.'

George gave up on custody. He went to his part of the station where his team were waiting. Paul Baern was standing at the kettle. 'Ah, Sergeant George, I remember you. How is life treating you since you left us?'

'Very funny, Baerny. I'll have a tea, please.'

Paul put his hands on his hips. 'Oh, tea is it now? Sure you wouldn't prefer a coffee with the chief superintendent? I mean, this must be a bit of a come down, mustn't it?' Paul was in his early forties, bald and with a paunch. He looked every bit the battle-hardened detective, but in fact had been a late joiner to the police, having spent his early working life running bars on large passenger ferries. Thanks to this, he was well rounded, good at communication and had the rare talent among coppers of being able to ask people questions without making them feel as though they were in trouble.

George laughed. 'Well, I don't mind slumming it with you mere mortals every now and then. Reminds me what I was lucky enough to leave behind.'

Paul echoed his laughter.

'What are we all laughing at?' The third member of the team, DC Samantha Robins, entered the room, her blonde hair tied back in a low ponytail that swung back and forth as she walked. Sam was the newest member of the team and added a much-needed woman's touch. Sam was more attractive than she knew, and could make the most sullen and taciturn criminal talk to her as though they were having a casual drink in a pub. Sam knew her strengths, and her investigative skills had already secured them several jobs that would have evaded them in the past.

'We're laughing at George here.'

Sam looked at George, now sitting at his desk. 'Oh, you've remembered where you sit, then?'

Paul grinned. 'Probably best he stays there. Outside's full of violent paedophiles, you know.'

George's smile widened. 'Tell you what, you've gotta watch out for them.'

Paul placed a mug of tea on George's desk. 'You off out again, boss?'

'I am. I'm at the hospital to speak to our bus victim. Sam, you able to pop up with me? She might talk more easily to you.'

'Because I'm a girl?'

'Nah, because she's horribly disfigured, so you've got something in common!' Paul called out. The team cracked up.

Chapter 16

As soon as George saw her, it was clear to him why the media had got so much mileage out of the story, and why the public outcry had been so huge. Sophie was seventeen, well on the way to being a beautiful young woman. She had soft features and mousey hair that fell over her face and looked blonde under the harsh hospital lights. Her large brown eyes were bright and inquisitive. She was wearing skinny jeans that emphasised her slenderness, with Converse plimsolls. She'd pulled the sleeves of her hooded top down over her hands.

'Can I offer you some tea? If I tell them it's for me, it'll be here quick.' Sophie giggled, and then raised a hand to cover her wound, her laughter dying away.

'I would love one, young lady, but I'll ask myself, thank you. I have a badge, you see — one look at this and you'll see just how fast a tea can be delivered.' George lifted his warrant card above his head, showing it to anyone passing by. No one took any notice. He turned to Sam. 'We're not in the blind unit, are we?'

'Don't think so, Sarge.' Sam smiled, shaking her head a little.

'Sophie, did you tell these people just *who* was coming to see you today?'

Her smile returned. 'You know, I don't think it got through.'

George looked around. 'It appears not. Sam, could you please go and find someone and tell them. And Sam, two sugars please.'

Sam got to her feet. 'Sophie?'

The girl pointed to a clear jug of water standing among three vases of flowers. George wondered if one of them was from Jamie. 'I'm fine, thanks. Make sure you let everyone know how important your sergeant is though, right?'

Sam nodded. 'Oh, I'll tell them *all* about him.'

The whole purpose of the visit today was to communicate with Sophie in a relaxed manner. As she beamed and dropped her hand from her neck, George cursed the piece of shit that had taken a swipe at her.

'Can't be nice being here, Sophie. If you're anything like me, you'll hate hospitals.' He stood and took off his jacket, and tugged at his tie to loosen it. 'I know you've already spoken to us coppers a couple of times so I wanted to apologise for coming back and bothering you again today.'

'That's okay, they said you might. The second time, they filmed it. It was just like having a chat. I forgot they were even police officers.'

'Good, and you don't mind talking about it, then?'

'No. It's weird. I don't mind talking to you about it, but it's a nightmare talking to my mum.'

George thought he understood. 'Happens a lot. Mums are the worst. They're too involved emotionally and it's difficult for them to hear.'

Sophie scoffed. 'You'd think it had happened to her! She's terrible, not been to work since, having a go at my dad, always on the phone to my auntie demanding that she throw her weight around. Really milking it, she is. Tells everyone she knows, and about how much it's affecting *her*.'

'Your auntie?' George pretended not to know about her connection to the mayor. Sophie sighed.

'She's the mayor, which my dad always says is pretty apt because she's *a* total *mare*. We've never got on, and yet now she thinks we should be best friends because I got attacked.'

'Maybe she thinks she can help?'

'She's a twat . . . Oops! Sorry, can I say twat in front of the police?'

'Well, let's hope so, eh, you just did — twice.'

'Well, if you do arrest me for it, I've got a powerful auntie.'

They smiled at each other.

Sam returned with two steaming plastic mugs. 'It's machine I'm afraid, and there's only coffee.' George sighed. He had to be pretty desperate to drink a vending machine coffee.

George turned to Sophie. 'So, what's the plan for you today?'

She shrugged. 'The plastic surgeon's coming in to see me and I might get to have the stitches out. I think that's all.'

'You already look a lot better than you did in that interview we filmed.'

'How did I look? Horrific, I would imagine.'

'You looked a little traumatised, Sophie, which is understandable. But all in all, you've handled this rather well.'

Sophie looked down. 'Some people get worse.'

'And most don't.'

She looked up at George. 'You look like you've been in the wars yourself, Sergeant.'

George had forgotten his own facial wounds. The swelling had just about gone, but the skin around both his eyes was dark. He pointed at himself. 'The eyes? Now let me tell you something, Sophie, if my wife asks you to do the washing up, you do the washing up, you understand?'

Sophie giggled. 'Got it. I think I'd like your wife.'

'I'm sure you would.' George decided it was time to get to the reason for their visit. 'In your interview you said that you didn't really get a look at his face, but you remember a tattoo?'

'Yeah, I saw it quite well — only bit I did see really. I didn't even know he was upstairs . . .' Sophie fell silent.

'There's nothing you could have done differently,' George said.

Sophie nodded. 'It was part of a tattoo. There was probably a lot more to it than I saw. It kind of reminded me of a crawling vine or something, you know? I think I said when I was videoed that it was really dark, like it was pretty new and I reckon that's right. Sometimes they fade, don't they?'

'You gave a pretty good description, good enough to give us something to go on. But what if someone far more talented than me sat down with you, do you think you could help them to draw what you saw?'

Sophie nodded again. 'Yeah, I reckon I could do that.'

'That would be great. I'll arrange for someone arty to be in touch, and we'll get it done sooner rather than later.'

Sam chipped in. 'I could do it. I used to be good at drawing.'

'Used to be?' George said.

'Still am. We could give it a go at least, the sooner the better while it's fresh in your mind.'

A shrill voice suddenly cut off any reply. 'Sophie, who are these people?'

'Oh, you're here. This is Sergeant George Elms and this is Sam, but I don't know her surname.'

Sam stood up. 'Robins.'

George followed suit, and faced a woman in her late thirties. She was wearing tight-fitting jeans with a white blouse that billowed out from her high waist. She carried a black leather jacket over one arm. George assessed it as being her *visiting her daughter in hospital* outfit.

'Mrs Hayward? I'm Detective Sergeant George Elms. I'm leading the investigation into the attack on your daughter.'

'And a fine job you're doing of it, too.' The sarcasm positively dripped. 'Sergeant George Elms, you said? I shall have to write that down for my sister.'

'We are doing all we can. We've just had a chat with Sophie here and have come up with a decent action plan. We'll do all we can to get a satisfactory result.'

'Action?'

Sophie sat forward, looking enthusiastic. 'We're gonna draw the tattoo I saw.'

Mrs Hayward sniffed. 'Drawing tattoos? You should be out there questioning people, looking at CCTV, getting fingerprints, not drawing pictures, Sergeant.'

'Rest assured, Mrs Hayward, we are doing all those things and more, but we do need to make sure we cover every aspect. The tattoo might turn out to be very useful, critical even.'

'Well, I'm sure that's something that can be done another day. Are you even supposed to be talking to my daughter without me here with her? I know the law, Detective Sergeant.'

'You're here now.'

'Lucky I am. She's very tired, she's had quite an ordeal and you people have already spoken to her at quite some length.'

Sophie raised her eyebrows at George, as if to apologise for her mother. George decided it was time to leave. He took a swig of his coffee, and grimaced.

'Well, Sophie, it was lovely to meet you, it really was. We'll be in touch soon. Maybe Sam here can take you out for a coffee, and a bun as well while you get some work done.'

'Are you paying?' Sophie twinkled.

George smiled back. 'We'll see about that.'

Mrs Hayward busied herself arranging the flowers, turning her back on the two police officers.

'Goodbye, Mrs Hayward,' said George.

'Yes,' she said, still facing away. 'Goodbye.'

Chapter 17

Huntington had been up for twenty minutes when the alarm rang at four thirty. He opened the door to the en-suite and reached through to turn it off. He had been awake most of the night.

Huntington's evenings followed a routine. He would watch the news while his wife sat reading a novel. Once in bed, they would both read silently for exactly fifteen minutes before Huntington switched off his lamp, followed soon after by his wife. Bed had once been the place where they would talk, sharing their day, exchanging news. Nowadays, there didn't seem to be anything to talk about. Huntington sometimes wondered if his wife missed those conversations.

Last night, the routine had been interrupted. It started with a call from Helen Webb. 'Graham, sorry to call so late. Hope you weren't asleep?'

'No, no, is there something wrong?'

Helen sounded flustered. 'The media are publishing stories tomorrow about Epping Hill. Two of the nationals are running them as their main item, but just about all of them have got some sort of coverage.'

'I didn't think it was quite so imminent. I could have—'

'There's going to be media at the station tomorrow. The BBC are certainly coming, but we should also expect others. The chief . . .' Helen sighed, 'The chief has just called me. He's going to be there first thing tomorrow and the rest of the day at least.'

'What story?'

'The girl from the bus. Her aunt, the mayor, knows people in the media and she's been making a lot of noise. They've got an interview with her as well as the mother. On top of that, they've got hold of the YouTube video. *The Sun* is running it as their main story. Their headline, Graham, is "The Land the Police Forgot." The whole piece is based around Epping Hill and the idea that it's some sort of no-go area for us. They've even got interviews with Epping Hill residents, with quotes like, "we don't see the police at all, the gangs run this estate."'

'Jesus!'

'Just when you think it can't get any worse, they finish with interviewing a police officer who has declined to give his name. He or she says that the police only go to Epping Hill if they are called, and are slow to respond, hoping that the residents would have sorted the problem between themselves before they arrive. The same officer describes it as "hell on earth."'

'Jesus!' Huntington said again.

'We need to be ready for the chief tomorrow, Graham. I'm expecting to have to answer some pretty harsh questions.'

Helen ended the call and Huntington checked his clock. 10:25 p.m., nothing to be done now. He sighed as he climbed back into bed.

His wife looked over at him. 'What's the matter, Graham?'

He ran a hand over his face. 'Just some problems at work, nothing major.' He got up again and went into the bathroom. There, he found himself looking at his reflection in the mirror as though he hadn't seen it for a while. His face seemed to be more haggard than he remembered, the eyes more sunken and the bags underneath larger.

He returned to bed and spent the next few hours going over everything he could think of to say about Epping Hill Estate.

* * *

Huntington stepped out of his front door into the freezing darkness. He could hear the faint hum of a milk float somewhere in the distance. He pulled out of his drive and headed for the station.

'Have you been in long?' Helen Webb made him jump. She was dressed to kill, in a grey suit jacket with matching pencil skirt ending just below the knee. The shirt underneath was a crisp white and fitted, open just enough to show a silver pendant.

'Is he here yet?'

'Not yet.'

Huntington glanced at the clock. 7.40 a.m.

Just before eight o'clock, Jean exploded through Huntington's open office door. 'The chief's here!'

'Okay, okay,' Huntington said, apparently quite calm.

'He's already asked for you,' Jean puffed.

Chapter 18

George took his time answering the phone. Paul had brought down a round of toast and he had ripped off a large chunk just as his desk phone lit up.

It was a familiar voice. 'George, me ol' mucka, you're in then?'

'Nope, this is a recorded message.'

'Oh, alright. Hello, George, this is PC Brian Appleby from Force Intelligence here, yeah. You said that I should let you know if I was ever able to get any intelligence from Effingell Estate. Well, we've had a bit of a result on that front and I was hoping to talk to you about it. No problem, mate, I'll catch up with you when you're next around. Oh, and I got the test results back. I'm sorry, mate, but I think you'll need to get yourself checked out. Okay, George, bye now.'

The line went dead. George laughed and called Brian straight back.

'Hello? PC Brian Appleby.'

'Piss off, Granny, you know it's me.' Granny was a reference to 'Granny Smith,' as in the apple in his surname. The name had stuck from the days when the two men had been at training school together.

'You know that no one calls me Granny anymore, don't you, George? You see, I'm kind of a big deal up here now . . .' Brian trailed off as George laughed louder.

'So I hear. So what is so important that you feel you can interrupt my morning toast?'

'We have a Lawrence Matthews in. He's downstairs.' Brian paused. If he was waiting for a reaction he got none.

'Downstairs? What, like in custody downstairs or he's stood at the front counter picking his nose?'

'In custody — under arrest and everything. He might be picking his nose though.'

'Okay?'

'You know him, right?'

'I know he used to be a bit of a knob in Effingell. Was on the junk when I was in uniform.'

'Yeah, the very same. He's now sat in the holding cell with a bust-up elbow or arm or something. Anyway, I'm down there on a separate job and he's in there gobbing off. Keeps saying he's called "Smith." All he says is, "Don't you know who I am? Everyone knows me, I'm Smith." There's some other shit, but nothing else of interest.'

George sat up, his toast forgotten. 'Smith? What, and you think he could be?'

'Well, it would fit. I mean, we don't know much about this Smith bloke really, do we? Just that the snouts keep telling us he's the supply chain to Effingell. I have to say we have a top four likely candidates, and Lawrence isn't one of them.'

'Too stupid?' George suggested.

'An element of that, sure, but mostly too much of a slave to the gear. Like you, I met him when I was uniform three or four years ago, and the man was a fucking mess. I don't know what surprises me more, that he's claiming to be Smith or that he's still alive.'

Sam plonked a cup of tea on George's cluttered desk and he gave her a thumbs-up. 'He was always out of it, I'll give you that.

'He's hammered today, too. He's in for possession of heroin. A couple of probies found him wandering around looking beat up and high as a kite. They searched him, and sure enough he had a load of H on him.'

'They searching his place?'

'Yeah, already made sure of that.'

'Are you planning on talking to him when he comes down?'

'That's another part of the reason I called. I've got a course today, top end of the county. I leave in about fifteen minutes. Listen, George, could you spin down there, see what he's got to say, and report back?'

George checked the time on the phone. He knew he already had a packed day.

'Problem I've got, Brian, is that he's off his head, so I'd need to get down there later. I can't guarantee I'll be around then, though.'

'Well, he's talking now. This might be the best time. If he is Smith, though I think it's more likely he just knows who this Smith ghost is, now might be the best time to get the information out of him, before he gets a bit more lucid and clams up.'

'All right, Granny, I'll head down there now.'

* * *

The last time George had seen Lawrence Matthews was in a bedsit at Peto Court. Lawrence didn't have a place there, or anywhere at all back then, but he had crashed out on a filthy mattress laid out over old food cartons, beer cans, bottles, tin foil and uncapped needles.

Lawrence had been stick-thin. His face was almost a skull, with heavy eyes, sunk in their sockets. George was investigating a sudden death in the flat next to Lawrence's, caused, it would appear, by a drug overdose. He'd gone in hoping for a witness, but had soon realised that Lawrence was painfully close to suffering the same fate.

George recalled feeling a tinge of sadness at the state the man had been reduced to. He had met Lawrence plenty of times as a uniform officer. Lawrence's only vice at that time had been a beer or two. He was a fighter, solidly built with a muscular torso, a denizen of the nightclub world. It had taken just two years to transform the angry fighter to the skeletal frame lying on a stinking mattress, barely able to even raise himself up.

So George was surprised to meet Lawrence's appearance today. The muscles had returned. His hair was worn longer than the shorn, almost military style of his drinking days, but was in good condition. Lawrence looked well. His skin was pink, and his face was full and shaven. The only visible clue to the substances working their way round his body was in his eyes. The pupils were pin-pricks and he blinked in slow motion. George also noticed his clothing. Although the leather jacket was torn and had fresh bloodstains on the chest and back, it looked expensive and fitted well.

The arresting officer looked up briefly from his paperwork as George entered the holding cell. 'What happened to your jacket? I thought your fighting days were over, Lawrence.'

'Fighting days, you say.' Lawrence's laugh went on too long.

George wasn't sure if he recognised him.

'Elm?' said Lawrence. 'PC Elm, or was it Oak?' He laughed again. 'And who is Lawrence?'

'It's Elms. Sergeant Elms.'

'Like Bond! It's Bond, Sergeant Bond. Or something.' Lawrence looked confused.

'You remember me, then?'

'I never forget a gavver. 'Specially the ones that nick me. You was all right though, man, don't get me wrong, I don't hold it against yer. You gotta do what you gotta do.'

'So you'll know that I know your name's Lawrence?'

The uniform officer spoke up. 'I think he's had a bit of a drink, Sarge.'

'It's not drink,' George said. Then to Lawrence, 'How long have you been back on the gear, then?'

Lawrence's smile faded. 'The gear.' His eyes did not quite meet George's. 'Would you believe me, Sergeant, if I said one day?' He leaned back until his head rested against the cold brick wall behind him, and stared off into the distance. 'Just one day.'

George nodded his head. 'I would. I do.'

'I never thought I would, you know? But what it is with the H, mate, see, you hear some people talk about the rush but it ain't a rush. It's gentler than that. You can be surrounded by piss and shit, your life ain't nothing, no friends, family hate you . . . nothing, and yet the H, mate. The feeling . . . It takes you over, you know? You're living here, man, and it's like you're surrounded by sadness, but take a hit and for just a little while it can be a *glorious* fucking sadness.' Lawrence closed his eyes.

'And this is how you're feeling right now, is it?'

Lawrence kept his eyes shut. 'Yesterday I was *somebody*, you know? I was the man, and today I ain't nothing. But it's fucking glorious.'

'And who were you yesterday?'

There was a long pause followed by a broad smile. 'I was *someone*.'

'Well, you look after yourself.' George took a last look at Lawrence and made his way out of the custody area. He left a voicemail message with *Granny*. 'Yeah, Brian, just spent some time in the company of Lawrence Matthews. He looks a lot better than I remember him. He's out of his face today but I reckon he's only just back on it. Something's happened to him for sure, looks a little beat up. No mention of Smith, mate. He hinted a couple of times, maybe, but nothing solid. I'll try and speak to him when he's thinking straight, but I don't hold out much hope.'

George hung up just as Helen Webb passed him on the stairs leading away from custody.

Her expression was tense. 'George. You got my message?'

'Message?'

'The chief. Haven't you heard? He's here.'

George said nothing, puzzled.

Helen tutted. 'The chief is here. This negative press coverage about the Epping Hill Estate, we're getting a lot of flack. He's talking to everyone that works the estate. I'll be directing him to you, George.' Helen moved on down the stairs, not waiting for a reply.

George rolled his eyes.

Chapter 19

'Tell me about Epping Hill — a summary.' Chief Constable Alan Cottage gestured to Graham Huntington and George Elms to sit down. Helen Webb was already waiting when they arrived. Cottage dominated the meeting room, leaning back against a desk.

'Well, it's an estate on the outskirts of Langthorne and it's always been a blight on the area. The council, well, I mean back in the seventies and eighties, they—'

Cottage waved a hand, cutting him short. 'I didn't want the whole history of the place, Graham.'

'It has a population of around fifteen thousand, sir,' George offered. 'There are just three of the old-style tenement blocks left, with plans to knock them down in the next ten years or so. All of these blocks are principal sources of trouble, but Peto Court seems to be the worst. It's full of junkies and drunks, those the council couldn't put anywhere else. The rest of the population live in small terraced houses, and larger ones divided into flats.'

Cottage nodded. 'I see. And how is it patrolled? Is there specific tasking for the estate, or is it part of everyone's patch?'

Huntington cut back in. 'Well, that really falls to the individual patrol sergeants, *sir*. I mean, that's not really our department.'

'Not your department?' The chief picked up a sheet of paper from the desk. 'I am led to understand that you are the appointed area commander. That *Effingell*, as it has been branded by the locals and coppers alike, falls very much within your area?'

'Well, yes, but—'

'And is there anywhere else in the area that gives you *more* problems than Epping Hill?'

'Well, no, sir, but—'

'No, there isn't. Hence the reason I am here, along with the world's entire media.' He stood up and strode to the back of the room. It was designated as the briefing room and was where all the frontline officers came before starting their shift. It had a map of the area, and the walls were lined with the latest intelligence including numerous mug shots under headings such as, "Disqual drivers," "Prolific burglars," and, "Where are they?" Cottage stared at one of the mug shots with his back to the others. He spun round and paced back towards them, perching on the edge of a desk.

There was a long silence. 'I think,' he said at last, 'I think, Helen, that I'll have a little ride out there. George here can take me round, and we can visit some of the hot spots so I can get a first-hand impression. I think it would be a good idea before I have to talk to the media. George, do you have an hour or so?'

'Well, yes,' George replied.

Huntington swung round towards the sergeant. His lips started to form words, but he said nothing.

'Good man, we'll take my car.' The chief began walking towards the exit. He stopped with his hand on the door handle. 'Graham, I'll come and see you a bit later in the day. I'd like you to give me your ideas.'

Huntington nodded.

Chapter 20

A uniform PC reluctantly handed George the keys to the chief's car. 'I'm his driver,' he said.

George shrugged, he had his orders.

George opened the door to the shiny Jaguar XF saloon car and slid along the soft leather. Behind the wheel, the bewildering array of buttons, dials, and knobs threw him into a momentary panic. He selected 'D,' and the Jaguar slid out from its space towards where the chief was waiting for him.

He took his place in the passenger seat. 'Thanks, George. Fuck me! Look at all these buttons!'

'Tell me about it. I reckon a jet has fewer settings. Are we taking anyone else, boss?'

'No, no, just us. Helen tells me there's a place that does reasonable takeaway coffee not far from here. I say we get some, and then we can head off into the badlands. To be honest, George, I'm just happy to be sitting in front. My driver normally makes me sit in the back.' Cottage gave a wide smile.

They travelled the first few minutes in silence. George was concentrating on not bouncing the fifty-thousand-pound Jaguar off anything else, moving or otherwise. Cottage gazed out of the window.

Suddenly he gave a laugh and turned towards George. 'I don't think Graham likes me too much, do you?'

'I don't know what Graham does like, sir. He has his strengths though. You've just got to know how to take him.'

Cottage chuckled again. 'A very diplomatic answer, Sergeant Elms. I think he's a bit of a prick.'

George felt the chief's eyes on him, checking his reaction. He smiled — but not too much.

'So, Epping Hill. Do you think Graham is a hindrance? I mean, would things on the estate be better under someone else's remit?'

'Well, sir, Epping Hill has had plenty of different people put in charge of it, both good and bad. Lots of ideas have been tried, and resources thrown at it. We have had a few successes, but on the whole we just can't seem to make any impact.'

'This is the worst it's been, though, surely? I mean, it's now front-page news. Epping Hill is about to be portrayed as the worst estate in Britain.'

'Nothing's happened recently that's any worse than what's been going on for as long as I've been working it. I think we've just been unlucky. I know that sounds like another diplomatic answer, but it seems to me that a couple of nasty incidents have been picked up by social media, making it look like we've completely lost control.'

Cottage rubbed his chin. The Jaguar bumped up onto a garage forecourt. 'You may well be right, George. I'm just not sure how this all ends. This is the place for coffee, is it?'

'It's the best place I know.' The chief already had his door open as George was putting the gear into Park and applying the handbrake. He watched as Cottage practically skipped across to the shop entrance, thanked a young lad who held the door open, and disappeared inside.

George was busy trying to work out the car's menu screen, when there was a tap on the window. He began a frantic search for the electric window button. The chief rested two cardboard cups on the roof and tugged the door open.

'Nice in there, aren't they?' The chief gestured at a petite brunette who could just about be seen through the condensation on the shop's glass front. The chief was still looking in her general direction as the Jaguar pulled away

'You married, George?'

'I am, sir, yes.'

'Happily?' There was a hint of mischief in the chief's smile.

'Yes.'

'No hesitation. I like that.'

'And you, sir?'

'Same, I'm happy to say. Twenty-two years — she's a good woman.'

'Then you did well to keep hold of her.'

'Keep hold of her? I knocked her up! What choice did she have?'

George smiled. 'Ah, I see. I used a similar technique. And then did it again, just recently.'

'Recently?'

'The wife's pregnant.'

'Really?' The chief seemed genuinely delighted. 'How pregnant?'

'Very. We're getting very close now, boss.'

'Well, that is good news.'

The two men sat in silence.

'Can you put us on the right radio channel for the area, George? So we can monitor the local patrols. Then you can show me the sights.'

George found the police radio neatly concealed in the armrest and powered it up. They listened to a random update about a drunk found lying in the middle of a town centre road, and both rolled their eyes.

They arrived at the place where the "Welcome to Epping Hill" sign had once stood. This had been free of graffiti for as long as it had taken the workmen to install it. It had remained in situ for almost a year, which was quite an achievement, albeit doctored to read "Welcome to Effing Hell." It had made George smile on his almost daily trips over the estate's threshold. Now the sign was gone, leaving two metal poles jutting out, possibly a more fitting emblem.

After the absent sign, the road became one way, leading downhill towards the seafront, where Peto Court was situated. The car park was on the far side of the building, making it necessary to circle round the building before stopping the car. All signs marking "Peto Court" were long gone.

They stared at the square, drab exterior with its endless identical windows sporting dirty net curtains or towels hung against the filthy glass.

The chief turned to George. 'This is Peto Court?'

'How did you guess?'

'It's pretty standard. We had a lot of places like this in Manchester. They were much bigger though. What is there, a couple of hundred flats in here?'

'Bedsits mainly. The top floor is all flats. There's actually only a hundred or so packed in there with three-quarters occupied. Although most of them aren't fit for humans to live in. No one complains. Most probably don't notice.'

'Are we stopping?'

George looked at Cottage. 'Do you want to?'

'Can we get in? Have a walk through, maybe?'

'I've got a fob for the main door.'

George slid the shiny Jaguar into an empty space between a Ford Escort with four flat tyres and a battered-looking Transit van. As they got out, George was suddenly aware that Cottage was dressed very much like a police officer — white shirt with epaulettes, black clip-on tie and black trousers with patrol boots. He began to feel a little nervous. Just then, a window, one floor from the top, slid open and a dark, square object flew out of it.

There was no time for a reaction, George emitted a noise that was meant to be a warning and the chief reacted by looking over to him just as the object smashed into the rear window of the polished Jaguar. The window gave with a deafening pop, and glass cascaded over both sides of the boot.

'We should leave.'

'Yeah we should, before they throw something that does some real damage.'

George peered up at the window, there was no movement, the chief was already tugging open the passenger door. George hurriedly checked the damage. The foreign object that was now part of the parcel shelf was in fact a microwave oven, and he was satisfied that it was stuck firmly enough to be transported back without any interference. He got back in the car and drove away from the building. Neither of them mentioned the sudden increase in traffic noise and the drop in temperature caused by the new vent in the rear window.

As the police station came into view, Cottage suddenly emitted a noise that sounded to George a lot like laughter.

'Are you laughing, sir?'

'I just realised that you've got to tell my driver about the window!'

'Why am I telling him, sir?'

'Because he gave *you* the keys.'

* * *

Helen Webb stood over George, who was sitting back at his desk. 'Who threw it?'

'Threw what?'

'That!' Helen pointed at the solid-looking eighties model microwave, freshly sealed in a see-through evidence bag tied off with a blue tag.

'Ah, that. To be honest, ma'am, I really couldn't tell you.'

'We have some idea, though? And forensics might be able to help?'

'We know that it was someone from Peto Court, or at least someone that was in Peto Court and who doesn't appear to like the police. I'll get it run through for prints, but if there is a match we still have to prove who threw it.'

Helen stood with her hands on her hips. 'Why didn't you call it in? We could have sent the tactical team in.'

'Ma'am, from what I know of Peto Court, most people would be so out of their face they would have no idea who threw it, and anyone that might have seen would certainly not be telling us about it. It would have been a waste of time.'

Helen huffed. 'That may well be, George, but the chief constable has been attacked on our patch, and we did nothing about it. That's not acceptable!'

'Nonsense!' the chief broke in.

Helen turned around, along with George and everyone else.

'Sir, I was just—'

Chief Constable Cottage raised his hand. 'No need, Helen. I asked George here to show me the sights, to give me an idea of what the Epping Hill Estate was like, and that's exactly what he did. Sure, we got attacked by a microwave oven, but I should know better than to park outside a place like Peto Court wearing this uniform.'

The chief beamed and for George at least the penny dropped. Cottage had once been a very active street copper where he would have enjoyed the banter with the criminals on the street as well as with colleagues. Being the chief constable made all that largely impossible and, for just a short time, the chief constable had got back in touch with just plain *Constable* Cottage, and he had loved every second.

Chapter 21

The first days of December had brought with them a noticeable drop in temperature. On his way into work, George passed three members of the uniform night shift who offered tired nods and grunts as they departed. Judging by the thick frost, they had suffered a cold night.

Paul and Sam arrived at the same time, but there was no time to talk to them as Helen Webb had followed them in and called out to George immediately. She sounded stern, and George wondered what he had done wrong.

'Morning, ma'am.'

'Where's your phone?'

Taken aback, George patted his pockets. 'I'm not actually sure.'

'Your wife has been trying to get hold of you. She's at the hospital. You need to go now. There's a car waiting for you in the yard.'

His face broke into a smile, but Helen remained serious.

'George, I'm afraid there are complications. You need to go now.'

* * *

George left the station at a jog and slid into the rear seat of a marked police car with two uniform officers in the front. It pulled away immediately. The lights and sirens fired up. The two men in the front had been told nothing more than to get their colleague to the hospital as soon as possible, and so the twelve-minute, white-knuckle journey passed in silence.

Helen had called ahead. A woman in green scrubs was shivering in the cold outside the A&E entrance. She flagged down the car and led George into the hospital. The walk beneath the neon strip-lights seemed to go on forever. The nurse was vague about why George had been called in.

'Your wife started having pains. We've done some scans and it appears there are complications.'

'Complications?'

'I'll ask the doctor to come out and explain.'

'Explain what?'

George was no wiser as he was led into a small room, empty, save for a coffee machine and five chairs lined up against the wall. He could feel his heart racing.

'Can I see my wife?'

'Soon, Mr Elms. I'll let the doctor know you are here.'

George was pacing the room when Dr Bondhi, a thirty-something doctor, entered. He spoke softly. 'Mr Elms, your wife was admitted to hospital this morning complaining of abdominal pains. We quickly realised that there was a problem with the unborn child. We could not find a heartbeat.'

George stared back, waiting for him to continue.

'Mr Elms, we performed an emergency caesarean. I'm very sorry. We were not able to revive the child.'

And there it was.

George slumped onto the chair. The woman in the green scrubs had come back and was hovering just inside the door. The motor clicked on inside the drinks machine, its hum the only sound in the room.

'Mr Elms, I know this is a shock for you. Is there anything I can get you?'

'What was it?' He shuddered at the word "it." 'I mean, a boy or a girl?'

'A girl.'

George almost smiled at the irony of it. 'A girl, ha. The things I said . . . the things I said about if it was a girl. I said if it was a girl it was no use to me . . . it was a joke. How could I?'

George was suddenly aware of the nurse kneeling beside his chair. 'You were joking, George, messing about. Men always joke about wanting a rugby player or a football player. It doesn't mean anything. Don't worry about it.'

George looked up at the doctor. 'How's Sarah?'

'Your wife's okay physically. She will need to stay in for a little while, we need to be sure there are no further issues, but she should be just fine.'

The nurse placed her hand on his arm. 'Shall we go through and see Sarah?'

'What do I say? I can't make this better, can I?'

'Just seeing you, just having you hold her hand, that will do more than anyone else in the world can do right now.'

Sarah lay staring at the wall. Her eyes flickered to George as he entered. He walked over to her and held her hand. She managed an exhausted smile. George sat on the edge of the bed, leaned over and held his wife. After a while, he pulled away and looked at her face. Her eyes were empty, there was not even sadness left in them.

Sarah sat up. 'You would have been outnumbered,' she said with a tremulous smile.

'All girls? I wouldn't have minded at all.' He forced a smile, even as his chest tightened. 'We'll be all right, you know. Just the three of us for now, but we'll be stronger than ever.'

'I know.'

'I'll spend less time at work, I promise. I don't think I realise sometimes just how wonderful a family I've got. We should all be together more.'

Sarah nodded, tears running down her cheeks. 'Charley would love that. She adores you.'

'I adore her,' George said. 'I adore both of you.' And they held each other, quietly sobbing together.

Chapter 22

Haden Skinner stepped out of the dimly lit gym, and squinted in the winter sunlight. Behind him, his brother Liam was fiddling with a large bunch of keys. He locked the door of the warehouse containing their armoury of weights, benches and mirrors. They were closing early.

Haden pointed a stubby finger at the brand-new, highly polished, four-wheel-drive vehicle sitting outside. 'VW Tow rag! What a name.'

'It's Touareg!' said Liam, missing the joke. Haden's T-shirt was taut across his biceps as he lifted his sports bag and dropped it into the carpeted boot. Liam started the vehicle, and the four-litre, turbo-charged engine stirred into life with a low growl. 'This sure do make you look perty,' he said in an atrocious approximation of a Texan drawl.

'Fuck you, bro. This is a fucking beast.' Haden rubbed the tops of his arms and glanced at his reflection in the side mirror. 'My arms are fucking burning, bruv, I hammered 'em today.' He flexed a bicep. The brothers were both into weightlifting, as well as the steroids that came with it.

Liam slid a mobile phone into the cradle on the dash and the Touareg moved forward.

'So, a Volkswagen?' Haden said.

'The lease people, they ain't doing the Q5s anymore. This is all right though, trust me.'

Haden looked round the interior, and stroked the leather. 'I would have demanded the Audi. I reckon they're playing you, bruv. They would have sourced one if you'd made enough noise.'

'Last thing I want to be doing is making noise.' Liam was peering at something behind them.

'Is it the usual?' Haden leaned forward to check the wing mirror. He saw a grey BMW following them at a distance.

Liam nodded. 'Yeah, same car too. It's like they ain't even trying anymore.'

'They want us to know they're there. The cops can do better than that if they want to.'

Liam glanced at his brother. 'So what do we do?'

'What we always do, bruv. Give 'em a bit of a run around, then head on out.' Haden pushed his feet out and sighed.

Liam took a number of left turns, and soon they were back where they started, with the BMW still on their tail. Haden leaned forward again to check on its progress. It was caught behind another car, unable to pull out. He waved a hand and gave a thumbs-up. The Touareg pulled away and the BMW dropped out of sight.

'You think we pissed 'em off?'

'Nope. Bored 'em, more like. Stick to the back roads though, Liam. We only got rid of the scum we were supposed to see.'

'We're nearly there.'

Haden peered out of the window. 'So we are.' He watched as the town of Langthorne merged into the Epping Hill Estate.

* * *

In the house the Skinners were heading for, the atmosphere crackled with tension. Ian Wells was pacing, increasing the irritation of his two companions. He stopped to light yet another cigarette, narrowing his eyes as he blew out smoke into a room already cloudy with it. Matty Cross sat on the sofa, fiddling with a baseball bat that he was trying to conceal underneath his jacket. Matty was squat, unlike the tall, lean, pacing man. He was to be at the frontline of the attack. The third man of the team was Deepak Hadhi, of Indian descent but born in Coventry, known as Dee. His long hair was tucked behind his ears and a gold chain with a boxing glove pendant swung as he sat forward. Dee had chosen a kitchen knife with a six-inch blade. He let it drop and it stuck upright in the exposed floorboards. Ian's floor was now criss-crossed with stab marks.

The sound of a diesel four-by-four heralded the arrival of the Skinner brothers.

* * *

Haden got out of the Touareg and stretched. He checked a chunky gold timepiece on his arm. Almost 2 p.m. They were right on time. 'Happy, bro?' he called out.

'Yes, mate.'

'Then let's get this done.'

Haden led the way to the house, lifting the gate which had fallen off its hinges. The path cut through a grassy expanse, littered with bits of bike, a partly deflated paddling pool filled with brown liquid, an upturned dustbin, and a square patch of brown, flattened grass. Haden thumped hard on the door. Liam looked back down the street to see if they had attracted any attention. Getting no response to his knock, Haden started kicking, until the door shook.

'Just a sec! Jesus!' Ian's voice called out, and the brothers could hear keys rattling on the other side of the door.

'What you fucking doing in there? Two o'clock, we said,' Haden shouted. The door swung wide, revealing a blinking Ian, who stepped back.

Haden's bulk blocked out the light. 'Ian, what the fuck?'

'Problems with the locks, mate.'

Haden grimaced. 'Whatever. We're here to get paid. We're already running late, so I ain't fucking about. Where is it?'

'There isn't any.'

'What do you mean, "there isn't any?"' Haden stared at Ian, then moved towards Dee who slid out a knife from behind his back. It hung from his hand as he stared back at Haden. Haden turned to Matty, who lifted the bat and tapped it against the palm of his other hand. Ian was now clutching a second baseball bat.

Haden held out an arm to stop his brother, who was trying to push past him.

Liam couldn't see what was happening inside. 'What did he say? There ain't none?'

No one answered.

Haden smiled slowly at Ian. 'It's like that, is it?' Ian made no reply. 'Cos there's still time to get the money, so we don't go down this road.'

Ian's voice was steady. 'There's no money.'

Haden nodded. He looked at each man in turn. 'Then I guess we're done.'

He turned on his heels and left, pulling the door shut behind him.

* * *

Ian let out a long breath, then twisted the keys hanging in the door to lock it. He pulled them out, placed them on the windowsill and stood to one side at the window, peering out. He saw the Skinners' VW pull away, and expelled the breath he'd been holding. 'They're gone. Just like I said.'

'You think that's it? They ain't coming back?' Dee's eyes were wide.

'Like I said to you, innit, these boys are a front, see, they're big boys and that intimidates people. Not us, though, not no more! Things are changing round here. If Smith's out of it, we've got to move ourselves up the line. Ain't no one going to do it for us.' Ian reached for a packet of cigarettes and offered them round.

* * *

Out of sight of the house, the Skinner brothers parked up. Haden spat. 'We go for the fucking Paki first, the cunt with the knife. He's sitting down — be on the left as we go in, so let me have him. We get him hard and fast, take him down, then we front the other two, see where their balls have gone. If they still want it, then we fucking have it there and then, but I want our fucking money first. Once we got that, they can have what's coming. Where are the tools?'

Liam crouched down in front of the bonnet and pulled at the grille. 'These cars have a space behind the grille, see. Just big enough for a few bits and where the filth would never look.' He stood up. The "bits" consisted of two Stanley knives, taped behind the large VW badge.

'Stanleys?' Haden took one and looked at his brother.

'They're effective and if you do get tugged with 'em, you can get away with them as tools. Not like the fucking meat cleaver you kept under your driver's seat.'

Holding their Stanley knives, Haden led the way back to the wooden gate, still hanging off one hinge. 'I still wish I had my cleaver.'

* * *

Back in the house, the three men began to relax, and the smoke thickened when Ian brought out the weed.

'So what do we do now?' Dee waved away the proffered joint.

'Now? We have a couple of spliffs, my friend!'

'And then?'

'Then?' Ian sat back and stretched his legs out. 'Then we have a conversation about what we want to do with the four grand.'

'What about getting Baurman his cut?' Dee picked up a cigarette and put it down again.

Ian turned to look at him. 'Stop worrying, man. Listen, I'll give him a bell, tell him we took him up on his offer and then go see him with his money. That gets us safe, he lets the Skinners know that we're working for him, and we ride off into the sunset with our prize.'

'Baurman told us to wait though, didn't he? He was going to make some arrangements.'

Ian sat up. 'Yeah, he did. But we ain't fucking kids now, are we? What happens if we let Baurman tell us what to do right from day one? We get to be in exactly the same fucking position as we were with the Skinners. Haden told me himself that they would never give us a bigger tab, because we couldn't be fucking trusted. We're doing five grand a week most of the time, and scraping by. Fuck that, man, I want out of this shithole and that means a bigger fucking tab. We turn up at Baurman's gaff with sweetener of a grand of the Skinners' money, he sees us for what we are, proper hardcore.' Ian felt around him for the remote, and Kanye West blasted out into the room.

* * *

Haden kicked the gate from its remaining hinge. Liam was carrying an iron bar from the car, and used it to block the front door, preventing it from being opened from the inside. The brothers made their way round to the back. The door there was made from solid wood, but Haden had come prepared. He carried a heavy iron tool, known by the police as 'the big red key.' He gripped the handles and swung the sixteen kilos of hardened steel into the door. Its three locks popped, Haden tossed aside the red key and the Skinner brothers entered the house.

Dee stood up and turned off the music. Ian made for the front door, and began struggling to open it, shouting, 'The fucking keys!'

But Haden had already reached Dee. Taking advantage of a moment's hesitation, he brought the Stanley knife up, slashing Dee from his abdomen to his armpit. Dee bent forward and stumbled. Liam came from behind his brother to deliver a coup de grace to the bridge of his nose, and he collapsed against the sofa.

Ian and Matty had found the keys to the front door. Ian fumbled and dropped them and had just unlocked the door when the Skinners turned their attention to them. Ian looked back at his stricken friend and gasped.

'So, Ian. I guess we didn't talk this through properly earlier. What did you think? That we would just fuck off? Leave our money here and fuck off?' Haden spat.

'He fucking cut me!' Dee had pushed himself up against the wall. One hand was pressed to his chest and blood ran out between his fingers.

'Shut the fuck up!' Liam moved back to Dee and sliced through his right ear and into the back of his head. Liam pressed the knife blade into Dee's neck. "Now *you* fucking listen! You ever pull a fucking knife on someone, you better know just what you're gonna do with it, understand?' Dee's breathing was erratic, and he tried to nod.

Haden stood close to Ian. 'Where's our fucking money, Ian? I don't have time to piss around.'

Ian appeared to hesitate.

'Listen, if I don't have my money in ten fucking seconds, then your Paki friend is gonna be the one to come out of this the best, you understand?'

'It's through there, in the bedroom . . . a . . . a loose board under the bed.'

Liam left the room. Haden stood staring at Ian, then caught a slight movement to his right. Matty was beginning to edge towards the baseball bat lying on the sofa.

'Pick it up if you fancy a go,' said Haden, waving the Stanley knife.

Liam emerged from the bedroom carrying a black bag.

'Thought so.' Haden turned to his brother, who was digging through the bag, sending the notes spilling out as he tried to count them.

'Forget it, bruv. If it's short we'll be back for the rest,' Haden glared at Ian, 'and we won't be so patient next time.'

'You've got what you wanted,' said Ian.

'Have I? You think this is just about the money? You're small-time, a fucking little gnat, so I expect some respect from you. How long we been doing this? I give you the gear, you sell it to your mates, take your cut and give me mine. We both earned out of this and now you've gone and fucked it up.'

'I'm sorry, Haden, I just—'

'Shut up!'

Ian looked down. There was a long pause and then Haden sprung to life. He leapt forward, thrust the knife into Ian's abdomen, and twisted. Ian let out a sigh and slid to the floor. Clutching the black bag, the odd banknote fluttering loose, Liam followed his brother out of the house.

Chapter 23

The smile on Inspector Craig Jacobs's face seemed a little forced. 'Sir, this is Ed Kavski.'

'Mr Kavski. I've heard a lot about you already. Inspector Jacobs here speaks very highly of you.' Graham Huntington shook the proffered hand.

'And so he should,' Kavski replied.

Ed and Jacobs both laughed.

'Please, take a seat.' Huntington indicated the table, covered with a crisp white cloth. He had chosen the venue after some thought. Paul's restaurant was at a distance from Langthorne House Police Station, and too expensive for most people who worked for the police. In fact, it was attached to his golf club. Huntington just hoped they didn't look too out of place.

Huntington wore a shirt and tie, as did Inspector Jacobs, now trying to loosen his. Ed was in jeans and a Hugo Boss T-shirt with the short sleeves rolled up over his considerable biceps. Huntington tried to avoid staring at the large, faded tattoo that wound around Ed's right arm. A waiter materialised, carrying three menus and a tea-light candle, which Huntington waved away.

Jacobs picked up the menu and flipped through it. 'And you said that coffee place was overpriced.'

'That coffee place *is* overpriced. I believe in value for money. I was also keen to keep Mr Kavski here away from Langthorne. It wouldn't do for me to be seen lunching with him at this stage. No offence, you understand.'

Ed waved a hand. 'Makes sense.'

'So you'll have questions for Ed here, I expect?' said Jacobs.

'Plenty, and not just for Ed, I might add.'

The waiter delivered their drinks — coke for Ed and water for the other two — and vanished.

'Fire away.'

'Okay then. Ed, I'd like to hear your view of this idea and the reasons why I should be trying it in Langthorne?'

Ed crunched ice and put down his glass, missing the coaster. 'I've had a very brief chat with Craig — with Inspector Jacobs here — about your problem. From what I've heard, the Epping Hill Estate is pretty much the same sort of area as we've worked in before. The guv'nor came up with the idea that we'd go in there as civvies and rattle some cages. It was amazing what results we got, and quick too. The civvy angle really works. It gives us real freedom in dealing with people.'

'And you were made aware that you would be treated the same as anyone else, if you were found using violence,' added Jacobs.

'That's right, we were.'

'I said no prompting.' Huntington wagged a finger at Jacobs.

'Well, we were anyway,' Ed continued. 'I mean, Inspector Jacobs explained to us beforehand that we could be a bit physical and that no one would make any complaints to the police, and he was right. I mean, we didn't go over the top, but more than you can do as a copper. Anyway, we knew that these sorts of places have pretty much the same structure. You get the junkies at the bottom, that have to fund their habit with all the petty crime that makes a mess of your monthly figures. Key Performance Indicators they were called in the Met.'

Huntington nodded. 'They're KPIs down here too.'

'Right, well, your KPIs for stuff like thefts, housebreaking, theft from motor vehicles, that sort of thing, are pretty much guaranteed to be your junkies, the bottom feeders, and we'd been targeting them for years without effect. You'd lock one of the fuckers up and two more would be waiting for you to turn your back so they could carry on. And because you're talking minor stuff, the ones you caught would be back out in twelve hours anyway. *And* because they'd been locked up all day, they would be desperate for their script, so there'd be people released from custody getting nicked for a street robbery on their way home.'

'Mr Kavski, you'll excuse me for reminding you that I know all this. This isn't my first day.'

Ed sniffed. 'Of course you do. You'll see my point, though. The idea is not a new one, but we did it by starting with the bottom feeders. We were put in with a backstory already in place, so everyone in the area thought we were badass gypsy types. Then we leant on a few of the junkies to find out where they were getting their gear from. The next layer up was those that dealt in order to source the stuff for their own use.'

The waiter reappeared. 'Gentlemen, are we ready to order?'

The three men sat back, each barked their choice in turn and the waiter picked up on their tone. He offered no small talk, just a firm underline on his pad and an accompanying nod and he was gone.

'So then,' continued Ed, 'We'd lean on the next layer, who were getting their stuff from bigger fish, usually a local with a bit of muscle or a screw loose. Someone everyone knew and everyone was intimidated by. We'd change our game plan accordingly and go in hard. The next layer would be based outside the estate in a nicer area, but close enough to keep control of their patch, and we needed to step up our game a bit more to earn our intel. After that came the proper bigwigs, the ones that were supplying all over the country. We got information on importations of large amounts of class A, the lot. It was beautiful.' Ed took a drink, the ice clinking against the side of the glass.

Huntington was beginning to respond to the idea. 'Easy as that, eh?'

'It didn't even take long. By the end, which was, what, five months or so, we had earned a reputation and the major players were coming to *us* with job offers. We could have formed links with major importers from all over Europe, the whole damned planet if the Met chief hadn't suddenly lost his balls. The man's a fool. He could have claimed all the glory and *what* glory it would have been. We had enough names and information to bring down the entire UK drug supply network. He was welcome to the glory too, as far as we were concerned. We just wanted a chance to get it done.'

Huntington sat back, already visualising himself as the man responsible for an operation that branched out into Europe and beyond.

'And you have a team of people all ready to go?'

'Four people, plus me. I found five has the dynamics right. We talked about us pitching up in caravans, but the problem in Epping Hill is that it makes us a little vulnerable. We need to be able to put in a fair amount of kit — computers, listening devices, notes et cetera, the sort of stuff that would make it pretty obvious that we're snouts. There are a few empty council properties on the estate. I wondered if there's any way of getting us housed in one of those?'

'I know a couple of people on the council,' Huntington said. 'One of them in particular owes me a favour. I'll make a call and see what I can do.'

'Great. I think it would make a lot more sense. There's still a fair amount of preparation to be done. We'll create our identities like we did last time — criminal records, warning markers, slides for the uniform briefing, fake police records for our vehicles, and so on. It's all set up from the last op. All we need from you is to sign some paperwork giving authority for the fake records to be entered onto the computer. It's done all the time with diplomatic vehicles and politicians to ensure—'

'As I said, Ed, this isn't my first day. I've signed off similar requests.'

'Of course.'

'Chicken Caesar salad?' The waiter had reappeared unnoticed with the meals, and they waited for him to leave.

Huntington tugged apart a granary roll. 'So, talk to me about timing.'

'Well, I'm supposed to give four weeks' notice at the moment, but I get the feeling they won't insist on it. I can assemble most of the team pretty sharp. The background work will take a week or so, and then we'll be good to go.'

'What sort of timescale did you have in mind, sir?' Jacobs said.

Huntington was aware that he hadn't yet agreed to the operation. He took the bait. 'Soon as possible. Inspector Jacobs, you will be running the op on the ground. I want you two to be in daily contact, and I will expect to be kept fully informed. I will have specific tasks for you to complete. There have recently been some nasty incidents in Epping Hill, and we need the culprits identified. I assume when you talk of "rattling cages," you can also get people to talk about who might be responsible for knifepoint robberies, for example?'

'No problem,' Ed said through a mouthful. 'Same tactics, just different questions.'

'Good. I'll make sure Inspector Jacobs here has all the details you need. Once that's done, you can turn your attention to the many layers of Epping Hill. You do have to understand, though, I am not authorising the use of force against any persons in Epping Hill at any time. If you choose to use those tactics, you are on your own. Understand?'

Ed nodded. He and Jacobs exchanged a smile.

'This total faith of yours in the culture of these places, and Epping Hill in particular, that they won't just go to the police when you exert pressure on them, you'd both better be right because I won't be backing you up in the dock if I'm asked. Do you understand?' Both men nodded. 'And, Ed, you will have no direct contact with me. You take orders from me via Inspector Jacobs. I will be running this thing day to day. If at any time and for any reason I feel that I need to pull it, then you immediately up sticks and leave the area. Do I make myself clear? No questions asked.'

'Clear as can be. You're the boss. I know this doesn't sit easy, but you will have full control and you *will* get results from this. You just have to take a bit of a punt.'

'A punt?' Huntington shrugged. 'A punt it is. Let's get the ball rolling.'

Chapter 24

'I knew you'd be in here.' George smiled at his wife, sitting in the easy chair that had been positioned next to the cot. They had both been expecting to spend a lot of time here, comforting their new addition and watching her sleep. When Charley had arrived, it had been one of George's favourite times. He would simply sit and watch how content she was, and listen to her gentle breathing, the occasional sigh. Mornings were also special — when Charley first woke up, she would still be a little sleepy and liked a cuddle. She'd lean into his shoulder as he held her in his arms, sometimes gripping on to his finger with her tiny hand.

Sarah shifted a little and the plastic cover crackled under her weight. 'We've not even taken the wrapper off this. We'll get a full refund.'

Not for the first time, George had no reply to this. Since that morning in the hospital, his heart had ached, becoming a sharp pain whenever he looked into Sarah's eyes. She wasn't coping well. The doctor had warned him that it would hit his wife hard. Sarah had carried their daughter for nearly nine months. Since coming out of hospital, she had been spending more and more time in this room, which had been meticulously prepared for the new arrival. They had considered everything. Except that it would never be needed.

'She would have been so happy here, you know,' Sarah said.

'Of course she would.' George looked round the room. It was all in neutral soft colours, they had been waiting to add touches of blue or pink.

'And so would we, George. We would have been happy too.'

George rested the palm of his hand against her cheek, and bent down and gave her a gentle kiss. 'We've always been happy, Sarah. Even when we've been tested, we've come back and been happy all over again. We've got so much going for us. I know we're hurting at the moment, but it will get better.'

'When?' Sarah snapped. She looked up at him through eyes brimming with tears. 'When will I stop feeling like this? It hurts so much.'

George put his arms round her and held her tight. 'It takes time. It just takes time. We'll get through this together.' He felt Sarah's shoulders shake with her sobs.

Chapter 25

It was six a.m. The front door to the basement flat of 72 Shellend Street was suddenly kicked open, crashing against the wall. Several people stumbled to their feet. A man crawled away from the sudden burst of daylight, still carrying his beer.

Flanked by two colleagues, Ed Kavski stood over the crawling man. The fourth was positioned at the back door, where a woman trying to stagger out, bounced off him. Next to Ed, a team member raised his Taser, the red dot on the chest of one of the room's inhabitants. It prompted him to a panicked question.

'What are you doing!? I got raided the other week and you found nothing. I drink, so what? I'm a registered alcoholic, all right, that's it.'

Ed feigned indignation. 'Raid? You think we're scum?'

'Of course you're police! You got them Taser things, and who else just fucking kicks their way into places!'

'Would coppers do this?' Ed brought his right boot hard up into the stomach of the man still on his knees. He rolled onto his side.

'Hey! There's no need for that!'

Ed gestured at the man on the floor. 'You call me scum again and he won't be the target next time, got it?'

'Look, what do you fucking want?'

'You're Elliot, right? You live here?'

'Yeah.'

Ed looked around. 'Nice place.'

'I'm on the sick, mental health.'

The room was dim. The filthy net curtains were stuck to the window with damp grime. Against one wall was a slowly collapsing sofa covered with numerous throws, each as filthy as the next. Music was playing quietly, coming from a small television in a corner. The flickering light from the screen provided the only brightness in the room. A wooden table took up most of the space between the sofa and the television, holding dust, food scraps, drink cans and fag ash.

'The sick? That should give you the time to clean up this shithole then.'

'What do you want?' said Elliot.

Ed looked down as the man at his feet retched and coughed up liquid. His lip curled. 'A young girl got a knife in the face on a bus. It weren't far from here. I've been talking to people round the estate, and your name's been bandied about. Seems you might know something about it.'

'Know something about it?' Elliot spluttered. 'Some girl gets knifed and you come here to ask *me*? I don't know what the fuck you're talking about.'

Ed smacked his lips. 'Well, seems we have a problem. You see, we have at least three people who said you are the person we need to talk to. Now I ain't too good at maths, but I know that three's more than one.'

'You are police! You can't just kick my door in and start accusing me of stuff I know nothing about! What you asking me about this for?' Elliot was beginning to stutter.

Ed nodded at the man with the Taser. He raised it and squeezed the trigger. The trap doors on the weapon blew apart, and two barbed prongs shot out. They carried a combined electric current of twelve thousand volts, which pulsed through Elliot's body with a loud clicking noise. Elliot crashed forward, yelping in pain. 'You fucking . . .'

Ed stood over him.

A voice sounded from behind Ed. 'You can't do that, come on . . .' Ed spun round and pointed his Taser.

'You want to know what it feels like?' The voice fell silent. 'Good choice.' Elliot's hand had reached round to feel for the prongs sticking into his back, metallic wires coiling back from them to the Taser.

'You wanna call us scum one more time, mate?'

'Jesus, what do you fucking want from me?'

'What do I want? You need to answer for what you did. What you did to that girl was bang out of order. So what I want is really very simple, even for someone with *disabilities*.' Ed knelt and brought his mouth close to Elliot's ear. He gripped the top prong. 'I want you to do the right fucking thing. I want you to crawl out of this fucking hovel and go down to the cop shop and tell them bastards that you were responsible for the girl in the bus. Got that?'

Elliot looked up from the floor. 'But I didn't! I didn't touch no girl.'

'That ain't the answer a man in your situation should give, do you understand?'

'Look, I heard about it. I've talked with people about it. We all know what happened, but I had nothing to do with it. You got to believe me. I had nothing to do with it, for fuck's sake!'

'All right, pal, no need to get emotional.' Ed twisted the metal prong and Elliot's face contorted into a grimace. 'It hurts, don't it? The police, you know, they fire these things but then they have to get a paramedic with some special tool to come out and remove the fucking thing, otherwise it can be very painful. You can't just wrench them out. They can do some real damage.' Ed suddenly pulled, and the prong popped out, taking with it a chunk of skin and leaving a hole which immediately filled with blood. Elliot screamed, and he felt behind him for the wound. Ed pushed Elliot's head into the floor and grasped the second prong, which was digging into his buttock. This one didn't come out as easily, it had buried itself deeper, and brought a lump of flesh with it. And more blood.

Elliot screamed.

Ed held him down as he thrashed about. 'Calm down. Calm down. Now listen to me. I'll be back every day until I know you've done the right thing. I'll find out whether you've been down there or not. Don't you think for a second you can pull the wool over my eyes, and don't think that you've had a rough time here either. You've got off pretty fucking lightly, my friend. And if I hear that you ain't been there, or that you've mentioned our little *meeting*, then I will make sure you realise just what rough can be, do you understand?'

'Yes,' Elliot whispered. 'Fucking yes.'

As the four of them moved to the door, Ed stopped. 'You made the right decision here, Elliot. Don't think you can change your mind now. You don't want me to come back, believe me.'

Some distance from Shellend Street, one of Ed's team looked at him, shaking his head. 'He ain't capable of knifing no one, Ed.'

'Who gives a fuck? He's a shit. He's guilty of something, you can be sure of that.' The men's laughter echoed down the empty street.

Chapter 26

George Elms stepped out onto his front doorstep. His Laguna waited silently on his drive, thick, freezing fog drifting around it. George pointed the fob at the car. Nothing happened, and George swore for the umpteenth time that he would get the batteries in that fob changed when he next had a day off. The ice in the locks was solid, and almost ten minutes of further bad language ensued until the interior light flickered on.

By now George was wishing he'd brought his coat, which he'd left hanging in the hall. The trouble was, saying goodbye to Sarah had been hard enough the first time. He didn't dare go back now. He'd told her that he was needed at work, and she had said she understood. In truth, he could have stayed at home, but he needed some time away, a break from home.

It was the first time he'd come into work since his compassionate leave, and he'd made sure to be early. He dreaded the thought of all the condolences, and he'd called Helen Webb to tell her to warn his colleagues off, but he had no idea if she'd done so. At least he didn't have to worry about his own team. Paul Baern was the next to arrive. He bowled in, took off his leather jacket and scarf, stared at George with narrowed eyes and belched.

'Breakfast.'

George smiled, leant back in his chair and rubbed his eyes. Paul was staring at him.

'What?'

'You're new here, are you? I'm Paul, nice to meet you. Now, the first thing a new boy has to do is make the tea.' Paul shook the kettle and switched it on. 'There you are. I've made a start for you.'

George's smile grew wider.

'Milk, one sugar please, stranger. I need a piss.'

Next to file in were members of the administrative team. Mostly, these were women who always stuck together — a "gaggle," as Paul called them. Usually, they ignored his team, but today each one gave George a smile and a wave as they entered. He didn't respond. Then Sam Robins arrived, shaking her blonde hair from a woolly hat.

She smiled at her sergeant. 'Sorry, are you new here?'

George smiled back. 'I know, I know, the kettle's already on. Whatshisname told me that the new boy has to make the tea. You know who I mean, erm . . . the bald, fat lad.'

They were still laughing when the bald, fat lad returned.

'What's so funny?' Paul asked.

Sam hung up her coat. 'Nothing, Paul.'

'You laughing too, new boy? Getting a bit above your station, aren't we?'

George made the tea, and quickly filled the awkward silence. 'Right, I need to get up to speed with all the good work you people have been doing. We'll take our teas into the CCTV room and have a quick chat. No doubt you just need to tell me that all the cases are complete, but it's got to be done.'

Paul stood up. 'You joke.'

For some unknown reason the CCTV room was always hot. It was where the officers viewed CCTV footage on two large plasma screens mounted side by side on the wall, and connected to various computers. There were DVD and tape players on the desktops in front of which was a collection of half-broken chairs that had once been out in the main office. None of them trusted the chairs enough to sit on one.

'Right then. It's been two weeks and I know we had a lot on when I left. So let's talk about where we are. Sam, you were talking to Sophie, our injured girl from the bus. Did you ever draw that tattoo? And where is the investigation now?'

'There was no need to in the end. Huntington took the case over, and we had someone walk in and cough it. Huntington pretty much closed us down. I did the interview and I had a few bits to check up on, but I was told there was too much going on to spend more time on it.'

'Who's our offender?'

'Elliott Tinsow.'

George frowned. 'Tinsow? The pisshead?'

'Yeah, Shellend Street.'

'We know him, don't we? He's a drunk and a shoplifter, but he doesn't slash seventeen-year-old girls with a blunt knife.'

Sam nodded. 'I agree. He couldn't give me any proper details. All he said was that he had been drinking all day and couldn't remember much about it.'

'The kids didn't say anything about their attacker being pissed.'

'They didn't, no. I was going to go back and speak to them both, and talk to Sophie again about the tattoo.'

'Does Tinsow have a tattoo?'

'Not so you'd notice. He's got one on his forearm that was a DIY job and has almost faded away. I think it was the initials of whoever he was drinking with at the time.'

George rubbed at his chin. 'I assume it was a charge and remand?'

'No, thankfully. We couldn't find any grounds to keep him in custody, so he was released on bail. He's got a curfew as part of the conditions. He's got to be indoors overnight, starting at six in the evening.'

'Thankfully? You're usually the first one to sling 'em in jail.'

Sam smiled. 'I know. I just wasn't convinced. I didn't push for the remand, to be honest, and I think you can expect Huntington to mention that to you. He wasn't a happy man at all when I let Elliot go.'

'I'll deal with that. When's he due in court?'

'Not sure yet. He's got to come in to get his date. He's on a short bail, seems CPS were thinking along the same lines as me. They wanted a few more things sorted before they'll authorise the charge.'

George slurped noisily at his tea. 'So you *will* need to speak to the kids again.'

'Huntington said he was going to organise uniform to do it. It's just a statement from each of them covering a couple of further points.'

George chewed his bottom lip. 'We'll do it. You say Tinsow's on a curfew?'

Sam nodded. 'Every night, all night.'

'I think it's only right we pop in on him then. I reckon we should have a little chat off the record, see if his memory's any better.'

'I said the same. Huntington wasn't so keen to hear my views.'

George guessed that the last couple of weeks had been particularly tough on Sam, having to answer to Huntington directly. He was not someone who took women seriously. That was a mistake. George respected Sam more than most people he had worked with. She was a first rate detective.

'Paul, you were involved with the taxi driver who got a beating. As I recall, we were struggling to get any information from the people there, and you were going to see the victim.'

'Yes, that's it. I spoke to him at the hospital — he's not long out actually. He didn't want to tell me anything at all, he's not even alleging that he was beaten up. He said that he was flagged down by someone and then he can't remember anything after that. Next thing he knows, he wakes up in hospital.'

'Okay. You intend to speak to him again, or is it case closed?'

'I spoke to Huntington and he said to sack it. There's no more lines of enquiry outstanding and the victim doesn't want police help. I was hoping to pop in on him again now he's back home and has had a little while to think about it.'

'I agree. You never know, his family might have been nagging at him to tell us more, and he could take the opportunity when you go round there. I've got a pretty clean slate at the moment, until they start loading the work back on, so I should be able to get out with you both. Sam, you and I will go see Sophie and the lad, see if they remember if the guy had been pissed. Have you got the tape of your interview with Tinsow?'

'Uh huh. It's in the file.'

'Good. Dig it out and we'll sit down and have a listen first off, and make sure we cover the content with the kids. We'll go and check Tinsow this evening, and try and get some more information out of him.' George paused. 'I remember he did a spell in prison, totting up for a load of shoplifting. You don't reckon he wants back in?'

Sam shrugged. 'It's possible, but he was weird in interview, really weird. He kept saying he couldn't remember any details about the robbery, but he was really angry about it. I couldn't tell if he was angry at himself or at us, but it wasn't what I expected. He said he came in to cough it because he felt guilty, but he wasn't showing any remorse.'

'We'll have a good chat with him. I'll need to catch up with Helen and then Sam's boyfriend, Mr Huntington.' Sam snorted. 'And then I'm all yours for the day. Before I start, is there anything I don't know about?'

Sam and Paul looked at each other, and Paul said, 'Oh, there was some stuff needed doing for Major Crime. They've got a murder at an industrial estate with a few cars burnt out at the scene. They've managed to ID the car and there's intel linking it to Effingell. They've given us three names with a few bits to do on them. There's no suggestion there's anyone from Effingell involved, but they are asking for it to be done ASAP.'

'ASAP you say? We've got enough rumbling on without assisting departments with more officers than desks. I suggest they send their own DC's out, assuming it's not beneath them.'

Paul nodded. 'Understood.'

They picked up their mugs and left the stagnant atmosphere of the CCTV room. George could have guessed that Helen would be waiting for him. 'How are you, ma'am?'

Helen tilted her head and pursed her lips. 'I'm fine, George, just fine, but how are you?' She placed a hand on George's forearm, and he was suddenly uncomfortable. 'Are you sure you should be back?'

'I'm more than sure, ma'am. I've just been getting up to speed with the team, and it seems like it's all been running well while I've been away.' Helen went on nodding long after George had finished speaking.

'Listen, ma'am, while I'm here, my mind is on my work. That's just what I need.'

'Okay, George, you know where I am if you need to talk to me about anything.'

'I do, ma'am, thanks.'

'It was good news about the young Sophie girl, wasn't it?'

'Certainly was. Do you know the offender, ma'am?'

Helen shook her head. 'I don't. Huntington said he did and he wasn't in the least bit surprised.'

'Oh, he knows him, does he?' George wasn't buying that for a second. 'I do too, and I must say I was surprised to hear him linked to it.'

'Oh, it's a bit stronger than being *linked*, George. The man came in and held his hands up to it.'

'Did we get much supporting evidence? I haven't had a chance to get completely up to speed.'

'Nothing forensically, but Tinsow was among those we were going to speak to. The bus station CCTV had picked him up on that route numerous times, and getting off at the same stop our offender did.'

'And did the CCTV have him getting on the bus on the night of the robbery?'

'No. As I recall, it didn't, but the coverage isn't comprehensive. It would have been quite possible for someone to get on the bus without being caught on the cameras. But I'm sure Graham will give you a lot more detail. He will want to see you this morning, so please touch base with him as soon as you can.'

"Touch base." George hated all that management-speak bullshit. 'First I'm going to buy these people some breakfast. Seems they've been working hard in my absence, so it's only fair.'

Chapter 27

Heading out for bacon butties, George was pleased to be on his own, and made a detour around Epping Hill. He had no idea why — he certainly hadn't missed the place.

He rounded a sharp corner at low speed and did a double-take. He thought he recognised a girl pushing a buggy as Elizabeth Wallis. Not long ago, he had broken news of her boyfriend's demise. She was walking towards Peto Court. George caught up with her as she arrived at the solid metal door of the communal entrance.

'Elizabeth!'

The girl turned round, obviously recognising him. She came over to George.

'How are you doing, Elizabeth?' he asked.

'It's Lizzie, Sergeant. I'm pretty sure I told you that last time.' Lizzie tossed aside her fringe which had fallen into her eyes.

George smiled. 'You did. I guess your memory is better than mine, Lizzie.'

'Sergeant Elms, right?' Even Lizzie's half smile lit up her face. She was wearing a black body-warmer over a long-sleeved black top and skinny jeans. Lizzie's mousey hair was held back in a ponytail, but her long fringe kept falling into her eyes. George was once again struck by how out of place she looked in Peto Court.

'George,' he reminded her, 'and I think I said that last time too.'

'So what can I do for you?'

'Nothing at all. I saw you walking along and just wanted to see how you were doing.'

Lizzie looked down at her sleeping daughter and then back at George. 'It's been okay. Not great, as you can imagine, but we're getting through it. To be honest with you, we were looking for a way out. It wasn't . . . well, it wasn't a happy relationship, not recently anyway, and we'd had enough.'

'You and sleeping beauty there?' George gestured at the buggy.

'Little monster, more like!'

'It's never easy though. Getting news like that is always a shock.'

'It was a shock, yeah. I won't be shedding any more tears for him though. He wasn't good to me or to her. I just feel sorry for his mum.' Lizzie rubbed her hands together. They were white with cold.

'Yeah, she didn't take it well. It's always harder for the parents, especially the mums, they only ever see their sons as angels.'

'That's certainly true of Jackie.'

'So I assume you will be getting out of this place pretty soon, then? Maybe let your parents help you out now?'

Lizzie swept back her fringe and curled her lip. 'I won't be asking *them* for any help. I can look after myself.'

'I'm sure you can Lizzie, but we all get a hand every now and then. I just meant that you could probably do with moving out of here.' George nodded at Peto Court looming behind her.

145

'And go where? I don't really know anyone in the town. At least there are people I know here.'

'Maybe they aren't the sort of people that you really want to know. I've worked this place for a long time and I've seen a lot of good people get sucked in. It's not a nice place to be, Lizzie, and you're far too good for it all.'

Lizzie gave the buggy a shove. 'Thing is, Sergeant Elms, you don't really know me, or what's good for me.'

Lizzie walked away and disappeared into Peto Court. George sat in his car, contemplating whether to go up to Flat 22 and apologise. Then he shrugged and pulled away.

* * *

George made his way to an industrial estate where he knew of a particularly good "dog van," the sort that cooked all the ingredients of a hearty English breakfast, then stuffed them into a bread roll as long as your arm. The woman behind the shiny metal counter had plump, rosy cheeks and a cheerful smile. George had once been a daily visitor to her van, and she remembered him.

'Sorry, sir, we don't serve traitors.' She turned her back and busied herself at the grill.

George pretended to be indignant. 'Traitors?'

'Well, you've clearly found somewhere else to go for your rolls. Tell me . . .' She turned back and looked at him. 'Are you cheating on me with another van?'

George patted his stomach. 'No, Carol, I wouldn't do that. It's . . . it's the muesli.'

'Muesli? That stuff'll kill you, you know!'

'The wife insisted on it.'

Carol looked George up and down, beaming. 'Well, I think she's a lucky woman.'

George straightened his suit jacket. All at once he was very self-conscious. Carol put her head back and laughed.

'I tell her that every day.'

'And what can I get for you today? And I must warn you that the muesli is off.'

'In that case, I shall have three of your filthiest breakfast rolls, please. And I mean filthy in a good way!'

'We don't do them any other way.'

The breakfast rolls had bacon sticking out at the sides, sausages at the ends and plenty in the middle. Back in his car, George had just unwrapped the end of one to sneak a bite when his phone rang. It was Graham Huntington. George swore. 'Hello?' he mumbled.

'George, it's Graham Huntington.'

George gulped down his mouthful of food. 'Hello, sir.'

'It's good to have you back, George.'

Thank you, sir. It's nice to be back working.'

'Yes, yes I bet. Terrible business.'

George smiled at the area commander's best effort at condolences. 'What can I do for you?'

'Ah, yes. I was hoping to catch up with you today. There's been a lot of work gone on in Epping Hill over the last few weeks, and we're looking to push on with it. You're a key man, George, you and your team, and I wanted to make sure you're up to speed.'

'Okay, sounds good.'

'Excellent. I understand you're out and about at the moment. Give Jean a call when you're back on station.'

'I will do, sir.'

As George drove away, he glanced across at the dog van. Carol flashed him a smile. George managed an awkward wave.

Chapter 28

When George returned with breakfast, Brian Appleby was there, talking to his female detective in full flirt mode. He was telling a long story featuring Brian Appleby in the role of hero. He was facing Sam, his back to everyone else. George shared a knowing smile with Paul.

'Is this the one that ends up with you saving the world again? And the hero always gets the girl, right?'

Brian spun to face the voice. 'George, you shouldn't have.' Brian pointed at the rolls, his face suddenly flushed.

'I didn't. Had I known you were going to be down here flirting with my staff, Brian, I still wouldn't have.' Brian flushed a little but maintained his smile. 'I was just talking to Sam here while I waited for you to get back.'

'Of course you were,' George said. He held out one of the wrapped rolls. Sam touched Brian lightly as she moved round him to take her roll. George and she exchanged a smirk. 'You seem to be the only one here not with your hands full, mate, and you're the outsider. That puts you on tea duty, right?'

'Tea duty?'

'You want a cuppa, right? Because I know I do. Sam?'

Sam held up her Disney cup. 'Ooh, yes please, Brian. That would be very nice.'

'I don't even know where the stuff is.'

'It's all there.' Sam rose to her feet. 'How about I go fill the kettle?'

Brian watched Sam walk out of the office and sighed. 'Never, ever will I listen to you complain about working conditions down here, George.'

George nodded at the door. 'You wouldn't know what to do with it, mate.'

'That might well be true, but I'd have a hell of a time working it out.'

'So, you just down here to admire the scenery, mate?'

'Not at all, that's just an added bonus.'

'You hear that, Paul? You're an added bonus.'

'I'm a what?' Paul said through a mouthful of bread and sausage.

'I came down to say hello really, welcome you back and all that.' Brian opened his arms and leaned towards George. 'And if there's anything you need, here or outside, mate—'

George cut him off. 'Thanks. It's just nice to be back, really. It sounds a little harsh but I've hardly had time to think about . . . things, you know, since I got here this morning.'

'I know what you mean. There's a lot to be said for keeping yourself busy.'

'So, two weeks is a long time in intel-land. What juicy information have you got to offer about everyone's favourite place?'

Brian visibly relaxed. 'Ah, Effingell. What can I say? It's the usual ebb and flow I suppose. Your team have been getting results left, right and centre.'

'So I hear.'

'Huntington's got a bee in his bonnet at the moment, and he's been putting on the pressure over there. You can't go down there now without seeing two, sometimes three panda cars, even at night. I think some of the players are getting pissed off with the presence. They seem to be applying their own sort of pressure on people to cough the jobs we're interested in, hoping we'll fuck off.'

George bit his lip. 'You think that's what happened with Sophie and this Tinsow lad?'

Brian shrugged. 'I'm pretty sure he wouldn't have coughed it otherwise. He wasn't even a suspect for us.'

'You think he did it?'

'He said he did.'

'Anyone can say that.'

'You don't think he did it?'

George eyed his roll and licked his lips. 'I'm gonna have a chat with him this evening. It doesn't sit right with me — there are quite a few bits that don't add up.'

'You told Huntington that you're speaking to him?'

'No, why would I?'

'Huntington's been all over this. Every stage since Tinsow walked into this police station has been micro-managed by him. He's not keen on people contacting him without first seeking his permission. He's even been bail checking Tinsow in person.'

George was puzzled. 'Why would he be so bothered, now Tinsow's been bagged?'

'Who knows with that man? He doesn't exactly give a running commentary on what he's thinking, either.'

George shook his head. 'Sam and I spoke to Sophie just after it happened and she gave us a pretty good description of the attacker. She said the offender had a tattoo on his neck. Our Mr Tinsow doesn't. Also the lad who was with Sophie is a bit of a fighter, big for his age and trained too. If he went head to head with Tinsow, I would put my money on the young lad. Not a stick-thin alcoholic who wheezes when he has to get up and answer the door.'

Brian shrugged again. 'I don't disagree with you, mate, but what can you do? There's enough to charge him with in court and if he stands up and goes guilty again, then it'll be case closed and yet another success for Sam here and your team.'

Sam looked up at the sound of her name. 'What was that? Did I hear something about making me a tea? That kettle will need boiling again — it goes cold after an hour or so.'

Brian got to his feet. 'Yes, miss.'

George called out to her. 'Sam, you going to be able to come out and see Tinsow with me this evening?'

She nodded. 'I should be able to make it out.'

Brian was frowning. 'Oh, one thing you need to be aware of is there's a new bunch of rogues for your people to deal with. They've been quiet, at least as far as the police are concerned, but our sources on the estate are having a bit of a hard time with them.'

George looked at him. 'New rogues?'

'Two brothers, and at least a couple others. We don't know much about them yet. Seems they've spent most of their time in other areas, but now they're here and have managed to get the council to house them in Roman Way. I forget their names, I've got them written down upstairs.' Brian stood up.

'What county are they from?'

'All of them.'

'Gypsies?'

'So it seems.'

George sighed. 'Just what Effingell needs.'

Brian had moved to the tea-making station, and was stirring the mugs. 'I agree,' he called back. 'We're putting on all our resources down there, to try and find out as much as we can. Like I said, from our point of view they've been quiet—'

'So far,' George cut in.

'So far,' Brian repeated. He brought three teas and put them on the three desks.

'You not made yourself one?' George asked.

'No, I've got to get back up there. I've my own team to make tea for.'

George raised his cup. 'Well, thank you for ours. Let me know if you hear anything interesting.'

Brian gave a thumbs-up and walked out, casting a last look at Sam.

Chapter 29

'Mr Tinsow?'

Elliot Tinsow opened the door to his flat. It was ten past six in the evening, and he looked as if had just woken up.

'What do you want?' Elliot grunted.

George smiled. 'I'd like to have a word with you, Elliot. I think we might be able to help each other out.'

Elliot hesitated. 'I think you people have done all you can to help me. Now you know I'm in, you can fuck off.' Elliot's gaze darted briefly to Sam before he shut the door.

George bent down with his mouth to the gap that had once housed a letterbox. 'Elliot, I know you didn't do what you said you did. You might think you don't have any options, but maybe you do have a choice.' George looked at Sam as they waited on the doorstep.

Elliot opened the door and looked at George.

'How about we step inside for a couple of minutes?'

Elliot turned away and walked inside. George and Sam followed him into the living room. Elliot stood and faced them, arms crossed. He was wearing dark blue jeans, made for someone with a much larger waist. His white vest looked as though it had been damp and dried several times since its last wash. A strong, musty smell emanated from somewhere in the room — or possibly Elliot himself.

Elliot's words were a little slurred and his eyes had the watery look of the alcoholic. 'I don't reckon I've ever seen so many cops.'

'Are you getting regular visits?'

'Three last night, four the night before, always two of you. You people obviously got nothing better to do. Makes me fucking laugh. I can't remember the last time I went out at night, and here you are checking on me every few hours!'

'That includes the night you were supposed to be riding the bus?'

'I've already said all I've got to say to your pretty assistant here.'

Sam looked at him. 'I wasn't sure you were telling me the whole truth, Elliot. You seemed to miss out a lot of the detail.'

'The whole truth and nothing but the truth, so help me God!' Elliot sniggered, and moved backwards. The backs of his legs touched the sofa, and he slumped onto it. He waved vaguely at a mound of dirty clothes on top of a couple of chairs. George and Sam remained standing.

'You didn't rob two kids on a bus at knifepoint, did you? I think you're a better man than that.'

'So what? I said what I needed to say to Detective Robins here, didn't I? You got it all on tape, too, no going back now.'

'That isn't true, Elliot. If there's a reason why you said what you did, you can tell me. We're here off the record. I can give you options. The police can protect you if that's what you need.'

'Protect me! Listen, mate, you should be happy. I see the news. The papers are ripping you lot apart for this. That girl is some politician's daughter or something. So I swan in and take it on the chin, it's problem solved.'

'Elliot, I'm not interested in locking up the wrong man for this. Yeah, we want a result, but you're not it. Whoever did do that to the girl is a threat to all the other girls in this area. You really want to go to prison? You'd be looking at seven years minimum.'

'We're all prisoners to something. I might as well be one for real — might just sort out a few things for me.'

George took out his notepad and scribbled on it. 'That's my name and my mobile number. I want you to have a think about what I've said, and I want you to help me. Anything you say to me is off the record until you tell me any different.'

Elliot stuffed the piece of paper into his pocket. George knew it was the only answer he was going to get right now, so he and Sam left the flat.

Back in the car, Sam said, 'What do you think then?'

'Well, it definitely wasn't him, he basically said as much.'

'So why would he come in and say it was him? That still doesn't make any sense to me.'

George stared out through the windscreen into the lamp-lit street. 'It doesn't make sense to me, either. Maybe Granny Smith was right. The area gets flooded with panda cars because of this job, and all the extra attention upsets some of the major players. They choose someone sufficiently weak and put pressure on them to cough the job.'

Sam chewed her bottom lip. 'He's not who I'd choose.'

'Really? He's not exactly going to put up much of a fight.'

'He's physically weak, sure, but what's the man got to lose? Look at him — you could give him a kicking but it probably wouldn't even register through all the booze. It's not like you can threaten to take away his cash, his wife or his quality of life, is it?'

'You've got me there. So what does he have?'

Sam shrugged. 'Does he have any family?'

'No idea, but give me a second.' George raised his phone to his ear.

Paul answered it on the second ring. 'What do you want? I'm trying to go home!'

'Sorry, man. You're good to go. I just need a quick favour.'

'What do you need?'

'Our man Tinsow. Can you bring him up on your screen, see if there's any intel about him having family?'

There was the faint sound of someone hitting a keyboard. 'There's a sister and a mother. They live together, according to the most recent intel — which is five years old by the way. Looks like the daughter's some sort of carer for the mother. There's an address on here, hang on a sec.'

George took down the details and ended the call. 'It's been a long day,' he said.

Sam turned to face him. 'Certainly has.'

'You mind making it just a little bit longer?'

'Supposing I said no?'

George grinned. 'I know you won't.'

Chapter 30

George looked out of the car window at the large detached houses that made up Cornwallis Avenue. It was a wide road, the pavements separated from the houses by a strip of neat grass with well-established trees. The rain that had started just a few minutes earlier was now heavy and looked to be set in for the night.

'Well, this wasn't what I was expecting,' George said.

'Me neither,' said Sam.

'Kettle's on,' George suddenly announced.

'You what?'

George was trying to make out the names of the houses. 'Kettle's on. It's the name of the house.'

Sam grinned. 'Of course it is.'

'And here it is.' A slate-grey sign with the word 'Kettallson' in white letters was recessed into a low wall. George bought the car to a stop.

'Nice touch.'

The rain was blown almost horizontally into the faces of the two officers as they stepped from their car. Sam put her A4 notebook over her head. As an umbrella it was pretty useless. The imposing wooden door, beneath an archway with benches running either side, did much to add interest to the plain exterior. A separate building housing a double garage was tucked away to the side, almost hidden by thick shrubbery. George lifted the heavy metal knocker. Sam stood next to him, shaking her hair and cursing the rain.

There was no answer, and he backed away from the porch to see if any lights had come on upstairs. 'There's a light on at the back of the house. Might be a security one, though,' he called out.

'Hmmm.' Sam evidently did not feel like moving from her dry spot. George moved back and knocked with more force.

'Have you pressed that?' Sam was pointing at the doorbell on the wall. She pressed it, and the two officers waited. Sam brushed the moisture off her notebook with her sleeve. George was just about to call it a night, when a bright light illuminated the porch. George heard a window open on the ground floor.

'Can I help you?' The woman sounded annoyed.

George went over to the open window. 'Good evening. I'm Detective Sergeant George Elms, and this is DC Robins. We were hoping to talk to you about Elliot.'

'I'm afraid we don't know anyone by that name.'

George screwed up his face. 'I see. That's a shame. We were led to believe that Elliot's family lived at this address. How long have you lived here?'

'I'm afraid we can't help you.'

'I understand.' George pulled out his notepad and scribbled on it. 'This is my name and my number. I'll pop it through your letterbox. I appreciate you can't help, but perhaps the previous owners left a forwarding address. If you know of anyone who's a friend or relative of Elliot's, can you please ask them to get in touch? I know he didn't do what he's accused of.'

George turned away. They heard the window being pushed shut, and the click of a locking mechanism.

Sam had remained waiting by the front door. 'We're going home, then?'

'Not just yet.' George stepped past Sam and pushed the piece of paper through the heavy brass letterbox. They walked back to the car

'I really need to wash my hair,' said Sam as she sat back in the car, where George was letting the engine run to clear the windscreen.

George smiled. 'Yes, you do.'

'Well, she was a great help.' Sam was peering back at the dark outline of Kettallson.

'Wasn't she?' George had been driving for less than a minute when he suddenly pulled the car over and produced a ringing phone from his trouser pocket. The screen displayed 'unknown number.' He clipped it into the hands-free device, and the ringing came through the car's speakers.

'Hello?'

'Detective Sergeant George Elms?'

'Yes?'

'My name is Marion Tinsow. I'm Elliot's mother. You were just at my house.'

'We were.'

'At the end of Cornwallis Avenue, if you turn right into Lynwood and drive a short distance up the road you will see a gap in the hedge with a stile. Park your car a little way from this stile and then walk back over it. There's a path that goes all the way along the back of the houses. We're twelve houses along.'

'Okay,' he replied, hesitant.

'Make sure you're not seen.'

The line went dead. George looked at Sam, who was peering out at the worsening weather, clearly unimpressed. 'Do you think it's far?' she said.

'I don't know. I just hope the kettle really is on.'

The route to the back of the house was longer than they had hoped. The path was narrow and dark. George

159

had managed to find a torch, but the batteries were almost dead. Each of the houses had windows lit, but they were not bright enough to light their way. On one side of the path were trees that would have provided shade in summer. On this winter evening, the rain came down through their bare branches. The two of them were soaked through.

'That must be it.' George pointed at an open back door from which a bright light spilled. Sam grunted. George had to hold back sodden branches to enable Sam to walk into the garden, and they both made a dash for the cover of a striped awning that was pulled out over the back door.

As they approached, George could see a woman leaning against the wall of the house.

'Here.' The woman stepped forward and offered a towel.

'Thanks.' Sam took the towel and rubbed at her hair.

'One for you, too,' said the woman to George. 'I'm Maggie, Elliot's sister.' Maggie took a last drag of her cigarette and squashed the butt under her shoe. She picked it up and dropped it into the dustbin. 'My mum doesn't approve.'

'Of the smoking or the littering?' George said.

'Come in, you must be soaked!' George saw the silhouette of another woman, moving back into the house.

They went into an open-plan kitchen, dominated by a large central island. A copper kettle sat on the hob.

'Cup of tea?'

'We would both love one, Mrs Tinsow.'

'It's Marion, please.' She went over to a cupboard and reached up for crockery. Her daughter moved to her side, but Marion brushed her off. 'Don't fuss, Mags.'

'My mother's not well — not that she will accept it.'

Marion huffed and put out cups and saucers on a table at the far end of the kitchen.

'Please, sit down.'

'You have a beautiful home,' George said.

'Thank you.'

'Though I must say it was a rather unconventional means of entry.'

Marion busied herself with the tea. 'I'm sorry about that. Just recently we've had to be a bit more . . . careful.'

'What do you have to be careful about?'

Marion shivered. 'Maggie, would you light the fire, please?' Above the fire was a small shelf, where George could see a framed picture of a younger Elliot wearing school uniform and smiling broadly.

George's question remained unanswered.

George pointed at the picture. 'That has to be Elliot.'

'It is. It's an old one. I don't have too many of Elliot as an adult.'

'Do you still see him?'

Marion gave a long sigh. 'I saw him recently but that was the first time for, oh, a long time. He had a bit of a fall-out with his dad and that made it difficult. His dad, Peter, died three years ago and I had hoped that Elliot would sort himself out then, but it doesn't seem to be the case.'

'I don't think Elliot's a bad lad—' George began.

'He isn't,' Marion cut in. 'He isn't at all. He's got his problems, but he would never hurt anyone. We did everything we could for him. He had a good education — or at least he went to the right places — but he just didn't seem to be interested in anything. Peter was in property. He built up a portfolio and did rather well. Elliot was never interested in the business. Peter wanted him to get a job and start buying property like he had done, build up his own portfolio maybe. But Elliot didn't want to know.'

'I imagine it's difficult when you have a vision for your kids and they don't share it,' George suggested.

'Do you have children, Detective Sergeant?'

George flinched. 'Just the one.'

'I guess that your child is much younger than Maggie here, and Elliot.'

'She's six.'

'Ah, yes. I remember those days — hard work. Maggie is a geography teacher. Elliot was just as bright although he was more into English and all types of art. The *whimsical* subjects, my husband called them. Peter tired of trying to get him to focus on further education and a career. He thought that getting him out of the house might be the best way to go. He said that if he got away from the home comforts, he would learn that he had to work for the things he wanted in life.'

'Sounds logical.'

'It backfired horribly, Sergeant. Peter chose to put him in the least desirable property we owned. It was a neat and tidy basement flat, but it was in a bad area. You have probably been there to speak to him — Shellend Street on the Epping Hill Estate.' George and Sam nodded.

'Well, I can assure you that when he moved in it was neat and tidy. We provided him with everything he needed. Peter thought that if he had to live among the down-and-outs of that estate, as he put it, Elliot would be inspired to go and fulfil his potential. Peter failed to appreciate the risk that Elliot would become one of those down-and-outs himself.' Marion's voice broke, and she coughed. 'People took advantage of him. We would visit his house and he would have all sorts of people staying there, drunks mainly, and these people soon became his only real friends. Of course, most of them just needed somewhere to stay and they knew that Elliot wouldn't throw them out on the street. It didn't take too long before he was sitting there drinking with them, and then one day he was just as dependent on the drink as they were.'

'So, Marion, you know why I'm here. Possibly you might have some information that could help Elliot.'

Marion expelled a sigh, and brought her hands up to her face.

'We're going to have to tell them, Mum. I don't know what else we can do.' Maggie was standing with her hands on her hips, looking down on her mother.

'They said they would come back if we said anything to the police.' A tear escaped from one of Marion's eyes and she wiped it away. She reached out and took George's hand. 'I can trust you, Sergeant Elms, can't I?'

George pressed her hand. 'You need to start calling me George. Yes, Marion, you and your daughter can trust us both. If someone has threatened you, then we can deal with that, but you must tell me what has happened.'

Marion stood up and grimaced, as if in pain. She walked over to a drawer, took out a DVD and switched on a small television on one of the kitchen units. The screen displayed a date, four days earlier. After a couple of seconds two men entered the frame. The man in front wore a cap, a light coloured short-sleeved shirt and jeans. He had a thick neck and broad shoulders. The man walking behind him had a similar build, but was shorter. The first man banged hard on the door, while the other stood with his arms folded.

'No sound?' George asked.

'No.'

After a short time, the door opened and Maggie appeared. The camera picked out just the top of her head, her slippers and tracksuit bottoms. While they watched the film, she had moved back to the wood-burner and was facing away from the television. On the screen, a conversation was going on between the three people on the doorstep. The first man was clearly agitated. He began gesticulating and moved closer to the door. Maggie reacted, and tried to close the door. At this, the man slammed his palm into the door to keep it from shutting. At this point, both men piled into the house and disappeared. Marion ejected the DVD.

'Jesus,' George muttered quietly.

'As you saw, they came into the house. They pushed past Maggie and knocked her over, and that man kicked her in the chest while she was still lying on the floor. It was all so sudden. You couldn't see me, of course, but I was standing behind her during most of what you saw and they made threats towards me and the house. They said they would burn it down and make sure we couldn't get out. And, Sergeant Elms, I believed them.' Marion's voice began to tremble.

'What did they want?' Sam asked.

'They were here about Elliot. They said that he had done something that he needed to take responsibility for. They said that if he didn't, they would be back. And when I spoke to Elliot the next day, he said that the same people had been to his house twice, and that they were trying to get him to confess to something he hadn't done. He said he would sort it out, and then I saw in the news that Elliot was being charged with attacking those poor children on the bus. You don't need me to say that there is no way Elliot did that, Sergeant Elms, no way at all.'

'Clearly not. Do you have any idea who these people were, and why they've chosen Elliot to be the one to take the blame?'

'None at all.'

George turned to Maggie. 'Maggie, can you add anything?'

Maggie looked at him, her eyes red from crying. 'Only that I was lucky not to have broken a rib.' She raised her shirt to reveal part of an inflamed, angry bruise.

'Let me take the DVD. Give me a statement about what happened, and I'll bring those low-lifes in,' George said, his fists bunching.

Marion shook her head. 'We'll do no such thing. The DVD is all yours, those people don't even know it exists, but we won't be taking it further. You can use that to help you find whoever is bothering my son. See if you can get Elliot to help you, but we will not become involved.'

Marion placed the DVD on the table in front of George. Sam picked it up.

George nodded. 'Thank you. But I beg you to reconsider. You have my number. If you change your mind, then call me, day or night. I will do all I can for Elliot, but he's got to want to help himself. I've been to see him and he didn't want to talk, so perhaps when you see him, try and persuade him to talk to me.'

'I'll try my best.' But Marion sounded unconvinced.

It was time to leave. Sam and George stood up and put on their damp jackets. They left the house the way they had arrived, walking in silence. This time they hardly noticed the rain.

* * *

'Of all the days!' Sarah's tone was quiet but very angry.

'Sarah, I'm sorry, it was a much longer day than I expected. I had to wait till after six to—' George began.

'I don't want to hear it. Charley has only just gone off to sleep. She's been hysterical all evening, George. She spent most of the day wrapped around me. She said she was sad and she just wanted to cuddle her sister. She's still asking why she's not coming home. What do I say to that, George?' Sarah's face contorted as she sobbed. 'What do I say? Because that's who you've got to apologise to, George, not me.'

'I'm sorry, I'll—'

'I don't want sorry! I don't want a word of explanation or apology. What I want is for you to tell Charley why you're late, to tell *her* how sorry you are. And I promise you, once you see her face you will never do it again. This is breaking her little heart and we both need to be here to put the pieces back together. She doesn't understand, George, so *you* tell her!'

Sarah's tears were flowing freely now. She turned and walked up the stairs. He listened until he heard her going into their bedroom, and sighed. He took off his jacket and

165

walked through to the kitchen. He had been saving some fine whisky for a special occasion but, certain that such an occasion wasn't about to happen any time soon, he poured himself a decent measure and threw it back. The liquid seared his throat and warmed his insides.

'Not as smooth as I'd hoped.' He considered having another, but left the glass in the sink and padded up the stairs, stopping at the open door to Charley's room. She was asleep now, lying on her side with her face towards him, her breathing deep and rhythmic. George stepped silently into the room and placed a soft kiss on his daughter's forehead. 'Night night, angel,' he whispered.

He tiptoed back out onto the landing, glancing into the third bedroom, where the outline of a baby's cot stood in the darkness like an accusation.

Chapter 31

'George.' Huntington rose to his feet and shook George's hand. He motioned to George to sit down. George noted that his desk was littered with paperwork. Normally it was almost empty. The area commander seemed tense.

'I was a little disappointed not to see you yesterday,' Huntington began.

'Yes, sorry about that, sir. I knew you wanted to talk to me but I got caught out on a job and didn't manage to make it back in time.'

'No problem,' said Huntington, 'you're here now.' He leant back in his tall leather chair and paused, fidgeting with his hands as though he was waiting for George to ask him something.

'What can I do for you then, sir?'

'Not much. I just wanted to see how you are and make sure you've not come back too early, that sort of thing.'

'I see. Well, I feel I've had long enough. Helen has said that I won't need to be on call for the next few weekends, and she's agreed that I work day shifts, which is great. That gives me evenings and weekends. I'll be spending enough time with the family and enough time away, if you understand me.'

'Ah, yes. So you can be out of the way while the women get their emotional bit out of the way.'

George felt himself flush with anger. 'Well, it's been an emotional time for all of us.'

'Of course.' Huntington rose to his feet and looked out of the window, keeping his back to George. 'You will have no doubt heard that Epping Hill has been quiet over the last couple of weeks — a considerable reduction in the number of jobs coming in and a few excellent results in the ones we had ongoing.' Huntington rocked on his heels, clearly pleased with himself.

'I have heard, yes. I see that Epping Hill is being flooded with uniform. That's having an effect, no doubt, but it isn't going to be sustainable. And I'm not sure about the Tinsow charge either, sir. I have information that he's been bullied into confessing. There are some real issues with—'

'Bullied?' Huntington spun round to face George. 'Elliot Tinsow is a shit. That is backed up by his criminal record.'

'Yes, he is a shit. But he's a petty shit — shoplifting, nicking booze and meat from the local Spar. Hardly armed robbery.'

'So he's escalated. Neither of us is surprised at that, surely? These people get greedy, they get desperate and they get stupid.'

'I spoke to Tinsow, sir. He hinted that he had been intimidated into confessing. I spoke to his mother, too. She gave me good evidence that she's been threatened on his behalf — that's how they are getting to him.'

'You spoke to Tinsow? To his mother?' Huntington looked horrified.

'Yesterday.'

'Why would you do that?'

'Like I said, there are things that don't add up. Such as the physical ability, or rather inability, of—'

'Let me tell you right now, George, you are not to be interviewing suspects outside this police station. That man has been interviewed formally under a police caution, and he has said that he was responsible for the armed robbery in which a teenage girl was callously disfigured. Now I suggest that whatever evidence you think you have is forgotten and disposed of before you fuck this up completely. Do you understand?'

'Not really, sir. This was a nasty incident, I agree, so are we not interested in making sure the person responsible is locked away? Not some poor sap that's had his mum threatened?'

Huntington sneered. 'Oh, spare me your moral code, George. The world is a better place with that man behind bars, irrespective of whether he's guilty of this job or not — and he is, I can assure you. I know there are still plenty of jobs out there that *do* need the attention of you and your team, and I don't expect to hear that you are wasting your time on cases that are cut, dried and closed. Do you understand?'

George considered arguing, but decided this was not a battle that could be won right now. 'Yes.' He deliberately omitted the *sir*.

'Good. Now, I remain in charge of the Tinsow investigation and I do not expect you to have anything more to do with it unless I personally request it, is that clear?'

'Yes.' George stood up to leave.

'Any questions?'

'Can I go now?'

'You may.' Huntington crossed his arms.

* * *

Detective Constable Paul Baern knew better than to ask how George's meeting had gone. It was written all

169

over his face. George answered a call on his mobile phone and looked over at Paul.

'Paul, you wanna grab your jacket? We're heading off.'

Paul looked up from the case file he was reading. 'Can do, Sarge. What's up?'

'Suspicious death. Uniform's got a suspected overdose at Peto Court. They want me to go down and cast an eye over it.'

Paul scoffed. 'Suspicious? Most likely another junkie with a bad batch.'

'Probably. I don't want to go on my own. You're on hand-holding duties.' George threw his car keys at Paul. 'And you're the driver.'

* * *

The old Ford Escort with four flat tyres was still in the car park in front of Peto Court, but it had now been joined by a marked police car, an ambulance and a stained mattress. George pulled up the collar on his overcoat as a stiff wind whipped off the sea. Paul was already at the door and held it open for his sergeant.

George shook his head. 'I'd rather wait outside.' He had his phone to his ear. 'Ah yes, hello, PC Waghorn. This is DS Elms, George Elms. I've been told to come down to Peto Court and call this number. Seems you have something here you want me to poke with a stick . . . righto. No problem. Oh, and PC Waghorn, when you can, you might want to pop down here and move your car. Yeah, past experience. Okay, see you in a sec.' George hung up and met Paul's expectant look. 'They're not coming out to us — seems they're not keen to split up, which is probably wise. We're to go up to the second floor and look out for the two men in uniform.' The men mounted the concrete stairs.

As in the past, whenever there was a death in this building the entire place was deserted. George and Paul were met at the end of the second floor corridor by PC

Waghorn, a squat, balding officer with a booming voice. 'Right, it's not been here long, apparently. The woman from the flat opposite raised the alarm — said she hadn't seen her in a while, looked through the letterbox. The needle's still in situ. It was in the right thigh when the ambulance got here.' PC Waghorn turned and started to walk down the corridor. Paul smiled at George but got nothing back. George was rooted to the spot. Finally, his legs began to move, as if by themselves. They walked the corridor, past number 18, past number 20 with the "0" missing. Waghorn stopped at number 22. Lizzie's flat.

George stepped inside. The flat was the same tidy, yet functional bedsit. Katie and her buggy were missing, with her nan, George assumed. The body lay on her back on the bed, her eyes almost shut, mouth slightly open, head tilted back where the paramedic had tried and failed to breathe life back into her.

PC Waghorn opened his notebook. 'PNC shows Elizabeth Wallis. She's a twenty—'

'It's Lizzie,' George said. Waghorn looked at him in surprise. George could feel his stomach tighten, his heart grow heavy. He had to leave the room. He stopped when he was back out in the corridor and put his hand on the wall for support. His other hand covered his eyes.

Paul rested a hand on his shoulder. 'You okay?'

George nodded. The door to number 23 squeaked open and both men turned to see a woman. Her greasy hair was scraped back and pulled at the skin on her haggard face. She wore tracksuit bottoms and a baggy Rolling Stones T-shirt.

'It's that cunt at thirty-three. He wouldn't fucking leave her alone. He likes the young ones, see. Gets 'em on it so he can have them.'

'Number thirty-three?' Paul said.

'Yeah. You ain't heard it from me though, I ain't no grass. I seen it before, though, and she was a nice girl, one of the good uns.'

'Thirty-three? Jamie Harper?' George asked. He knew the name. He'd known Jamie for a long time. He had plenty of previous for drugs. Dealing wasn't really his thing but he was a known addict and he had sex offences on his rap sheet, always teenage girls and the vulnerable, impressionable sort — runaways, truants and undoubtedly recently bereaved single mothers. George felt the knot in his stomach tighten.

Number 33 was along the same corridor as number 22, and George was there in seconds. He thumped on the door, following it up with a kick, and then stepped back to give it another. The door swung inwards, crashing against the wall. Jamie Harper was standing wide-eyed against the window, holding a baseball bat. When he saw who it was, he put it down.

'What the fuck? You can't just kick my fucking door in! What you got? Show me the fucking warrant!'

For answer, George smashed his fist into Jamie's nose. He felt it give, and Jamie stumbled back hard against the window, where a crack formed in the single glazing. For a second it looked as if Jamie was going to go through.

Then Paul shouted from close behind him. 'George! George! Jesus. We'll get him, mate, but not like this.'

George ignored him. His hand went forward into Jamie's face, again and again until his knuckles were covered in blood. Paul tried to grab his arm as he pulled it back for another hit. Jamie had fallen to the floor and George stood over him. The bat had landed against the wall, and George started to reach for it, but an arm held him tight around his middle. Paul hauled him backwards and pushed him towards Waghorn and his colleague, who had been attracted by the noise.

'Hold him!' At Paul's furious shout the two PCs took hold of an arm each. They wrenched George's arms up behind him and pushed his head forward.

They met no resistance. George was done. He allowed himself to be hauled out of the flat and held against the wall in the corridor. The woman who had given them the name stood watching from her open door.

Waghorn sounded both puzzled and concerned. 'You all right, Sarge?'

George caught his breath. 'Yeah, I'm fine. I'm fine.'

'Right, we're gonna let you go, Sarge, all right?'

'You can let me go.' George's voice was almost calm. The two men released him, and George inspected his knuckles. They had already started to swell.

* * *

Still in the flat, Paul picked up the baseball bat and pushed it into Jamie's neck as he lay slumped against a filthy radiator. Jamie smiled, showing bloody teeth, and spat out of the side of his mouth. 'I'm gonna have him for this. He's lost it. That was well out of order.'

Paul pushed the bat harder into Jamie's neck. 'You fucking listen to me. If you want to make a formal complaint about what's happened today, then you go right ahead. But you should know that if you do, we're both gonna come back and we're not gonna stop until we've done the world a favour, you hear me? Do you hear me?' He rammed the bat harder into Jamie's neck, and Jamie managed a nod.

Paul threw the bat at Jamie and turned and walked out, slamming the door behind him. The two officers were standing in the hallway, and George was nowhere to be seen. 'Where'd he go?' Paul asked

Waghorn nodded at the doors at the far end of the corridor. 'Gone to get some air, I think.'

Paul turned to the two men. 'Listen, gents, about Detective Sergeant Elms—'

'We didn't see what happened,' Waghorn cut in quickly. 'You guys turned up, then left for a short time, then came back.'

Paul nodded. 'We will be back, just give us a few minutes. He's had a tough time.' He turned and strode away.

* * *

Paul Bearn found his sergeant sitting at the bottom of the stairwell. Paul swept away foil, cut-up plastic bottles and an empty bottle of citric acid before taking his place next to him. There was a short silence. 'Maybe you're not ready yet, George. No shame in that, you know.'

George sighed. 'No, that's not it, you're wrong.'

Paul nodded towards the stairs. 'That up there, that wasn't anything like you. You don't react like that.'

'I knew her,' George said quietly.

'I guessed that. Did you know her well?'

'Not at all really, she's just some girlfriend of a loser who killed himself in a nicked car. But she didn't belong here. There was hope in her, you know? She had a chance to change her life. If she'd just listened to the right people, she could have been in a better place. She could have really been something.'

'But she chose not to, George. It's sad, very sad, but she had choices and she made the wrong ones. Life's shit. In our job we see it time and time again, and mostly we shake it off.'

'But I let it get to me because I just lost a daughter, right?'

Paul spoke softly. 'Well, maybe that is what happened. Doesn't make you a bad person. You're human just like the rest of us . . . and just like the rest of us, sometimes your personal life spills over into what you do for a living.'

'You have no idea what it did to us.'

Paul was silent for a while. 'The seventh of March 1990, me and Karen lost our baby girl, Anna. She was our first born and she was everything to us.'

George stared at him in amazement.

'We'd struggled to get a house and to get it right in time, done it all by ourselves. Bit of a shithole it was, tiny little terraced place right up against a fish and chip shop. But it would have been just fine. It was a start at least. After we lost Anna we never went back. My mum cleared the place for us and we moved back in with her till it was sold. When she was born they needed to work on her quick, so she was snatched away from us the second she arrived. That was the only time I actually saw her alive.' Paul's voice shook. 'We had a funeral for her. Didn't invite anyone else, just me and Karen stood by her tiny grave. Neither of us could find any words, you know, we just stood there. That two-foot tall piece of granite is the only evidence that she ever existed — but she did, George, and we loved her.'

George hung his head. 'I had no idea.'

'How could you, mate? We don't mention it, me and the missus, but every year we always book it off work, seventh of March, and we head back down that way. Next door is still a fish and chip shop. We go in there and get some chips and then walk to the beach, the same place we used to go when Karen was pregnant and we were talking about all the things we were going to do with Anna. The first few years it was hard. We nearly packed it in, but now we actually look forward to it. We take the mickey out of each other, and what Anna would have become with both our genes combined. I'm a fat lad and the missus is a bit ditsy. But we've also had two beautiful daughters since, and we talk about them, and what they're up to and how we can help them out. It does get easier, George. It probably doesn't feel like it now, but it does, and trust me, you'll be a better dad to young Charley, too. You'll move heaven and earth to make sure she never goes without.'

'It's not me I'm worried about.'

'Sarah?'

'Yeah.'

'Thing is, she's probably thinking the exact same thing. You've got to look after yourself before you can look after anyone else. That, back there, it wasn't you, and the last thing you want to do is get yourself in trouble at work. You're too good at your job.'

'Thanks. And I'm sorry. It must have been painful for you too, hearing about what happened with us.'

'Yeah, it does bring it all back to you, but I know what you're going through. And there are enough DSs on today to cover this, there's no need for you to go back.' Paul stood up and made for the door.

'No, no, I want to go back. Make sure she's treated with a bit of respect. We all know how overdoses are treated down here.'

'I'll give you a minute. And, George? You know now, so if you need a chat or to vent, I've been there.'

'I might just take you up on that.'

* * *

George remained seated on the stairs. He waited until Paul was out of sight, and then he opened up his left hand which had been tightly closed. Lying face up was a tiny plastic wristband bearing the handwritten name, 'Macie Elms.' He made a fist, brought it up to his mouth and kissed it.

Chapter 32

Ed Kavski stared out from the Range Rover at the village of Acrise. It was situated in the leafy part of the county of Lennokshire, where cities and towns gave way to acre after acre of farmland, narrow country lanes and woodland. It was rich land, and housed the wealthy. Acrise was hardly a village, more a smattering of generous country manors, most of which were secluded behind high walls and sturdy electronic gates.

Ed and Inspector Craig Jacobs were facing one such gate right now. The driver pushed a button and the gate slid open to reveal a long, straight driveway, flanked by well-kept lawns and woodland. The drive opened out to a large, gravel parking area in front of a new-looking house. An eight-foot-high wood sculpture, resembling a bass clef, stood in the centre.

The Range Rover crunched over the loose gravel and pulled up outside a chunky wooden front door. The front door swung inwards to reveal Oscar Baurman, wearing a loose, short-sleeved shirt over a plain white T-shirt and baggy, knee-length shorts. His feet were bare. His hair, damp and combed straight back, was black with a hint of grey. The untidy beard appeared to be longer under his chin and on his neck than it was on his face.

'Mr Baurman, how are you?' Ed Kavski made his way through the front door into the large, open-plan ground floor. A lounge area to their left had large flat-screen TV fixed to the wall, opposite a sofa in black and silver.

'Well, I must say, gentlemen, this is a first for me,' Baurman said. 'I can't say your kind are usually welcome here — no offence, Inspector.'

Jacobs appeared to flounder a little. His face flushed red. 'You have a lovely place. It's warm in here too.'

Baurman looked down at his feet. 'Underfloor heating. I don't like to wear shoes.'

The men crossed the heated floor and sat down facing the muted television, which was showing Sky News.

'Coffee?'

'Sure,' Ed replied, and Jacobs nodded. Ed stared around the open space and high ceilings. He could see a mezzanine floor, reached by wide stairs to the rear. Beyond, Ed could see a fenced-off field with two horses, with hills and more woodland in the distance.

Baurman walked into the kitchen area, which was a small step down off the lounge. 'My wife got me this new coffee-making machine,' he called back, against the sound of a gurgling noise. He padded back to Ed and Jacobs, who was perched on the edge of the sofa with his legs crossed and his hands clasped tightly together.

'You okay, Inspector?' Baurman looked amused.

'Fine.'

'You seem nervous.'

'I do feel a little exposed here,' Jacobs said. 'I mean, coming here, this meeting. We know you've had cops watching this house. They take photos of your visitors, and that means me.'

Baurman sighed. 'We discussed this. You do know I'm not new to this, don't you? The car I sent is totally blacked out. That car comes in and out of here most days, sometimes several times a day, so I can't imagine why they would take any notice of it today.'

'I know it's stupid, but—'

'Yes, it is stupid,' Baurman cut in, 'but I am not. Like I said, I'm not new to this and I know how to protect my investments, which at this time happen to be you two.' A beeping noise issued from the kitchen and Baurman walked through to tend to the coffee.

'Relax,' Ed whispered to Jacobs.

Baurman made his way back to them carrying two small coffee cups. Ed looked down at the dark brown liquid. He noticed that Baurman didn't have one himself.

'Are we all clear on what we're doing?' Baurman said.

Ed nodded. 'I'm clear on what you need from us, sure. It's just how you want us to do it.'

'Hence the reason we're here drinking my nice coffee.'

Baurman stood looking down at them. 'Basically, I'm looking to get control of Lennokshire as a whole. I already supply large areas of the county, but Epping Hill is the key and it appears I have some competition.'

'The Skinners?' Ed suggested.

'Exactly.' Baurman finally took a seat. 'Those two thugs seem to have established quite a foothold in Epping Hill, as well as the surrounding area. That's not something that would normally bother me much, but they are causing me problems with my own supply.'

'They're a pretty small operation from what I can tell. How are they interfering with you?'

'Yes they are small, but they are ambitious. Recently they made contact with the very supplier that I use. He has a rather novel way of importing large amounts of substances into the country using the passenger ferries at Dover Docks, which they are now taking advantage of. So, our mutual supplier now has to transport larger amounts and as a result, his risks increase too. The Skinners are paying a higher premium for their goods, far higher than I am, and they have been for six months now. Not surprisingly, I'm now being asked to pay the same.'

'That's not good,' Jacobs said. Ed stared at him.

'It's not great, no,' Baurman said. 'Normally, I would simply look to remove them but they have become a large enough interest for my supplier that if the brothers were to disappear, he would stand to lose a lot of money. And the suppliers tend to react to losing money in much the same way as I do. At best they would hike the price up even further, so that I was making up the difference, and at worst our working relations would become very sour. I cannot afford either of those things to happen.'

'So you want them put away?'

'Exactly. If the Skinner boys get clumsy and become the subject of police activity, then they are out of my way and everything goes back to normal. There should be no way they would know that I was involved in putting them there. I would be in a far stronger position when it comes to negotiating my ongoing price, and I lose a competitor along the way.'

Ed grinned. 'Makes sense. We can get them nicked, no problem. We're already working our way through Epping Hill. We'll get hold of the people on the streets that are doing the selling for them and force them to give their evidence to the police. We can find out where they keep their gear, set up a raid and—'

'I've got a better idea,' Baurman cut in. He stood up and walked over to the large front window. 'I had a man working for me in Epping Hill — "Smith" — who was responsible for coordinating my operation on the estate and beyond. Recently we had a bit of a falling out. I was hoping I had delivered a sufficient message and he would fade into the background but I'm hearing that this isn't the case. He's back on the gear and coming to the attention of you lot. He's now a liability and I intend to remove him from the picture altogether.'

'Remove him from the picture?' Jacobs questioned.

'Someone in my employment will pay him a visit. The weapon used will then need to find its way to the Skinner brothers. Needless to say, this will be your task. I don't care how you do it, but it needs to be linked very strongly to both brothers.'

'A plant?' Jacobs said.

Baurman shrugged. 'Call it whatever you like. I need to be sure that the Skinners get put away and that the evidence is damning enough to keep them out of the way for some time. I just need my man to lose confidence in them so that he sees me as the best long-term option.'

'We can do that,' Ed said, ignoring Jacob's bemused expression.

'Good.' Baurman walked to a cabinet under one of the spiral staircases and returned with an A4 envelope which he dropped into Jacobs's lap. 'You'll also need to drip-feed this Huntington fella with intel after the incident, to keep up the momentum of the police investigation. Up to you how you do that. Ed, I suggest your task is to make sure my man gets away clean, and then the inspector here will take charge of getting the weapon to the right place.' Baurman looked at them. 'Do we see any problems with this?'

Ed shook his head. 'Not at all.'

'You want me to organise a raid and then *plant* evidence?' Jacobs said.

'Unless you want to be involving someone else?'

'Jesus, I wouldn't know where to start,' Jacobs said.

'Then, yes.' Baurman leaned towards Jacobs, who was looking down at the envelope as though Baurman had dropped a snake onto his lap. 'Unless you have a problem with that?'

Jacobs shook his head. He uttered a weak, 'No.'

'Good. The envelope contains fifty thou and you'll get the same again when the Skinners are nicked. There's also a mobile phone on which you will be contacted so you know when the event is taking place.'

Ed snatched the envelope from Jacobs's lap. 'No problem at all,' he said.

Jacobs and Ed bid their host farewell, and walked out of the front door and into the waiting Range Rover.

'I didn't realise this was going to involve conspiracy to murder,' Jacobs said.

Ed looked at him. 'We were always going to have to break the rules, Craig.'

'Breaking the rules is one thing, but conspiracy to murder, perverting the course of justice and God knows what else? We're not talking about losing our jobs here, we're talking about going to jail.'

'We always were, Craig, so we might as well jump all in. We just better be sure we don't fuck this up.' Ed turned up the envelope, tipping out bank notes in five-thousand-pound bundles. He threw half of them at Jacobs. 'Sometimes the risks are covered by the rewards,' he said, and watched Jacobs scoop up the money and slip it into his jacket pocket.

Ed flipped through the notes. 'This is just the start. You have any idea how much money we can make out of this? It's literally endless, mate. Once this Smith is out of the way and we've earned Baurman's trust, we are in a perfect position to become his main link to the area. How could he say no to that? Him with the supply contact and us with the backing and resources of the police under our control via the chief superintendent — the sky's the fucking limit!'

Jacobs had his head turned to look out of the window. 'Sky's the limit.'

'You think you can handle Huntington?'

'Well, the difficult bit is over. Once he gets the Skinner result he'll be so full of himself he won't give a shit. And then I'll tell him what we're *really* looking to achieve in that estate. By that time he'll be in so deep he'll have no choice.'

'You really have got him all worked out, haven't you?'

'He's perfect. He's obsessed with his rank and his stature. Once he realises that rumbling us would see him lose everything, he'll be very much on board. We'll give him his cut if it makes him feel better, keep him sweet.'

'Sweet indeed!'

Jacobs was still turned to the window, but Ed could see just enough of his face to make out a wider smile forming. The cash had done it. The inspector was now fully committed.

Chapter 33

'George Elms.' This was said with some impatience into his desk phone. George was running late. Sarah had hassled him for going into work today and then the Laguna had frozen shut.

'Is that the way you were taught to greet people on your Community Contact course?'

'Yes,' George said, 'I believe it was.' He recognised the voice but he couldn't quite put a name to it.

'I'm coming back down to Langthorne today, George. I was hoping to catch up with you again.'

The chief! Shit, it was the chief! George sat up automatically. 'Sorry, sir, I didn't recognise the voice there at first. Eh, yes, I'm sure I can make the time.'

'Well, if you're too busy, George, then forget it. I'll go have a chat over coffee with the girl at the petrol station instead.' The chief chuckled.

'Probably best I don't drive this time though, sir, wouldn't you agree? Did you ever get that window replaced?' George winced a little at the memory.

'Of course, but I'm under strict instructions from my driver not to let you anywhere near the car this time, I'm afraid.'

'Fair enough.'

'I'll be with you about two this afternoon I would imagine. I have some bits to do this morning. I want to catch up with the state of play on Epping Hill and show my face around.'

George sniffed and rubbed his nose. 'Well, I can understand that, but I might not be the best person to update you on Epping Hill. I've not been around for a couple of weeks really, and Mr Huntington has been quite hands-on in my absence. He seems to be the man in the know.'

'George, I'm not coming down to talk work with you. I know you've been off. I just wanted to make sure you're okay, that you're getting the support you need and all the rest of it. I was so sorry to hear your news.' The chief's tone was warm and sincere.

'I appreciate that, sir, that's very kind. I'm fine, though. We're getting through it.'

'Of course you are. Doesn't mean I can't buy you a coffee and get us both out of the office now, does it?'

'I'll look forward to it, sir.'

George checked the time. It was coming up for ten already, and he had a full day's work stacking up. He looked across at Paul and Sam and could see similar mounds of casefiles in front of them.

'Sergeant Elms, good morning.'

George looked up. 'Morning.'

'I'm Inspector Craig Jacobs.' The man shot out a hand, and George stood up to shake it.

'Hello.' George was pretty sure he had seen him around. The inspector paused as if waiting for something, and George did his best not to look blank. 'I'm sorry, am I supposed to have something done for you, or . . ?'

'I'll be your direct line leader going forward.'

'Going forward?'

'Well, by that I mean from now on.' Jacobs put his hands in his trouser pockets.

'I see. Inspector Ascott has been—'

'When was the last time you saw Mr Ascott?' Jacobs cut in.

George couldn't recall the last time he'd seen the old man. 'Well, I know he's had a few problems with his health, but—'

'Mr Huntington has decided that this team might benefit from a more *hands on* style of management. Look, George, Mr Huntington's happy with the results this team has achieved, and the way you have been getting on with it. He just doesn't think you should have to. All the teams here have an inspector they can lean on a bit, get support from, someone to fight their corner, that sort of thing. He's asked me to do that job. I really thought he would have spoken to you about it by now.'

George looked down at a forgotten post-it asking him to go and see Huntington. Suddenly he found himself warming to the idea. Perhaps it would be nice to have another layer in between him and Huntington, and also Helen Webb if it came to it — someone who could deliver the bad news and take the repercussions.

'I'm sure he meant to.'

'Right.' Jacobs clapped his hands. 'I see there's a desk free over there. Do you mind if I move my stuff in?'

George frowned. This was going a bit far. 'We don't usually have the higher echelons of management in among us, sir, with respect. Do you not want one of those fancy offices? I'm not even sure that computer works.'

'I've been in one of those sweat boxes for the last three months. I like the idea of sitting in with the team. That way I can be on hand for any issues.' Jacobs was already clearing scrap paper and old pens from the desk in question.

'That's true,' George said. This was no good at all.

'I'll get my stuff moved in then,' Jacobs said, dragging his finger through a layer of dust.

'Okay. Let me know if you need any help.' George watched the inspector walk back between the desks and out of the door. Sam and Paul had been listening to the exchange.

He shrugged for their benefit. 'I know, I know.' The day was quickly going from bad to worse.

Chapter 34

George had spent the day working on a pile of paperwork. He had been so determined to get it finished that he had hardly taken any notice of the new inspector in their midst. Inspector Jacobs had begun setting up his desk, but had been called away into meetings for most of the day. This seemed to be the way for inspectors in George's experience.

George hadn't taken much notice of the time either, and he didn't look at the clock until just before four o'clock, technically his clocking off time. Alan Cottage was strolling in through the double doors and past a suddenly very interested Inspector Jacobs.

'George!' The chief's voice boomed across the office. His handshake was that of a friend rather than a work colleague. George found himself smiling warmly at the chief. He became very aware that just about everyone in the office, including his new inspector, was watching them.

'So, we out for a coffee then?'

'Sure,' George replied.

'Do you have a car? Only I wasn't joking earlier, my driver really doesn't want you to have mine.' The chief laughed.

'I do, but you'll have to slum it, I'm afraid. No heated leather seats.'

They left the office together. The chief said 'hello' to just about everyone, including Inspector Jacobs. George nodded and said, 'See you tomorrow, sir,' as he passed.

They both got into the freezing interior of an unmarked Skoda Fabia. Cottage didn't breathe a word of complaint and even commented favourably on the controls of the heating system. 'Finally, a heater that you just have to twist round to make it warmer. So, like I said to you earlier, George, I wanted to see how you were, just check that you haven't come back to work too early. There's no shame in saying if you have.'

'I really don't feel like I've come back too early. To be honest with you, boss, the job gives me something to think about. I found that when I was off I was just mulling over . . . things, you know.'

'I think I do. I have to say I'm very similar. We all have these traumas in our lives. I lost someone very dear to me too, once — of course we all do, more and more as you get older. Anyway, I went back to work for the same reasons. One thing I did have, though, was a very supportive sergeant. I was a PC at the time, you see.'

George nodded. 'That does help.'

'Have you got that? I mean, we've all got our opinions on the area commander down here, and I'm not sure how he would be in this kind of situation.'

George laughed. 'Awful! He's really bad at the personal stuff, sir, but to be fair to him he did exactly what I wanted him to do. He had a brief try and then he moved on.'

'I didn't really have you down as one for prolonged expressions of sympathy, George.'

'Nah, it's nice to know that people care enough to try and make me feel better about what happened, but it's just time, sir. There's nothing anyone can do. We just need to spend as much time as possible together at home, as a family.'

'I agree,' Cottage said. 'But are you back full time?'

'I am, but I'm doing eight till four weekdays. Helen Webb sorted that for me, and it gives me every weekend off.'

'That makes sense. I'm glad Helen did that but if you need to be working reduced hours-'

'Actually the shifts work well sir. I have been doing some late shifts with my team. I didn't see the point in sitting in an empty office for four hours waiting for them to come in.'

The chief nodded. 'Okay. Makes sense, I suppose. Hang on . . . eight till four?' He made a show of checking his watch. 'Are you doing a late shift today?'

'I'm not, sir, no.' George was almost apologetic.

'Then you should be home right now!'

'It doesn't matter, sir, it's not a problem.' George chuckled, though he knew he was in a lot of trouble.

'Here we are talking about the importance of you spending time with your family, and I'm taking you away from them.'

'Honestly, sir, it's really not—'

'Don't make me pull rank!'

George turned right into the same garage they had visited before. 'Pull rank all you want, sir, but I'll tell you now you're not getting out of buying me a coffee.'

George sat in the car while the chief went in to get the coffees. A police-marked BMW X5 had also pulled up to fill up at the pumps, and two armed response officers stepped out of the car and began stretching and yawning. Both returned the chief's nod and watched him as he walked back to the car. They did a perfect double-take as they recognised Cottage, who was opening the door of the three-year-old Skoda.

'I think it would piss me off.'

'What's that?' Cottage passed one of the cups over.

'People's reaction, especially other coppers. Everyone immediately on their guard, just because you're there. I really wouldn't want that.'

'Of course you wouldn't, and that's why you'd make a good chief constable, George. There are those who do enjoy it, who see other people's reactions to their rank as one of their main reasons to move up. It's not me.'

George chuckled. 'I don't know anyone like that.'

'I'm sure you don't. How has our Graham been? He appears to be getting some results on that estate, finally.'

George stirred his coffee and tried to think of a tactful response. 'There have been some good results, that's for sure.'

'But?'

'But nothing that I know for certain.'

'You can't talk in riddles to me, George. That's one of my rules.'

George took a sip of his scalding coffee. 'The big result was getting Tinsow in.'

'He's the bus robbery fella, right?'

'That's right. I had a bit of an issue regarding Tinsow. It just didn't fit for me or for Sam — she's a decent detective and was leading the investigation.'

'He came in and coughed it, right?' Cottage's eyes narrowed.

'He did, yeah. But Sam and I went and saw his mum and sister. They live together in a nice house, a million miles from how Elliot lives. Anyway, they had a visit from three heavies who basically roughed them up as a way of getting to Elliot and forcing him to cough the job.'

'You know this for certain?'

'As certain as I can be. They had a camera covering the front door that filmed these lads when they paid them a visit. These are normal, decent people. They weren't lying to me about the facts and they were genuinely scared.'

'You have the camera footage?'

'I did get that, but I got no support from the mother or the sister. They want nothing to do with it and I can't get back to talk to Elliot. He's the key. If he would tell me what happened and support us, then we might get somewhere.'

Cottage wiped a splash of coffee froth from his chin. 'I was told he got bail. Why can't you go round there?'

'Sam and I did go round and we spoke to him. He hinted that he had been pressured into it, which was why we went and saw his mum. He might crack with a few more questions, but I mentioned all this to Huntington and he wasn't happy at all.'

'I can see why, I suppose. This job is still all over the media. I get asked about it on a regular basis. If someone walks in and holds their hands up to it, I think anyone in Graham's position would not be looking that particular gift horse in the mouth. I'm not happy, though, not happy at all. If this Tinsow fella isn't the right man, then it could really come back and bite us on the arse. It would be far worse for the force if it came back a second time.'

'So what do you want from me, sir? I mean, I've told Huntington what I know, so the ball's in his court really.'

Cottage paused. 'Go and see Tinsow again and have a word. I'll tip Graham off so you don't get your ear chewed, and I want you to report back to me directly with what happens. I'm due back here on Monday, so you can fill me in then, in person. If we get any solid evidence, or a statement from Tinsow that he was pressured into a false claim, then we'll act on it. As it stands, there's not much more we can do.'

'Sounds fair.'

'Now, driver, take me back. We're eating into your family time. Is your wife going to be okay with you being late tonight?'

'Judging by the way she reacted last time, sir, I'm in a lot of trouble.'

'Oh dear! Do you have much on tomorrow?' Cottage said.

George slowly pulled away across the grey forecourt. 'I always have a lot on . . .'

'Take the day off, with my blessing. I feel bad about making you late. I'll fudge it with Helen, I'll tell her you need it for some reason.'

'Well, that's very kind of you, sir, but I couldn't do that. I mean, it wouldn't be fair on the team to just not turn up, and I have stuff to do — going to see Tinsow for a start.'

'You don't need to impress me with your dedication, George.'

'You're right, I should have already impressed you enough,' George laughed at his own cheek. 'I tell you what, though. I could do with Friday off. That would please the missus no end. My girl's school is having one of those staff training days.'

'Oh, I see. Taking advantage of the boss, are we? Think he's a soft touch?'

'Well, it's worth a try!'

'Do you think you can talk to this Tinsow tomorrow?'

'I'll make sure of it.'

'Yes, do that. We need to know what we've got there, if anything. And I'll have a word with the lovely Helen about your long weekend. Can't have the wife upset now, can we?'

'We certainly can't, boss, and that's very kind of you.'

George took the chief back to Langthorne police station. Helen Webb had been waiting for their return at the side entrance. She came clip-clopping out of the building as soon as she spotted the chief stepping out of the car.

'Oh, you didn't take that one, did you, George?'

'Yes, ma'am. I thought it was the best one to take, for security reasons, so we could blend in,' he lied.

'I see.'

Cottage was laughing. 'It worked perfectly, too. We're back in one piece and George here didn't stop to pick up a microwave.'

Helen wasn't laughing.

'Sir, will you be needing your driver? I remember you said you wanted to get off promptly.'

'Are you trying to get rid of me, Helen?'

'No, sir! Of course not'

'Oh, Helen, I was just winding you up. I'll pop in and grab him myself, and then I'll be off. I have a meeting at HQ to get to, I'm afraid. The working day is far from over for me.'

'Very good,' Helen replied, and turned away.

'Oh, and Helen. George here will be needing Friday off.'

Helen looked back. 'Oh, right. I'll let Inspector Jacobs know.'

George couldn't resist a dig. 'You know that we've got ourselves a new guv'nor then, ma'am? I only found out when he turned up this morning.'

'Yes, er . . . yes, I do know. Graham did tell me that he was speaking to you about it.'

'Maybe we missed each other.'

'George and his team have a new inspector? I don't recall Graham mentioning that to me. I would like to say hello myself. Don't worry, Helen, I'll let this Inspector Jacobs know about Friday. Enjoy your day with the family, George. Lord knows, they are priceless.'

'They are indeed, sir. And thank you.'

* * *

George shook his head as he parked on the drive to his home. The clock on the dashboard read 18:09. He was over an hour later than he'd said he would be.

George stepped out onto ground that was already icy. He gingerly made his way up the slight incline towards the front door. He decided that he would forget the apologies

194

and launch straight into a story about how he had spent most of the day with the chief constable. If he was casual enough, he might just get away with it.

As he pushed his key into the lock, the door was flung open. Sarah stood, hands on hips.

George forgot everything he had planned to say. 'Sorry, Sarah. I was all set to get off—'

'Don't you *fucking* sorry me *anymore*!' Sarah's face flushed, her eyes widened and she clenched her fists. George almost cowered.

'Listen.' He spread his arms, palms up — his best submissive stance. 'Listen, I got Friday off, that was my payoff.' He took a step backwards, as Sarah filled the doorframe. 'You told your sister you couldn't go out with her, but you can now. I'll look after Charley. I thought you'd be happy.'

'What?'

'I can look after her on Friday. I'll take her out for the day. We bought those zoo passes and I've never been there with her. It's supposed to be cold but dry. We'll wrap up — she'll be fine.' George was babbling, but it seemed to be working. Sarah turned and went back into the house. George followed her inside, rubbing his hands. Sarah stuffed some clothes into the washing machine, keeping her back turned to him.

'I was with the chief constable today. He was supposed to pop in and see me at two this afternoon, but he didn't get there till I was about to leave. Thing is, you can't just tell the chief constable that you've got to go home.'

'Why not? What's more important, George, the chief constable or your family?' Sarah spoke into the tumble dryer.

'Oh, come on, I didn't realise I had to choose between.'

'And if you did?' Sarah turned to face him.

'I'll give it up, the job, everything, if you want me to. If you want me to be here all the time and you think it's the best thing for our family, fine, I'll do it.'

'Don't be ridiculous!'

George put his hands on her shoulders. 'Is she still up?'

'She's watching a DVD in her room.'

'King Julien?' George laughed.

'Isn't it always?'

George held her from behind. 'Why does she always like the characters with a screw loose?'

'I blame her dad. If you really are going to take her out on Friday, then you'd better go and tell her.'

George kissed the back of her neck and walked away. He stopped at the kitchen door. 'Do you think the zoo is the right idea? I don't know what these young women like to do with their dads these days.'

Sarah smiled. 'George, she's six.'

'Really? But how come she's always organising *me*?'

George went up the stairs to his daughter's room. She was lying on her bed, head hanging down, watching her television upside down. She smiled broadly as her dad walked in.

'Hello, Daddy!'

'Hey, sweetness. I like your pyjamas.'

Charley righted herself and sat up on the bed. She tugged at her pyjama top so George could make out Princess Rapunzel on the front.

'They're new — Mummy bought them for me.'

'I see. Mummy's very good to you, isn't she? Seems like maybe it's *my* turn now.'

'What?'

'You fancy the zoo?'

Charley squealed. 'When?'

'Well, I'm afraid the next day I have off is after two more sleeps. Is that okay?'

Charley leapt to her feet and was hugging his legs before he had time to react. He laughed as she let go and clattered down the stairs.

'Mummy! Mummy, Daddy's taking me to the zoo where the animals live!'

'I know. Daddy told me he would.'

'Do you think King Julien lives there?'

George appeared behind his daughter, smiling. 'Well, Charley, I happen to know that there are lemurs there, and what do we know about King Julien?'

'He's the Lord of the Lemurs!' Charley clapped her hands and jumped up and down.

Sarah looked at George over their bouncing daughter, and smiled. 'Right you, back up to bed. You still have to do a day at school tomorrow before your zoo trip.'

'Oh, but Mummy,' Charley whined, 'Daddy's just got home.'

George opened a kitchen cupboard. 'Tell you what, if you'll just pop back to bed, Charley, me and your mum are gonna light the fire and polish these off.' He produced a large bag of marshmallows.

Charley was bouncing again. 'Nooooo! Can I have some marsallows, Mummy, please can I, can I?'

'You'd better ask your dad.'

Charley spun round to face him.

'Definitely not, unless . . .'

'What, Daddy, what?'

'Unless you can beat me in an arm wrestle.'

Charley yelped and sprinted through to the dining room. Sarah met her husband's gaze, and sighed. 'Every time.'

Chapter 35

Graham Huntington swore. The sound of his ringing phone had interrupted the weather report. Huntingdon always listened to the weather on his way into work. He edged a foot closer to the temporary traffic lights in the distance.

'What?'

'Sir, it's Inspector Jacobs.'

'This had better be fucking good. It's six thirty in the morning, Craig. I'm not on the clock yet.'

'Sir, I know, and I'm sorry to bother you. It's just that the chief constable visited me last night, last knockings.'

'So? He came and saw me, too. It's no surprise he's down here after the recent issues with the press. He seemed pleased with some of the results.'

'He said that to me, too. The other thing he said was about George Elms. It seems to me that those two are working very closely. I had no idea—'

'I agree. It's unprofessional,' Huntington growled.

'He said that they'd spoken about Elliot Tinsow. The chief was asking me what I thought about Tinsow, and what I knew about his history. I couldn't lie to him. I said I had no idea. I said that you'd said you weren't surprised in the slightest by him holding his hands up, that he fitted as the culprit.'

Huntington thumped the steering wheel. 'This again! I spoke to George. He came to me with it and I *told* him to move on, there's plenty of jobs out there that need a lot of work doing. I just don't understand why he's so fixated with this one.'

'Neither do I, but it could cause some problems.'

'You think I don't know that? Now he's got the fucking chief asking about it! That was a big success, a real positive message to get Cottage back onside, and George Elms is fucking it up.'

'What do you want me to do, sir?'

'Nothing for now. I moved you in there so you could put the reins on him, and that's what we'll do. Let me have a think. Hopefully I'll be out of this damned traffic before Christmas. We'll speak later.' Huntington ended the call abruptly, and thumped the steering wheel again.

* * *

'CSI came down earlier,' Paul began as soon as George walked in.

'Go on,' George said, still in his jacket.

'They cleared the scene. All their work is done and they gave this to me to pass on to the parents.' Paul held up a bronze door key.

'Scene?' George was scrabbling round in his drawer for his notebook. 'Whose parents?'

'This is a key to Elizabeth Wallis's flat.' George stopped rummaging. 'They asked if I could make sure the key got to her parents. They can go and collect her things if they want. I'm going to drop it round this afternoon.'

'I'll do that, Paul. I'll drop it round to them.'

'You sure?'

'Definitely. I'd like to.'

Paul nodded and thrust the key into George's hand.

George turned to Sam, car keys jangling in his hand. 'We never drew that tattoo, did we?'

'No, there wasn't the need in the end.'

'We're going to see Sophie.'

'We are? You want me to draw the tattoo now?'

George stopped his rummaging. He had found what he wanted, and stuffed it into his bag. 'I'll be in the car. Soon as you can.'

* * *

'Read me out that address again,' George said. It was the first thing he had said in half an hour.

'Forty-seven Ingles Road,' said Sam. 'Is this Ingles?'

'Yeah. I've been here a couple of times for domestics. Not to number forty-seven, I should add. Nice area.' George was driving slowly, looking at the numbers. The road reminded him a little of his own: well-kept, semi-detached houses, each with its own drive and garage, typically middle class.

Sam counted down the odd numbers. 'Should be this one.'

They stepped out of the heated Skoda into the freezing fog.

Sophie answered their knock. 'Hey!' She looked pleased to see them.

Sam stepped inside ahead of George. 'How are you, Sophie?'

'Good, thanks.'

'You here on your own?' George asked.

'Yeah, my mum's just popped out.'

'Okay. You okay talking to us without your mum? We won't do anything formal until she gets back, but we can have a chat, right?'

'No problem.'

'How's your injury?' George asked.

'Fine. I'm all done for now. There's no pain or anything. I've just got to wait for it to finish healing and then the plastic surgeon's going to have a look at the scar.' It was now a long white gash punctured by red dots, pale pink along its length. Sophie had covered it with make-up, but it was still very visible.

'Tea?'

George pretended to consider this. 'Is it better than the hospital tea?'

'I make *great* tea.' Sophie led them through the hall to the kitchen.

George and Sam leant against a tall breakfast bar. 'You have a nice house,' Sam said.

'It's okay, a bit boring. So do you still need my help? I got your message saying that you wouldn't need to draw that tattoo, and we've been told that someone is in prison for what happened.'

George nodded. 'Someone was arrested, yes. We might still need to draw that tattoo, though, but I want you to see something first. Do you have a DVD player?'

'Yes of course, there's one in the lounge.'

Sophie led the way, and George produced a DVD from his bag. Without a word, he inserted it into the DVD player. Sophie and Sam sat on a sofa, facing the TV. Sam shifted uncomfortably as the picture appeared. It was shot from above, looking down at a doorstep. George watched Sophie. She leaned forward in her seat, waiting for something to happen.

She didn't have to wait long. Two men appeared at the door to "Kettallson." The image was a little grainy and shot from an awkward angle, but Sophie immediately recoiled. She pointed a shaking finger at the screen.

Sam put an arm round her. 'It's okay.'

'That's him,' Sophie whispered. 'That's the man.'

George ejected the DVD and put it back in his bag. He dropped onto his knees in front of Sophie, whose head was bowed. 'I'm really sorry, Sophie. But that helps us massively.'

Sophie looked up, her eyes puffy and red. 'It's okay. I take it that's the man you arrested?'

George and Sam exchanged glances. 'No, but we will,' George replied gently, 'soon.'

* * *

'So what now?' Sam asked. They were still sitting outside Sophie's house. Sam's sergeant sat staring out of the front of the car, and she guessed that he didn't know himself.

'The way I see it, we've two options,.'

'Two?'

'Yeah. We go see Tinsow today as planned, and then take everything we have to the chief on Monday.'

'Yeah . . .'

'Or we give Huntington another go.'

'You were planning to go and see Tinsow again today?'

'Yeah, sorry, it was only decided late yesterday. The chief practically told me to, and then he asked me to go see him on Monday and tell him what was said.'

'Well, do that then.'

'We have to be careful though, Sam. Now we know for definite that Tinsow isn't the man responsible, and we also know that the man that was responsible is desperate for someone else to take the rap. Desperate enough to beat up an old lady in her own home. It doesn't make sense to me. We weren't anywhere near getting anyone in for it. We had no idea at all. In fact, all we could prove is that Tinsow *wasn't* the man responsible.'

'Maybe the man on the film thought we were closer to him than we actually were.'

'Maybe,' George said, but he looked far from convinced. The car began to move.

Sam tugged at her seatbelt. 'What are you going to do?'

'Tinsow first, then I think I'll see Huntington.'

Chapter 36

Ed paced the main bedroom of 5 Roman Way, talking on his phone. 'This Elms is becoming a proper pain in the arse.' He looked through the dirty net curtains at a group of four men in hoodies swaggering by, their breath visible in the freezing cold.

'And you say he has the ear of the big chief?' Oscar Baurman's voice was perfectly calm.

'So it seems.'

'Well, then, you have to deal with it, don't you? I still don't understand why you're calling me with this. We have our arrangement and you have your instructions. I don't need to be told about the problems you're having. You just get the job done.'

Ed looked around him and lowered his voice. 'The reason I called is because I have a proposition for you. One that delivers the same result, and also removes any future problems with our arrangement.'

'You need to be more direct, Ed. This isn't a fucking movie trailer. What do you want to do?'

'Change the target, Mr Baurman — to George Elms.'

'You want to wipe out a gavver? Smith is one thing, but we take out a copper and we'll have everything they've got after us. It's also a lot more difficult to pin something like that on the Skinners and let's not forget, that is your primary concern.'

'I hear what you're saying, but listen. I've given it some thought. I do explosives — that's my bag, so I do the job. I can make something real crude, real simple, like you could make after an afternoon on the internet. Our inspector organises the raid on the Skinners based on the information I give him, as per the original plan. All he needs to do different is plant components similar to the ones in the device I use on George Elms. Explosives have a massive bonus — there's no forensics, because everything they would normally look for is incinerated. The cops know a bit about the Skinners and they've been looking to get something on them for years. Trust me, if they think those brothers have targeted one of their own, they will lap it up. There's no risk to you — you have complete deniability.'

The response came after a lengthy pause. 'I want the Skinner boys out of the way and I need them to go inside. You can target the Pope for all I care, as long as the Skinners get fingered for it. My problem is that you've got to get that soppy inspector on board. He's not going to be happy with something like that.'

Ed smiled. This was the answer he was hoping for. 'Don't you worry about Jacobs. He's on his way over now, and I think he'll understand why it needs to happen.'

* * *

'This is madness!' Jacobs sat with his hands clasped tightly together, trying to control his breathing.

'Craig, this has to happen. If we don't remove Elms now, he might well destroy everything we've worked so hard to achieve. We have control of the area commander, for fuck's sake — we've got Huntington by the balls! We could give him the big picture right now, and there would be nothing he could do about it. He made this possible. He put us here. He kept us off the books, invented false personas, endorsed illegal use of force and, as far as the courts would be concerned, he knowingly allowed a man to be bullied into admitting to something he didn't do, *and* he did it all for cash.'

'Isn't that enough, then? I mean, that's all we needed to do, right?'

Ed sighed. 'It should have been enough. But this Elms, he has the chief's ear, and he won't let this fucking Tinsow thing go. It's a house of cards, mate, and if Elms gets to Tinsow, questions will be asked and Huntington will be taken off Epping Hill. Then it's curtains for us, and we *can't* let that happen.'

Jacobs was looking down. 'George Elms has a family. There are pictures of them on his desk.'

There was no reply and he looked up. Ed grabbed him by the scruff of the neck, lifted him to his feet, and shoved him back against the wall. Jacobs's head hit the wall so hard that his eyes flashed white for a moment.

'You need to wake up, you hear me? Do. You. Hear. Me. This was never gonna be a walk in the fucking park! You knew what you were getting into!'

Jacobs closed his eyes. He could feel Ed's breath on his cheek. Ed lifted him again and banged him into the wall. He threw Jacobs over the bed, and he landed heavily on the bare floorboards.

Ed towered over him. 'You're either fully committed to this, or you become as much a risk as Elms. Understand?' Ed's lips curled in disgust.

'Okay, Ed. Okay. It was just a shock. But you're right, you're right. I can deal with it.'

Ed snorted and stalked out of the room. 'Let yourself out, *Inspector*,' he called back.

Jacobs felt the back of his head for blood. There was a lump, but nothing more. Gingerly, he got to his feet, using the wall for support, and limped away as quickly as he could. He found his car and sped off. He needed to get back to the station and speak to Huntington. A man's life depended on it.

* * *

Graham Huntington was in a meeting — with George Elms. Jean apologised again to Inspector Jacobs. She noticed that his suit jacket was torn and dirty, as were his trousers, particularly at the knees. He seemed to be limping. He also seemed to be under some kind of stress. His eyes were wide, his lips dry, and beads of sweat dotted his brow.

'Are you okay, Inspector? You look a little upset. Do you want to sit down, sir?'

'No, no, thank you.' He wiped at the sweat on his forehead. 'Could you just tell the chief super for me, Jean, could you tell him, please . . ?'

'Yes, sir?'

'I'm not feeling well,' Jacobs said at last. 'Just tell him that I've had to go home.'

'Oh dear.' Jean put her head to one side in sympathy. 'Nothing too bad I hope, sir?'

'No, no. Just a twenty-four-hour thing, I'm sure.'

Jean made a note on her pad. 'Very good, sir.' When she looked up, Jacobs was already gone.

* * *

George emerged from his meeting red-faced and angry. He was tempted to ring the chief right then, with Huntington in earshot. George could prove without a doubt that Tinsow was not the man responsible for the robbery. Tinsow hadn't answered when he'd called, but George knew that when he eventually spoke to him, Tinsow would crack. He would wait, though, until Monday when he would have a report ready for Cottage, detailing everything he knew. He would show him the DVD, too, like he had just done with Huntington. He could bet that the chief's reaction would be quite different.

'Sergeant Elms, are you okay?'

George had stopped dead in the corridor, thinking through his options. 'Oh, hello, Jean. I'm fine, thank you. I was in a world of my own there.'

'Ah, that's good. I've just seen Inspector Jacobs. He looked awful. He's had to go home. He said it was a bug, but he looked sort of shaken.'

'Oh, really? He seemed fine earlier.'

Jean shrugged. 'He said he thought it was just a twenty-four-hour thing. Hopefully he's not given it to anyone else.'

'I'm sure he'll be fine, Jean. Thanks for letting me know.'

* * *

The slamming of the door as George left his office was not lost on Huntington. He let out a long sigh. 'Fucking amateurs. Why the fuck do I have to work with them?' He called Inspector Jacobs, but it went straight to voicemail.

Next he called Ed Kavski, on an untraceable pay-as-you-go mobile.

Ed did not sound pleased to hear him. 'This is unexpected.'

'Why have I just watched a video of you forcing your way into some old lady's home and giving her a beating? You fucking *stupid* prick!'

'Video? What video?'

'Welcome to the modern world, where people have security cameras watching their doorsteps, you fucking idiot!'

Ed let out a little laugh. 'The cheeky mare!'

'You think this is *funny*? Elms just brought this DVD to me. He knows that the person on that film is guilty of perverting the course of justice, but that's the very least of it. He also tells me that the man with you on the DVD has been identified as the suspect for the robbery Tinsow himself has claimed. Now maybe you want to tell me how that can be, Ed? How the *fuck* can that be?'

Ed laughed again. It wasn't convincing. 'You weren't supposed to find out just yet, *sir*, but it does no harm at all.'

'Find out *what*?'

'Well, you see, this has all been a bit of a game. Jacobs and I tried it first in the city, but they got suspicious. They knew we were up to something but they couldn't work out what, so they shipped us out. Got rid of the risk. They were right, too. If they'd pushed it they would've shown themselves up very badly.'

'What have you done?' Huntington glanced nervously at the door to his office.

'That's its strength, you see. You senior bods, and the police as a whole, you're all about public perception. It's your biggest weakness and so it's very easy to play on. What we did was give you a chance at that promotion, and you snapped it up without ever thinking where it might lead you. All it took was a little provoking on our part.'

'Provoking? It was you who organised the bus attack?' Huntington slumped back in his chair.

'Jacobs's idea if I'm perfectly honest. A good one, too. I thought we carried off the junkie look rather well. The YouTube thing, now that was all me. I even had the contacts in the press, who were more than happy to run with it. Let's be honest, we didn't create the problem, we just exposed it to the world — forced your hand.'

'I still don't see why. What do you stand to make out of this?'

'Well, *sir*. *You* have put us in a quite enviable situation. We are now in a very good position to remove all of the competition for the supply of drugs in Epping Hill and much further afield. We've been working our way through the dealers, drip-feeding you information. And, like the good little boys in blue that you are, you've been scooping them up, getting them off the street and out of the way. Most of them come straight back out, but by that time they've lost their patch to the competition. To us. In a nutshell, you, and only you, have created the single most powerful drug supplier in the county.'

'I . . . I didn't . . .' Huntington had no response. The enormity of what Ed had been saying was just beginning to register. He put his hand to his brow.

Ed hadn't finished. 'You kept all this off the books. You sorted us with fake identities and you endorsed the use of violence . . . which has been considerable, by the way—'

'I did not!' Huntington's fist slammed down on the table. 'That is one thing I said from the start! I never wanted innocent men through the doors. I wanted the whole drug scene extinguished, the top men brought to justice. I didn't want this!' He sounded desperate.

'What would a jury say? That's what you need to be thinking about from now on, *Graham*. If you look in your bottom drawer, you'll see a white envelope. Have a look.'

Huntington pulled the drawer open. 'There's no envelope.'

'Taped to the bottom of the one above, if my instructions were followed properly.'

Sure enough, Huntington's fingers touched paper. He found the tape and tugged at it. He brought the envelope up to the table, where the contents spilled out. 'Money?'

'A good amount,' said Ed, 'and now with your dabs all over it. There are a few more packages like that dotted around, all in places that . . . well, let us say they are definitely attributable to you. And they are where you asked me to put them should a prosecutor ever get round to asking me about them in court.'

'You bastard!' But Huntington's voice lacked conviction. He knew he was beaten. 'You made sure there's no way out, didn't you?'

'We did, yes. But rest assured, life on the inside can be sweet. Your role going forward will be to provide us with police resources when required. Generally that will benefit us both. You'll be removing my competition, and you'll be getting massive results — like you've never had before. That secures your promotion, and let's face it, that's all you wanted out of this. You'll also be rewarded with more envelopes. You've been played, Graham, but it could've been a lot worse for you.'

'I don't see how.'

'I'll give you some time, Graham, but not much. You're an intelligent man, so you won't need long to realise that we haven't given you any choice. I will be calling on you soon — something will happen in the next couple of days. A major job will come in and you'll need to divert resources the right way. You'll understand what I mean when I explain it in detail.'

Huntington sat up. 'You listen to me, you prick, you don't own me just yet, so don't think you do. And don't think you can just tell me what to do, you understand? *I* say what I do.'

Ed chuckled. 'Maybe you need to sit and think about the position that you find yourself in. I expect your attitude to be very different the next time we speak.'

'Oh really. And what are you going to do? Attack another old lady?'

'Ah, not this time.'

* * *

Ed hung up the call with a satisfied smile. His moment was interrupted by the arrival of four men — his team.

One of them had clearly been chosen as the spokesman, and he wasted no time in getting to the point. He stood with folded arms. 'Me and the boys, we was wondering when we were gonna get paid.'

'Twenty-fifth of the month Huntington said the wages go in, didn't he?'

'You know what we mean, Ed.'

'Yeah, I do. Fair enough. I just got off the phone to Huntington. We're now in a stronger position than I even imagined. The proper money — and the real work — starts from tomorrow. You have my word.'

The man stood firm. 'We were hoping it would be coming in by now.'

Ed's smile suddenly dropped. He drew himself up to his full height. 'What did I just fucking say?'

'All right, boss, we just want to get paid is all, you know. That's why we're here.'

'Get the fuck out. You heard me. I don't lie and I *don't* fucking repeat myself!'

The men filed out. Ed pressed Jacobs's number. The call went to voice mail, and he cursed. He sent a text message:

ITS MVING FST NOW. DUN 2NITE. CALL ME 4 INSTR.

Chapter 37

George's wife opened their front door and gave a mischievous smile.

'I'm sorry, we don't accept door-to-door salesmen.'

'But I'm not a salesman, I'm your husband.'

'You can't be my husband — he's never early and he would certainly *never* bring me flowers.' George came into the house and hugged his wife tightly. Charley sprinted along the hallway and grabbed her parents' legs to join in. The flowers were squashed somewhere in the middle.

'Aah, three whole days with the woman I love.'

'Where is she?' Sarah teased. 'I'll kill her!'

'Must be around here somewhere . . . I'm sure she was here.' George received a playful punch on the arm.

'You want a cuppa?' Sarah asked.

'Of course.' George looked down at Charley, who was bobbing around beside him.

'Daddy! Daddy, we have to be up ever so early in the morning because we need to go to Tesco. Mummy said we should buy a picnic, and then we can be first in line for where the animals live.'

'Did she now?'

Sarah grinned. 'Well, it was kind of both our idea.'

'I'm sure it was. You know how much I love Tesco.'

'You always say that, Daddy, but it will be good tomorrow because we can buy cheese and ham and bread and crisps and sweets.' Charley bounced as she listed each item.

'Sounds lovely, young lady, but more importantly, what do we have for nowsies?' George went over to the stove and peered into the pan. 'Bolognese?' He poked it with a fork, receiving a light slap on the hand from his wife.

'Maybe. You'll have to wait. I didn't know you were going to be early.' Sarah smiled.

Charley grabbed him by the hand and led him into the lounge where she had been colouring. As they left the kitchen, she tugged his hand and whispered, 'It is Bollock-nays.' George stifled a laugh.

* * *

At ten o'clock that evening, George was lying on the sofa with Sarah tucked into him, watching the credits on a movie that was just finishing. George's mobile phone began to ring from his jacket pocket, hanging over the banister in the hall.

'Are you on call?' Sarah asked, rubbing her eyes.

'No,' George said.

'What are they calling you for then?'

'I have no idea.'

'Leave it.'

'I was planning to. I'll go switch it off or it'll wake the beast.'

George patted the pockets of his jacket and found the phone. The screen displayed a missed call from Graham Huntington.

'Strange,' he said, and immediately the phone rang again.

'Hello?' George kept his voice low and walked through to the kitchen.

'George?'

'You okay, sir?'

'Yes, well, no. Look, sorry, I know it's late but I need to speak to you.' His words were short and sharp, as if he were out of breath.

'It's not a problem,' George lied. 'How can I help?'

'You said you spoke to Tinsow.'

'Well, I did, yes, but that was a few days ago now and—'

'Today! Did you speak to him today?'

'With respect, sir, you told me not to.'

'Don't play games with me, George. We both know you headed out to talk to him after our meeting. Listen, I don't care. I'm not pissed off with you, I just need to know what happened when you saw him.'

'I did go out there — I took Sam along — but he wasn't in. That was early afternoon and it was probably for the best, to be honest.'

Huntington swore and then let out a long sigh. 'Uniform went round there at half six. Someone was in the house but it wasn't Tinsow — some lad who is staying there. Anyway, this lad said that Tinsow had been dragged out of the property earlier in the day and had not been seen since. We've got real concerns for him here.'

'Kidnapped?'

'That's a drastic word, George. Certainly there's cause for concern.'

'It's unlikely Tinsow would breach his bail. Do you think it has something to do with the men on the video?'

Huntington snapped back, 'I don't know. Look, don't worry. I was just seeing if you had spoken to him today, to see if you knew anything. I'll let you get back to your evening.'

'You know I'm off tomorrow too, sir?' George screwed up his face, waiting for Huntington to suddenly declare it an emergency situation, demand his attendance and ruin his day.

'Ah yes, yes of course. Have a good day.'

The call ended and George was left staring at his phone looking puzzled. Sarah popped her head round the door.

'*Modern Family*'s on the telebox — you fancy it?'

'Sure.'

Sarah smiled. George knew why, his wife was expecting him to tell her he had to go out.

'Who was that?'

'Work.'

'I guessed that.'

George followed Sarah through to the lounge and sat on the sofa. 'There's a missing person come in, that's all. High risk by the sounds of it.'

'Did they ask you to go in?'

'No. For once it seems like the boss is in control.'

* * *

Ed Kavski had been waiting some time, and at 11 p.m. he was happy to finally be able to step out and stretch his legs. Light snow fell around him, adding to the hushed atmosphere. Finally the light had gone out in what he was sure was the Elms's master bedroom. Now he could complete his task.

Ed pulled off his leather gloves, and typed a simple message into his phone: *Lights off.*

The residents of Broadacre Avenue generally went to bed early. They had jobs that got them out of their beds early, in order to earn the sort of wages needed to live on such a street. Ed had no intention of staying long. He opened the back door of his Audi, and took out a black leather suitcase. He closed the car door quietly and strode across the road, making prints in the snow. He stopped at the Elms's Renault Laguna, which had been backed onto the drive with the offside close to the front door. Ed walked round to the driver's side. He would be able to work in the shadow of the house, and the car would screen him from the road.

Ed had once been regarded as a specialist in the deployment of improvised explosive devices. Ed had already prepared the explosive package, complete with a magnetic base that held it to the underside of the car, level with the driver's seat. The IED was a home-made hand grenade-type device carrying twenty pounds of explosive. It was sufficient to consume the car and anyone in the vicinity. It worked on the same principle as a grenade — the IED had a pin that had to be removed from the body to set off a three-second delay before detonation. To finish the job, Ed needed only to fit a simple and almost invisible clip by tucking it underneath the door sill, which was attached to the bomb itself by a thin length of wire. Opening the driver's door would pull the pin, detonating the bomb.

Inside the house, the Elms family slept soundly. After just two minutes of silent activity, the grey Audi A4 pulled away into the night.

Chapter 38

Charley creaked open the bedroom door and whispered to her dad. Losing patience, she bundled into her parents' bed and crawled up George's prone body.

'It's half six, Charley. The zoo doesn't even open for another four hours.' George pleaded with his daughter, whose face was less than an inch from his.

'But we have to go to Tesco first, Daddy.'

George buried his face in the pillow. It was hardly the best thing to say to get him out of his warm bed.

Finally he relented. Sarah had stirred and complained at Charley's constant fidgeting, so George had no option but to get up. He took a leisurely shower and, feeling suitably warmed, opened the bedroom curtains and had to squint against the brightness of the sun glinting off the snow and frost. Stars still twinkled above the houses.

'Have you got the membership card for the zoo?'

'No idea,' he replied.

'It should be in your wallet. I lent mine to Kate so you'll need yours.'

'My wallet?' George patted down his work trousers and suit jacket, lying over the bedroom chair. 'Have you seen my wallet?'

'No. Have a look downstairs, or maybe your car.'

George snapped his fingers. 'I got petrol.'

'Good for you.' Sarah rolled over.

'I assume you're not going to be in too much of a rush to meet Kate this morning?'

'Yep. How often do I get the chance for a lie-in? Kate's done the same. She's lumbered Dave with the kids, so we're both enjoying a rest.'

'Is that what you're doing, then? Lumbering me with our daughter?'

Sarah turned over again and flashed George a sleepy smile. 'Definitely! Close the curtains, George, and piss off.'

She chuckled and buried herself under the covers.

* * *

George was taken aback by the wall of cold as he opened his front door.

'Are we going now, Daddy?' Charley appeared in the doorway. She had doubled her normal size by putting on all of her winter clothes, complete with pink gloves and fur-topped boots. She skipped over to where George stood at the driver's door of the Laguna.

'Not yet, hon. I'm just going to grab my wallet and then finish my cup of tea. Wait inside for me, young lady, it's too cold out here.'

Charley pouted, stomped a foot and stood still. George couldn't be bothered to argue with her and turned back towards the Laguna, pressing the button on his fob.

'Shit!' He turned to his daughter to see if she'd heard him. She was busy trying to scrape frost together in a pile. He pressed the fob again. Still nothing. 'Shit thing,' he said again, under his breath. He stepped forward, his daughter watching, banging her padded gloves together to shake them free of ice.

George slid the car key into the driver's door lock where it stopped less than halfway in, the metal end pushing against ice. With increasing frustration, he pulled it out and jammed it back in again. There was some give but not enough to unlock the car. He tried again, and it sunk in a little further — it was almost there. He tried to turn it, hoping to hear the lock clunk open. Instead, he heard the distinct sound of a key snapping.

It broke at the base of the black plastic handle, leaving a barely visible piece of polished metal protruding out of the lock. George swore through his clenched teeth and bent down to inspect the damage. There wasn't enough of the key to grasp it with pliers. Still muttering under his breath, he stormed back into the house, leaving the front door open for Charley to follow.

'Are we nearly ready to go, Daddy?'

'Not now, Charley!'

'Everything okay?' Sarah called down from the bedroom.

'Yeah, fine. I need to call the AA out for the Laguna. Nothing major — I just can't get into the damned thing.'

'Do you want to take mine? Kate's picking me up in an hour or so. I can sort the AA man for when you're back.'

'I'll give them a call. If time starts to get on, then I'll take yours.'

'Suit yourself,' Sarah called back down. 'You can bring me a coffee, too, seeing as you seem determined not to let me have my lie-in.'

George dialled the AA while he put the kettle on.

* * *

'DC Baern?'

'Yes?' Paul said, but didn't look up.

'Yes, good morning. I was hoping to speak to you, Paul. I'm Graham Huntington.' Huntington held out a hand and Paul suddenly sprung to his feet and took up the handshake.

'Sorry, sir, I was miles away. Good morning.'

'Please sit down,' Huntington continued. 'I know George is away today, but I wondered if you knew anything about Elliot Tinsow?'

Sam could see Paul was floundering, so she came to his aid. 'Sir, we've all had some involvement with Tinsow, but I interviewed him and did a follow-up with the sergeant.'

Huntington had walked straight past Sam and addressed the male DC. He turned to look at her. 'Ah, Sam, isn't it?'

'That's right. I might be able to help with Tinsow.'

Huntington smiled. 'Very good. Bail checks were carried out on our friend Tinsow last night, and it appears he was not there to answer them. We now suspect that he had little choice but to breach his bail — someone may have . . . got to him.'

'Got to him?' Sam said.

'Indeed. From what we understand, Mr Tinsow had been under pressure to come in here and hold his hands up for this job. The fear is that his disappearance is related to this.'

'Disappearance?' Sam bit her lip. This was not the time for a told-you-so.

'His mother has reported him missing, and we have been unable to locate him at this time. That is a disappearance in name at least. Of course, this wouldn't be the first time someone's gone missing on bail . . .'

'But you don't think this is a simple breach of bail, do you? I have to say, sir, from what I know of Tinsow, I would agree. He is not a man who would breach his bail lightly.'

'Quite. I'm here because of your team's involvement with Tinsow, and your knowledge of Epping Hill. If there's anywhere you think we might try, and if you can fit some time into your day today to assist with the search for Tinsow, then I would very much appreciate it. We have uniform checking each of his listed associates but unfortunately, due to his lifestyle, Mr Tinsow has been associated with just about everyone within five square miles of his home at one time or another.'

'I don't think he would have gone far,' Sam mused.

'Our thoughts exactly. There was a male at the address when police called, who said that someone took Tinsow away, and there is some suggestion that it was against his will. We couldn't get much sense out of him at the time, so uniform went back at around midnight last night and arrested this male for Tinsow's abduction.'

'To sober him up?' Sam smiled.

'Exactly. An old trick indeed. Our colleagues in Major Crime should be speaking to him in the next hour, so hopefully that will give us something to go on.'

'We can help out today, I'm sure. I've met Tinsow's mum. That might be a place to start,' Sam offered.

'Very good.' Huntington turned smartly away and was gone.

'Didn't that strike you as odd?' Paul asked.

'He's a very odd man.'

'I meant the way he was acting.'

Sam nodded. 'Whenever I've met him before there were no airs and graces. *Get it done and get it done now.* That's how he works. What was all this "if you have the time" crap?'

Paul chuckled. 'Maybe he's just a bit misunderstood.'

'Or maybe he knows he was wrong about Tinsow?'

'And maybe he doesn't give a shit about that.'

'I didn't know how much to say to him, you know. I don't think he wanted George to go out and speak to Tinsow, so I didn't want to say too much.'

'I know what you mean. Perhaps we should check with the skipper how much he's told the boss.'

'Call him on his day off? This time in the morning?'

'He won't mind. He might appreciate knowing that Tinsow is missing, and that Huntington is personally leading the search.'

'And maybe he won't!' Sam said.

'And mention that he's gone a bit weird on us, too. George might be able to shed some light on it, or tell us if that's a danger sign.'

'Oh, I'm ringing him, am I?'

'You're his favourite!'

'Whatever. Maybe Huntington's speaking to us like that because he really needs our help.' Sam began scrolling through her phone for her sergeant's number.

'Who knows.'

Sam pushed the call button then thrust the phone at Paul. 'It's ringing!'

Paul shook his head and took it.

* * *

'Morning, sir.' The middle-aged AA man emerged from a hi-visibility orange Transit van. He was decked out in the same colours, and wore a name tag reading "Stan." George came out to greet him, looking a little sheepish.

'Morning. I'm sure you get called out to idiots like me all the time.'

Stan smiled. 'You'd be surprised what we get called to. Our operator said you'd snapped the key off in the ignition?'

'No, no, I didn't even get that far. I've snapped it off in the driver's door.' George pointed to where what was left of the key could be seen jutting out.

'Ah, I see. Then you'd better put the kettle on.'

George was a little taken aback at the man's cheek. 'Tea or coffee?'

'Oh, thank you, coffee . . . if there's any water left when we've poured it over your lock.'

'Oh, I see! I didn't think of that.'

'Well, it wasn't like I was doing much.' Stan laughed heartily. 'Of course, the later models of the Laguna don't even use a key.'

'Oh, really?' George said, uninterested.

'No, no. You get a card you slide into the dash. The car starts with the push of a button. It's all very high tech.'

'Hmmm. George shifted from foot to foot as he struggled to pay attention to a lecture on starting devices.

'. . . You sit down and the car knows exactly what driving position you want and everything, the seat just adjusts.'

George checked his watch. They were getting to the point where they would have to miss out Tesco and go straight to the zoo. This could actually work in his favour.

'I might not need the kettle after all.' Stan had pulled the front of the driver's door handle away, leaving more of the key exposed.

'Daddy!' Charley called out from the doorstep. She had refused to take her boots and coat off, apparently believing that if she did so, they would never leave. She stepped back out onto the frozen drive. 'Mummy's asking how long it's going to take.'

Stan re-emerged from the rear of his van with a pair of pliers and a grin. 'Women, eh? I should have this out in a jiffy. Do you have a spare key?'

George felt his mobile phone vibrate in his pocket. It was Sam.

'It's here,' George called out, and placed the key down next to Stan. 'I just need to take this.' He ushered Charley back inside.

'Sam?'

Paul answered. 'Sorry to bother you on your personal phone.'

'You may just have saved me from the most boring man who's ever fixed a car,' George whispered. Charley started to walk towards the kitchen.

Five metres behind them, with a little brute force and some wriggling, the front part of the key finally slid out. Stan took the spare key and inserted it into the thawed lock. 'I think the ice has cleared!' he called to George.

Stan pulled at the door handle. He had to use his considerable weight to pull the frozen door open. 'We're in!' he called out triumphantly. George half turned in the doorway to give him a thumbs-up.

The blast surged upwards and the fuel tank immediately caught alight. The Laguna was engulfed in flames. The shock wave tore Stan apart before the flames could even reach him.

The blast lifted George off his feet, through the internal double doors and into their living room, where he struck the far wall. His phone was thrown free and smashed to pieces. Charley was thrown against the doorframe and she fell to the floor.

* * *

Sarah had just dozed off when she heard the explosion. She struggled to get out of bed and put some clothes on, to the sound of falling debris.

She heard Charley wailing at the bottom of the stairs, and the sound tore through her. Sarah flew down the stairs, to her daughter, who was bleeding from her leg and the side of her face. She heard a rumble above her, another loud thud and the roof tiles smashing. Was the house about to fall down?

'Charley, honey, we have to get out of the house, but I need to find Daddy first. Where is he?'

Things were falling from the shelves and walls, each crash making Sarah jump.

'He was here, he was here,' Charley managed to say through her tears.

'Okay, baby, okay. Where are you hurt, Char?'

'My leg hurts, Mummy.'

Sarah looked down at Charley's left leg. Her foot was twisted round at an impossible angle, making Sarah wince.

'Okay, honey, it's okay. Anywhere else, Char? This is important. Is there anywhere else that hurts?'

'Where's Daddy?' Charley screamed as the pain increased.

'Listen, baby, we're going to have a quick look and then we've got to get out of the house.'

Sarah got up and made her way to where the lounge door had been. All the windows in the room had been blown out and a weak breeze rustled through the broken blinds. The room was littered with broken furniture and other debris. Charley clung to her, weeping quietly. Then Sarah saw her husband's leg over the back of the sofa. She moved forward to look, bracing herself for the worst.

George's face was black. Fresh blood ran down his cheeks and trickled from one of his ears. His shoulder looked as if it was pushed too far forward. He had come to rest on the back of his head and shoulders, his body twisted upwards. Sarah couldn't tell if he was breathing, but he was lying so still she knew he must be dead. She began to sob.

Something large and loud gave way in the kitchen. Realising that she needed to get her daughter out, Sarah made for the gap that had been the front door. Holding tight to Charley, she stumbled over the debris and past the smouldering shell of the Laguna, the thick smoke stinging her tear-filled eyes.

Her neighbours met her at the end of her drive. The couple had rushed out of their house at the noise, and were in shock themselves. Sarah, wearing nothing but bed shorts and vest, ran over to them and fell to her knees.

'My husband!' she managed, 'he's dead.'

Chapter 39

Sam and Paul had given up trying to call George, and they continued with their day. Sam was frustrated. It was just as Huntington had said — everyone knew Elliot Tinsow, everyone was an associate, just about everyone had a different opinion on where he might be, and every one of them was too drunk or high to care. She'd contacted the office for an update on the man arrested for his abduction, and the story was the same. He could remember nothing about his movements the night before, except going to the Co-op with Tinsow early in the morning to stock up on cider, and a blurry recollection of a man banging on the door, who Tinsow seemed to be scared of.

Sam and Paul had spent hours going from dosshouse to dosshouse and were ready to quit.

Paul and Sam were eating hotdogs purchased from a van in a shopping centre car park. 'I say we phone Huntington and tell him that we're done with it,' said Paul.

Sam was busy picking out the onions from her roll. 'We don't even need to do that, really. He didn't ask us to do anything specific. We've done above and beyond, as far as I can see.'

'Yeah, *we* know that, but *he* doesn't. I don't want him thinking that we just didn't bother.'

'Oh, I see. You after a promotion, Mr Kiss Ass?'

'Bollocks, Sam.'

'No, you're right. Give him a call and tell him what you've done for him.' Paul took out his mobile phone. 'And don't forget to ask him if he wants an apple brought back. Tell him you'll make sure it's well polished.'

Paul stuck two fingers in the air. 'Hello, sir, it's Paul Baern. We've been out all day and I'm afraid . . .' Paul stopped talking. 'Sorry, sir, go ahead.' He hunched forward in his seat. 'When? Where is he now?' Sam put her hotdog down. 'We'll head over there . . . I don't care, you tell them who we are or you come out and get us yourself!' He ended the call and started the engine.

'What's happened?'

'There's been an explosion. George and his daughter were caught up in it. They think it might have been a car bomb.' Paul revved hard as he pulled away.

'Jesus!'

They drove to the hospital in silence.

* * *

Armed police with Glocks strapped to their legs, and carrying assault rifles patrolled the perimeter of Langthorne General Hospital.

Huntington had been assigned two personal armed guards but had told them in no uncertain terms to fuck off. He ducked under one of the many fire exits and called Ed Kavski. Jacobs was still not answering.

'This was it? This was what you'd planned?'

'How did it go?' Ed sounded as if he were smirking.

Huntington was incredulous. 'How did it go? How did it *fucking* go? A police officer is fighting for his life, and his six-year-old daughter may never walk again.'

Ed took a while to reply. 'Attempted murder will do just fine if the girl's involved too. Even GBH with intent would be a reasonable result.'

'Reasonable . . .' Huntington's voice shook with emotion. 'A reasonable result is you strung up by the *fucking* neck for what you've done.'

Ed laughed. 'Jacobs said you were a bitter old fossil. Now you listen to me, Graham. Your part of the job kicks in now. You need to make sure that the investigation into this ends with the arrest of two brothers from the estate. Jacobs knows all about it. He was going to take care of it himself, but it seems he's become a little unreliable of late. Get in contact with him, get the information you need, and get the job done.'

'Fuck you! What's to stop me making a phone call right now and getting the whole lot pointed at you? You'll never see the light of day again.'

'Graham, we've been through this. We both know you won't do that. You don't seem to understand that it's you who's made it possible. You're now involved in conspiracy to murder. You just maimed a six-year-old girl. Graham, your career is over the second you make that call.'

'This is nothing to do with me! I'm utterly outraged—'

'Listen, let's not play this game. We both know you're never going to expose our little arrangement. You would be better off putting your efforts into working out just how you're going to get those Skinner brothers in the frame like I've asked. It really shouldn't be difficult. I already have a crate of components for you — all you have to do is organise a walk round their property and make sure they're found. Easy.'

'You think that with one of my men lying in a hospital bed fighting for his life I'm going to help you?'

'No, Graham, I think you're going to help yourself.'

The call was ended.

'God dammit!' Huntington kicked out at a rubbish bin which toppled over. In an instant, three armed guards appeared. Two dropped to their knees facing in different directions, rifles levelled, and the third scanned the commander and his immediate vicinity.

'You okay, sir?'

Huntington waved them away and marched back into the hospital.

* * *

Sarah Elms could tell something was happening. Most of the east wing of the hospital had been closed off to all but police and medical personnel. All of a sudden they seemed to be hurrying, and there was a flurry of radio chatter. Her husband and daughter were in separate but adjoining rooms. The medical team were keeping both unconscious: Charley so they could work on her shattered knee and protect her from the pain, and George while they assessed his head injury. They now suspected a perforated eardrum — a common injury in someone exposed to an explosive device.

Sarah was struggling to make sense of it. Someone had planted a bomb under her husband's car. A man had died, killed by a bomb intended for George. Whenever she thought of George and Charley standing by that car she began to retch.

Sarah peered through the door of the room where she waited. The armed men were now standing in line along the corridor. A grey-haired man walked through, flanked by several more armed personnel. He stopped in front of her and removed his hat. His armed escorts stood just behind him.

His deep voice carried authority and warmth. 'Sarah, I'm Chief Constable Alan Cottage, a personal friend of your husband.'

Sarah shook his hand. 'Thank you for coming. George has a lot of respect for you.'

'How are they both?' Cottage looked beyond Sarah, through the adjoining window at the two unconscious figures.

'Stable.' Sarah's tone hardened. 'Do you know what this is all about? Because no one seems to have a clue.'

'We will find out,' Cottage said.

'They should both be fine. As long as the scan from George's head comes back with no issues, he'll be out of the woods. Charley's knee will need some work — they can't assess just how bad it is until the swelling goes down. Apparently they've both been incredibly lucky. I'll be sure to tell them that when they regain consciousness.' Sarah broke into tears. Cottage stepped forward and she rested her head on his shoulder.

He spoke soothingly into her hair. 'We're going to be in the way for a while, Sarah. When George comes round we'll need to speak to him straight away, Charley too. It's your family and you tell us to leave whenever you feel you need to, but remember we're here to catch the bastard that did this. I personally will not rest until it is done. You have every single resource of Lennokshire Police at your disposal.'

Sarah moved back a little. 'The police have been fine. I know they're going to need to speak to George. I just want to see him wake up. They said they would wake him up within the hour if his results were clear. They said they examined his head and couldn't feel any soft bits — which if you know George will probably surprise you.' Sarah managed a laugh, but it faded quickly. 'He should be okay.'

'I'll be sticking around. I'd like a chance to take the mickey out of him myself when he does decide to open his eyes,' Cottage said.

Sarah nodded, wiping her eyes. 'Could you do me a favour?'

'Anything.'

'They told me that a couple of George's colleagues were here, from work. Paul and Sam? They stopped them coming through but I'd like to speak to them, to see if they know anything about why this has happened. George talks about them a lot, they're all very close.'

'Paul and Sam are here?'

Sarah nodded. The chief turned and opened the door, where his two armed shadows snapped to attention. 'DC Baern and DC Robins, where are they?'

One of the officers spoke into his radio, and then turned back to Cottage. 'They've been taken to a secure room in the hospital, sir. They're being spoken to by Major Crime.'

'Get them here now,' Cottage barked. 'We need to speak to them too.'

Chapter 40

George sat up in his hospital bed. His return to consciousness had been slow and confusing, and it had been more than an hour before he had been able to have a conversation with Sarah that made any sense. Her relief at seeing him awake and talking soon gave way to anger at the evil he had brought into their home. He had spoken to the chief too, who had been gentle, barely touching on what had happened or the reasons behind it. George had managed to tell him where he was in the investigation, and had directed him to Paul and Sam. The chief confirmed that George and his family were to go into protective custody until the police could be sure of the motive at least.

George just wanted to go home — but to what? Alan Cottage had told him that most of the front and all the windows had been destroyed. The building was so unsound that structural engineers had had to be called in before forensics could enter. The house was lit up by floodlights and covered by a large canopy, to prevent any evidence being lost but also to keep photographers away. Media interest was high.

George was alone for the first time since the explosion. Sarah had gone to check on Charley and to get some rest. A bed had been set up for her in Charley's room. He had been told that his daughter had suffered a broken shin and possible damage to her knee. He had been told they were lucky to be alive. He ran through all that had happened to him — his car destroyed by a bomb, the house a ruin, the injuries to him, to his daughter, and the mental anguish his wife had suffered. He didn't see how any of that could be described as lucky. A high-pitched ringing noise sounded constantly in his right ear. In both, in fact, but the right one was worse. The doctor had told him it was tinnitus and said that it could last anything from five minutes to five years. George had thanked him for his precision.

Sighing loudly, he sat up and removed the various monitoring devices attached to different parts of his body. He went over to where his coat hung at the door, and found his work mobile phone in a pocket. Taking the phone, he pulled the door open and came face to face with an armed guard.

'I'm just off for a walk,' George said.

'Sorry, sir, I'm afraid I can't let you do that right now. I'll radio through and get a walk organised.' The man began to lift the radio to his mouth, but George stopped him.

'I don't want a walk authorised. I just want to stretch my legs. I'm going stir-crazy in there.'

'Sorry, sir. Security protocols.'

'Do you have armed guards on the outside doors and the perimeter?' George cupped his hand over his right ear to see if it made a difference to the ringing noise.

'Yes, sir.'

'And this part of the hospital is also sealed off by armed guards?'

'Yes, sir.'

'Then I think I'm quite safe walking around this part of the hospital without any babysitters, don't you?'

'Sorry, sir—'

'Don't be sorry. I'll be going for a walk now, unless you want to explain to your boss why you were wrestling the man you were sent to protect.'

'Well, no, but I—'

'You stay here. I just want a short walk on my own.'

'But, sir, we're here for your protection. I had orders from—'

George pointed to his right ear. 'Sorry, can't hear you.'

Chapter 41

For Graham Huntington, it had been dark all day. He stood still on his drive, oblivious to the biting cold. He leant on his sports car and faced his house, looking at it as though for the first time. He expelled a long sigh and shook his head. He'd been coming home from his job as a police officer for many years — a job that had often been hard — but he had never felt so low, so desperate, so unsure as now.

Tinsow was still missing, and when Huntington had tried drumming up resources to look for him, he had received nothing but shrugs. 'He's probably just gone out somewhere and got smashed. He'll have no idea what time it is anyway. He'll turn up thinking he'd only been gone a couple of hours. Typical pisshead.' Huntington knew there was more to it than some pisshead getting lost on his way home from the off-licence. But it was impossible to convey the seriousness of the matter to his colleagues without saying *how* he knew. And then there was George Elms, his little girl, and the conversation with Ed Kavski. Just when he was beginning to get to grips with the Tinsow crisis, George had been hospitalised and damned near killed. And somehow Huntington himself had been put in the position of accomplice. How could he have let himself be played so easily?

The downstairs windows were in darkness, except the porch, which was lit up for his return. The master bedroom light was on, so he knew his wife would be sitting up in their bed, a novel in her hand, lost in a make-believe world. He shook his head. 'Rather that than the real world,' he said, and watched his words drift away in the cold night air. Still slowly shaking his head, he trudged towards the house.

'Graham, there's a dinner in the microwave. It's on the right setting, just give it three minutes.' He smiled. His wife had called down before he'd even closed the door. In the kitchen, he opened the microwave door to reveal sausages and mashed potato with vegetables. The microwave whirred into life and he stood watching the timer count down, suddenly realising how hungry he was.

Fifteen minutes later, he headed wearily up the stairs to bed and, sure enough, his wife was sitting up under the bedspread, a novel on her lap.

'You okay, Janice?' She stopped reading and looked at him, a little taken aback.

'Fine. Are you okay?'

He pointed at her glasses. 'Are they new?'

'Not really — more than a year.'

He looked down at his wife. Her eyes were her best feature. He'd always been confident around women, too much almost, but all his self-assurance flew out of the window the first time Janice looked at him. Those eyes could make him forget everything. Even now, as he looked at her properly for the first time in a long while, he still found her beautiful. Yes, her face had aged, but those high cheeks and sparkling eyes were still very much there. She had little dimples in her cheeks that only appeared when she really smiled. He felt a pang of shame when he realised that he couldn't remember the last time he had seen her dimpled smile.

His wife lowered her book and peered over her glasses at him. 'Are you sure you're okay?'

'I do love you, Jannie.' He hadn't uttered those words for almost ten years and even now they had just tumbled out, unbidden.

Janice looked surprised. She removed her glasses, revealing those eyes in all their beauty. 'And I love you too.'

'Why?' he said.

Janice recoiled slightly.

'Why would you still love me, Jan? I'm not a good husband and, you know what, I don't think I have been for quite some time. I don't deserve you. I don't deserve for you to still be here at all.' He let out a breath, an incoherent young man again. 'You're everything I ever wanted, you still are, Janice, and I take you for granted.' He sat down next to her, tugging at his shirt buttons to keep his hands busy, facing away from her. She said nothing. 'I just want you to know that I'm sorry. I've put work first for so long. I thought the career was all I wanted but it wasn't, Janice, it really wasn't. It was you, and it was here.'

'You don't need to be sorry, Graham. I always knew you wanted a career.' Janice placed her hand on his arm and he looked at her.

'No,' he said. 'When we were first together I kept a diary. It was all about you, how you made me feel, how lucky I was and how I wanted to spend the rest of my life with you.'

'I remember.'

'Where did I go wrong, Janice? How could I have let myself change so much?' Tears welled in his eyes, and he shut them tightly. Janice leant forward, placed a hand on his cheek and kissed him gently on his eyelids, and then on the lips. He did nothing at first, but then began to kiss her back. Her book slid off the bed and onto the floor where it was covered by his discarded shirt.

* * *

Huntington lay still. It was now 11 p.m. and he had been staring at the clock for almost an hour. Janice was sleeping soundly against his chest, something as rare as their lovemaking. His mind raced with thoughts of work, of George Elms and Ed Kavski and how he had let the last twenty or so years slip by without making the sort of impact he had wanted to, in or outside work. How had he let this happen? How had Kavski and Jacobs been able to play him like a fool?

He got out of bed and padded down to the kitchen. Somehow, he was slipping on his work shirt and trousers, followed by his overcoat and scarf, before taking his keys from the kitchen table, closing the front door and starting the BMW. He had started to drive in order to clear his head, but soon he was heading in a familiar direction, and at 11:09 p.m. his car came to a halt in his allotted parking space at Langthorne House Police Station.

The police station was silent, even the uniform patrols on night shift seemed all to be out. On his way into the station he passed a blackened window that reflected his face like a mirror. Huntington found himself stopping to look. The white of his hair stood out in sharp contrast to the black background of the glass. His face was pale and drawn, his eyes hooded, above bags that were more pronounced than usual.

'Looking good,' he said out loud.

It was a short walk to his office from the lift. He went straight over to a tall fitted wardrobe and opened the doors, taking in the familiar sights and smells of his policing past, hanging on individual coat hangers.

He rubbed the coarse material between his finger and thumb, feeling the heavy navy blue material that made up his dress suit or "number ones," as they had become known. When he had first joined they had been the standard uniform and he still had the original trousers, complete with a long, thin, concealed pocket running down his right leg for the stowing of a wooden truncheon.

A smile flickered across his face. He could still remember putting it on for the first time. His training complete, he was sent out on foot patrol with a shithouse of a man, Constable Hart, brash and impatient. He recalled Hart picking up a child and throwing him like a bowling ball at the poor lad's chums. 'Any one of these little oiks can become a crim. So you've got to make sure they realise what they're up against right from the start if they want to go down that route,' Hart's voice would boom out across the town centre. The kids would hear him coming and scatter, picking up their litter and throwing it hurriedly into bins. He demanded respect, that man. Kids, crims, and colleagues alike. He was a real copper, and wouldn't have lasted five minutes in today's police service.

Huntington lifted the uniform out of the wardrobe. He put his arms into the sleeves and pulled the jacket closed. It still fitted him well. Janice had let the trousers out a couple of times but his chest and shoulders were about the same, although he couldn't hope to do up the oversized brass buttons with the force's crown symbol on them. His force number was pinned proudly to the chest. He pulled open the blinds and once again used a window as a mirror, this time seeing a younger, healthier version of himself. The very man who had first stood in this jacket twenty-four years ago, with his entire career ahead of him.

He sat back in his chair and began to compose an email message. It was addressed to Chief Constable Alan Cottage, cc George Elms and bcc Craig Jacobs. He wanted Jacobs to know that there would be no playing along and nowhere to hide. He paused. Where to start? His cursor flickered in the subject box and he finally wrote: *I've been a fool.*

Soon the words came pouring out. First, Inspector Jacobs's role, then Ed Kavski and his team and how they were set up in Epping Hill, the violence he had sanctioned and how this had been acted upon. It ended with the disappearance of Elliot Tinsow and the attack on George

Elms and his family. He started to explain how this had happened, how he had been duped and how very sorry he was, but deleted it. He ended with the sentence:

I have created this. I have brought this on us all and tonight I will take responsibility.

He clicked send and waited for confirmation. He switched off his computer and sat back in his chair. He let out a breath and flexed his chest and shoulders against the stiff material of his dress jacket. He rose to his feet and went to the wardrobe whose doors were still open. He lowered his head and began to cry. Abruptly, he turned round and took up a pad of yellow post-it notes. He scribbled on the top one, pulled it off and stuck it to his desk. He ran his finger along the words on the note and turned round a picture of the smiling face of Janice, holding him round the waist. He went back to the wardrobe, lifted his dress suit jacket above his waist and removed his belt. Pushing aside his spare work shirts and trousers, he looped the belt round the wardrobe's rail and curled it back on itself, fixing it on the first notch.

Clumsy in his number ones, Huntington stepped into the wardrobe, and turned to face outwards. He took hold of the looped belt and pulled it to test its strength. Satisfied, he stopped still. His eyes scrunched tightly shut and then he opened them to look at the picture of him and his wife. It had been taken years ago on a beach in Mali. They were drenched in sunlight, their smiles genuine and bright.

He closed his eyes, his knees gave out and he rocked forward into his makeshift noose, which sunk into his neck and cut off his air supply.

His eyes bulged and secreted a single tear as he uttered a moan, a forced expulsion of his last breath.

Chapter 42

George had been watching his daughter sleep. Now he was sitting in bed in his own room. The shrill alert of an incoming email message to his work phone made him jump to his feet. He had left it turned on, it was the only means of contact since his own phone had been destroyed in the blast. The sudden movement worsened the ringing in his ears and sent a searing pain across the back of his eyes. He scrabbled in his inside jacket pocket and squinted as the phone lit up and announced the arrival of a new message.

He had to read the email from Graham Huntington twice. He read one particular passage several times in order to make sure he'd understood it correctly:

> . . . *And, George, Ed Kavski had the idea that you would be a far better target. He set the explosive under your car at your home and he told me to make all the evidence point towards the Skinner brothers. I couldn't do it. It was never my intention for decent*

people to get hurt and when I heard
you and your daughter had been
injured, that was when I knew for
sure that this whole thing had gone
too far. Please believe me when I say
that I didn't know this was going to
happen. If I had, I would have
stopped it.

George paced the room with the phone in his hand. The armed guards outside would certainly not let him pass. He knew that he should just tell them what he'd found out, but he wanted to deal with this himself. And he didn't want the police anywhere around when he finally got hold of Ed Kavski.

But how to get out of the hospital? It would need to be tonight before the contents became known to everyone. He would call the only person who could arrange for it to happen. George checked his watch. It was nearing 11.30 p.m. He lifted his phone to his ear, opting to call his personal number first.

* * *

Alan Cottage was at a charity auction. The three-course meal and auction were over, and the DJ was now demonstrating his poor taste and even poorer hearing at the disco. Cottage received an apologetic shrug from his wife, who knew just how little he liked these things. She nodded as he pulled out his mobile phone and slipped through the mostly drunken throng into an empty, brightly lit corridor.

'Hello?'

'Sir, it's George Elms.'

It sounded urgent. 'George? You okay?'

'You haven't read the email?'

'What email?'

'Huntington sent us both an email, just a few minutes ago. A man called Ed Kavski tried to kill me and my family. Huntington set it all up in Epping Hill with Craig Jacobs. They need stopping, and you have to get me out of this hospital, now!'

'George, I'm sorry, you've lost me, mate. Have they had to sedate you this evening? How about I pop back in the morning and you can—'

'It has to be now! We have to go to Epping Hill right now, don't you see? He didn't get me and we have no idea what that means. He might come back for my family. You need to get me out of here, now, make a call and—'

'George, George! Slow down. I don't know what you're talking about, or who you've spoken to but we can deal with this. You're safe there in the hospital, your family are there too, so let's deal with this tomorrow morning. First thing, I'll bring you a bacon sandwich.' The door to the main hall opened and his wife walked out. She fired a questioning gaze at him and he waved.

'There are people that want to meet you,' she mouthed. He gave her a thumbs-up.

George groaned. 'Look, can you access your work email from your phone?'

Cottage stopped to think, puffing his cheeks out. 'Er, no.'

'What about personal email? You must have that on your phone?'

'I think there is, but it's a bit fiddly and I'm an old man.'

'Tell me the address. I'll forward you Huntington's email. He sent it from the office in the last few minutes. He's at work right *now* — what does that tell you about the seriousness?'

The chief stayed silent.

'Look, I'll send the email. Call me back when you receive it and if you still tell me to wait till the morning, then that's what I'll do.'

'Fine, George. Look, I'll text my email address through. I have to type the damned thing out to remember it. Give me a second.'

The chief ended the call and made apologetic eyes at his wife.

'Let me guess. Work?' she said.

'Nothing urgent I'm sure,' he said, his fingers tapping at his phone.

'Are you coming back in?'

'Two secs.' His wife rolled her eyes and disappeared back into the darkened, noisy disco room. Cottage squinted at his phone's screen. He selected his email and it immediately demanded a username and password. He failed with the first two attempts and swore as he tried to remember what it was. 'Everything has a ruddy password,' he said, then clicked his fingers as it suddenly came to him.

The email took just a few seconds to open and he saw the message from George Elms. It took a few pushes for it to open, and his frustration increased when his wife reappeared at the door.

'I just need to read this, Rose.' She stood with her hands on her hips, but Cottage had forgotten she was there. He leaned back against the wall.

She nudged him in the arm. 'Alan, what's wrong?'

'Rose, can you get a lift home?'

'A lift home? Why would I need to—'

'Something's happened. Can you get a lift home?'

'Well, I can probably sort something. Why can't you take me home?'

'I'm sorry. I have to go.'

'Go? Now?'

Cottage shook his head and felt for his car keys.

'Now,' he said, and ran to the exit.

* * *

Cottage gripped the wheel of the Volkswagen and glanced at George. 'You look like shit.'

244

'If you recall, I got blown up recently,' George said quietly, facing forward.

'So you did.'

Cottage paused, the car idling. 'I'm fine,' George said. 'My ears are ringing a bit and I've got a headache that gets worse when I'm stressed, which is now, so if we could get going, I would really appreciate it.'

'What are we doing? Just so I know we're on the same page.'

'We need to put a stop to this. I say we go to the address on Roman Way. We have the advantage of surprise, so we should be able to get to this Ed without too much trouble.'

'And once we do?' George turned to the chief but said nothing. 'Only you haven't unclenched your fists since you got in the car.'

'He tried to kill me! Not only me, my daughter too! He chose to bring it right to my door and make it personal. There was no reason, no justification, no nothing . . .' George stopped and inhaled deeply.

'We have to do this my way, George, you know that. I can't go outside the law. Once this Ed knows he's been rumbled he'll fold and I can get it dealt with properly.'

'Fold? What, because you're the chief constable?'

'Yes.'

'From what I understand, he's not a copper anymore so he doesn't have to answer to you. The very fact that you'll be there in person, and not some uniform tactical team sent on your behalf, tells a story.'

'What story?'

'The story of Ed's strength. In his email, Huntington described the power this guy has. It's all about Lennokshire Police hiding the fact that they've been had. Ed's playing the media game — he knows that's what policing is all about these days. You turning up on your own just confirms it — you want to keep this all quiet, brush it under the carpet.'

Cottage turned to face George. 'I can't have it known, the things a senior member of my team has sanctioned on this of all estates. The media has already torn us a new one over Epping Hill. If it gets out, then I'm out of a job and Lennokshire is a laughing stock. All the work that we've done in there — that you've done — will be for nothing.'

'That's going to happen whatever we do. Just promise me one thing. I reckon I know the best way out of this for you, and I want you to promise me that you *won't* take it.' The chief looked at him expectantly. 'Promise me that you won't make a deal with this man.'

Cottage looked out to where a light rain had activated the windscreen wipers. Eventually he said, 'Let's just get there and see what we've got. Hopefully that old fool Huntington hasn't gone himself and made it worse!'

The chief drove away from the hospital grounds. George's fists were still tightly clenched.

* * *

By the time Craig Jacobs's phone alerted him to the arrival of Huntington's email, he was in no position to read it. He was lying on his side, tied to a chair. His arms were trussed up behind his back, fastened to the chair's wooden slats with rope. The right side of his forehead leaked blood.

Jacobs's phone was lying on a nearby table. Ed Kavski and three of his colleagues were waiting for Jacobs to regain consciousness so that they could continue to make him see that helping them was in his best interests. When the email alert sounded, Ed picked up the phone. He narrowed his eyes against the smoke of his cigarette as he studied a message also addressed to the chief constable and Detective Sergeant Elms. He finished reading and put the phone back on the table. He looked down at the stricken inspector, and then turned to the three men who waited with him.

'Change of plan.' He got to his feet and strode out of the room, ran up the stairs and grabbed a sports holdall from the bottom of a wardrobe. Downstairs again, he put it on the table and unzipped it.

The men exchanged confused glances. 'Change of plan?' one of them asked.

'Change of plan. We should expect a visit — tonight.'

'Visit? Who from?'

'The chief super, possibly Sergeant Elms, if he's up to it, and who knows, maybe even the big chief himself.' He smiled at this. 'But whoever knocks on that door,' Ed pulled a matt-black pistol from the holdall, peered down the raised metal sights and slid out the clip, checking it was full before pushing it back into the handle, 'We need to be sure we're ready.'

Chapter 43

'Bear left here.' George raised his right arm to point and winced. The medical team had been able to slot his dislocated shoulder back in place, but he had been warned that it would be tender for a few weeks, and then a further month before it would be back to full strength. His arm had been riddled with shrapnel, and glass shards had penetrated the skin. The bandages were stained with blood. The wounds had opened during his escape from the hospital.

'You going to be okay?' The chief sounded concerned.

'Fine,' George replied. Adrenalin was keeping the pain at bay for now, but it also had the effect of increasing the ringing in both his ears.

'How close are we?'

'The turning for Roman Way is at the end of this road. If you drive past and take the next right you can get round to the back. It's not a proper road so it should be quiet and there'll be places to stash the car.'

'Sounds good.'

George had looked at the address using the chief's smartphone, and they knew the target property was three houses in on the left-hand side. They could also see the unmade road that ran behind it, with garages for the residents. The road was as dark as they had hoped, but rougher than they had expected, and the firms sports suspension bucked and kicked its way through huge potholes. Cottage found a place to pull over. He switched off the engine and the lights went out.

The stones underfoot crunched as George made his way round to the chief's side. Both men looked back along the road. They had deliberately overshot the rear entrance to the property so as not to be seen. They made their way back through the shadows, using the cover of the tall fences that marked the end of the gardens of Roman Way. The rain began to pelt down. George was first to the gate, which clicked open with ease. George had expected decent security, and the two men exchanged a glance before he slowly pushed the gate inwards, hoping that most of the small backyard would be in shadow. Once through the gate he came to a halt. He pushed the gate open wider, so that Cottage could also see what had been prepared for them.

The sliding patio door that was the rear entrance to the property had been fully opened. Craig Jacobs had been positioned, tied to his chair, just outside it. He was partially lit by a security light fixed to the wall above him, which had been activated by their arrival. Jacobs was struggling against his restraints, apparently oblivious to where he was. His white shirt was ripped open and spattered with blood. One of his trouser legs was torn off up to the knee and his feet were bare, filthy, and stained with dried blood.

As the two men stood, shocked, in the damp garden, the security light went out leaving the patio in darkness. A voice rang out. 'The chief constable himself! And in his very best suit. Welcome to my home and, of course, I should thank you for picking up the rent.' The light came on and Ed Kavski emerged. He glanced down at the stricken inspector and smiled at the two men standing out in the rain. 'And Detective Sergeant George Elms, I believe. You look different to how I imagined, more in one piece.' George and Cottage could discern figures moving behind him.

'We're here to bring this to an end, Ed. It's over. Graham's told us everything,' Cottage growled.

'Ah, yes, "Confessions of a Superintendent." Well, let me make it clear. This is far from over. For the last couple of hours I've been trying to convince this man here that he should continue as planned.' Ed disappeared inside, and then re-emerged with something in his hand. He threw the object at the chief, who instinctively reached out and caught it. He opened his fist to reveal something soft and soaked in blood. George realised that he was holding a big toe. The chief recoiled and dropped it.

'This has gone far enough! I'm sure you didn't mean for it to all get so out of control. I can help you stop this before it gets any worse.'

'And there you are.' Ed smiled broadly. 'There you are. Before tonight, I had Graham and the inspector here to do my bidding but they became a little difficult. Now I have the chief of police himself wanting to discuss a deal. This couldn't have worked out any better!'

George looked sideways at Cottage.

'Don't misunderstand me. I'm not discussing any deal.'

'You will. You see, I'm holding all the trump cards. The fact that you're here means that no one besides you and the sergeant know anything about our little situation, and if you want that to remain the case, you're gonna need me on side. I have a job to do in Epping Hill. All you need to do is assist me with it. The people of your *Constabulary* never get to hear what you, the chief of police, sanctioned, and we all get to keep our jobs.'

'There will be *no* deal,' Cottage said again.

Ed's smile disappeared. He chewed at his bottom lip. 'Let me remind you of your situation. You three are the only people that know about me and my merry men, with the exception of Graham, and we all know that he's too pissed on himself to go public. Now as I see it, that means you either get on board *or* you become my only obstacles, and that makes you highly vulnerable.' Ed stood behind Jacobs, one hand resting on his shoulder and the other out of sight. 'You're running out of opportunities to make the right decision here, *chief*. Now give it another go.'

'There will be no deal,' Cottage said without hesitation.

Ed let go of Jacobs's shoulder and raised the other hand. It held a pistol. Ed pushed the barrel into the back of Jacobs's head. The inspector's eyes flickered open briefly, sparking with recognition as they rested on George.

Ed pulled the trigger. At such close range the bullet tore through Jacobs's head, shattering the skull, and out the other side, narrowly missing George's left arm. Pieces of bone, teeth and brain spattered George's face and chest and he recoiled in disgust, clawing at himself.

'Jesus! Fuck!' Cottage roared. His eyes widened and he raised a hand in defence as Ed pointed the pistol at George, then the chief, then back to George again.

Ed seemed to be talking to Cottage but the gun was aimed at George. 'You had one opportunity and you blew it. I don't need to tell you what'll happen if you don't take this one, do I, boss?'

George stood still, facing the gun barrel. At this range there would be no missing.

'Okay, okay, wait!' Cottage still had his hand up.

Ed kept the gun levelled at George. He kicked at the chair in front of him and it tipped forward. Jacobs's body landed, sprawled, at George's feet.

'We can make a deal, then?' Ed lowered the pistol slightly. His gaze darted to the chief and he licked his lips. The standoff continued for several seconds, long enough for the security light to switch itself off.

George took his chance. The armed police officer the chief had sent to escort him out of the hospital, had also unwittingly donated his sidearm. George had stuffed it down the back of his trousers, happily imagining Ed Kavski at the other end of the barrel.

George had to fire from the hip as the light came back on, but the movement was clumsy. The end of the pistol got caught in his jacket and he fired a shot off to the left. The shot missed Ed, it couldn't have been by much. The round surged through the dark interior of 5 Roman Way, where a scream suggested it might have found someone, at least.

Ed had disappeared inside the house and George fired blindly towards the patio doors. He and the chief stood illuminated under the spotlight of the security light, which concealed all movement inside. George was suddenly aware of return fire. It was coming at them from floor level. One of the rounds smashed the security light, throwing everything into darkness. George fell down, still pulling the trigger. The garden was lit with flashes from his pistol, and return flashes coming from inside the house. He hit the ground, his shoulder shooting pain as it popped out of its socket.

All sound was muffled. George could feel Cottage tugging at his clothes. The gunshots had worsened the ringing in his ears to the point of deafness. He was aware of being pulled to his feet, and he didn't resist. He wasn't sure if he heard another gunshot as he was hauled out through the back gate and pushed to the left, away from where they had parked the car. He began a shuffling run, still clutching the pistol, with his other arm flopping limp and useless at his side.

* * *

Cottage's ears were working just fine. He could hear men shouting. He couldn't tell how many men were following, or if they carried more weapons. Their footsteps were close behind him, too close for the car to be a viable option, so he led them in the opposite direction, towards the centre of Epping Hill Estate. He had noted the terrain when they had driven in — tight streets with plenty of parked cars, alleyways and narrow pavements. Maybe they would provide cover.

They reached the end of the unmade road. Cottage still had hold of George by his sleeve. The footsteps were getting closer, and he made a decision.

'George! We need to split up — it gives us a chance.' Cottage got no answer so, as they arrived at a four-way junction, he pushed George to the left and carried straight on. George started to try and follow him. He pointed. 'That way. We'll meet later.' The chief turned and ran away.

Chapter 44

Paul Baern had been sitting at home, bored and tired, until he received a short message from George. It hadn't made much sense:

> *Baerny,*
> *I'm going to Epping Hill. Long story,*
> *I'll explain when I can. If anything*
> *happens forward this to whoever you*
> *need to . . .*

Paul had opened the attachment. It was a detailed admission from his area commander. Paul knew George well enough to understand why he was heading straight to Epping Hill and when his calls went unanswered, he had made his own way there.

He sat in his car four streets away from Roman Way. He had no idea what he was hoping to achieve, or what he should do next. He decided to try George's number again. If George didn't answer this time, he would give up and head back home.

He lifted the phone to his ear, thinking that it was not his place to be interfering. The chief constable had also been sent the email, after all. Waiting for it to ring, Paul was attracted by a movement to his right. He recognised his sergeant, lit up by the orange glow from the street lights and sprinting past him as if his life depended on it.

'Shit!' He fumbled for the key and got out. He shouted out, but George didn't look round and he didn't slow. Paul checked around him. He couldn't see or hear anything that would have made George run like that, and he set off after his fleeing boss.

* * *

The chief constable licked his lips and tasted the salt. His shirt clung to him. At last he felt he was able to slow to a walk. His highly polished brogues striking the pavement was now the only sound that could be heard among the densely packed houses.

He looked over his shoulder. All he could see was dimly lit pavements, shiny with moisture, and the terraced houses decked with Christmas lights seeming to huddle together to keep warm.

He turned a corner and paused to catch his breath. He looked around him. Nothing moved but his shadow, which had appeared in front of him before sliding under and behind him as he walked beneath the yellow street lights.

He shook his head and shivered as the sweat on his back turned cold.

A voice cut through the night. 'You done yet, old man?'

He whirled round. Illuminated by the streetlamps were two figures, their faces concealed under hoods. They came towards him. As he broke into a run, they followed.

Their footsteps reverberated through the Epping Hill Estate. It was a warren of dark alleyways and boltholes. From one of these emerged a third hooded figure, surprising the sprinting man, and forcing him off the pavement and out into the road. He stumbled over the kerb, where a pool of water had collected in the gutter, and lost his balance, falling to his knees. Sodden and bruised, he looked up to see a car approaching at speed, throwing up sheets of water from the wheels. The driver failed to notice the man on his knees, or the look of horrified surprise on his face, his arm raised in self-defence.

It all happened in slow motion. The car hit the stricken man even before the brakes were applied. He fell under the front grille and was dragged along the tarmac, shredding skin and clothing. The vehicle lurched sideways into a row of parked cars.

The driver's window rolled down and a teenage boy leant out, his eyes wide. 'What the fuck was that?'

The passenger door swung open and another boy put a foot on the ground, peering back through the drizzle. 'I think it was someone.'

'Connor! Shut the fucking door.' As the passenger struggled to close the door, the car scraped other cars and accelerated away into the warren of the Epping Hill Estate.

The three men on foot stared at the crumpled figure at the kerbside. One of them nodded at the others who, without a word, turned and ran off into the darkness. The remaining man looked up briefly at the lights flickering on in surrounding houses. Swiftly, he crouched down and patted the fallen man's pockets. He swore and peered at the ground around the motionless figure. A small, oblong object caught his eye, lying against the wheel of one of the parked cars. It was the casing of a mobile phone, the battery part nowhere to be seen. He stuffed it into his pocket and, as the front door to one of the houses opened, he slipped back into the shadows.

* * *

George's head throbbed, the pain in his right arm made him groan with every step, and his lungs felt as though they were bursting. He'd heard a muffled shout, and knew he wouldn't be able to outrun Ed and his people for much longer. He needed a plan B. He knew this estate well, but pain and confusion had caused him to lose his way. Then he saw the shape of Peto Court ahead of him.

'Lizzie's flat!' His hand went to the inside pocket of his jacket. The key was still there. At the metal door of the communal entrance stood two men, swigging from cans of beer and propping the door open. They stepped out of his way as he ran through. George started up the steps.

He could hear muffled footsteps echoing through the empty stairwell, and as he reached Lizzie's floor he heard someone call his name. If he could just get there and get the door locked he could call for help.

He disappeared into Flat 22, he could hear heavy footsteps behind him in the corridor. George slammed the door shut, cursing the pain in his shoulder as he struggled to lock the door. He felt it click just as a voice shouted from the other side, and began banging the door.

George couldn't make out the words. All he knew was that they would kill him this time. He was a sitting target in here. He backed away from the door, his head still throbbing. The buzz in his ears blocked out almost all sound.

George backed away, stumbling over a discarded laundry basket. Sprawled on his back, he was aware of a thump at the door and a splintering sound as it caved in. The flimsy wood buckled and a figure appeared silhouetted in the doorway. Without hesitating, George lifted his pistol and pulled the trigger.

Chapter 45

George sat on his bed. He'd tried lying down but it had just increased his discomfort. And his frustration.

He was back in the same hospital room that he had left a few hours earlier. Back when everything was different. It was no wonder he couldn't sleep, despite his utter exhaustion. The events since leaving this room kept playing over and over in his mind — particularly how it had all ended. Uniform cops had arrived almost immediately, he still had the pistol raised when they entered, he damned near pulled the trigger again but he saw the blue writing just in time and discarded the weapon. He had been so relieved. He pointed at the man still lying in the doorway, ordered them to make sure he was dead. They'd calmed him down and walked him out. George reckoned he would remember that walk for the rest of his life. One of the officers held his arm as he looked down at Paul Bearn's face, his eyes shut, bleeding heavily from his chest. George's last vision as he reached the end of the corridor was of Paul's upturned palm laid out on the floor, spotted with blood. It was that image in particular that he couldn't shake.

Helen Webb entered his room. She was with a man in a suit.

'George, how are you feeling?' Helen asked.

'Like shit, ma'am.'

'Physically? Are you injured?'

'Nothing major. My ears have calmed down thankfully, my shoulder's giving me some jip . . . how's Paul?'

Helen sighed. 'He's stable, George. He took a big hit in the shoulder. There was a scare over damage to his lung, but they seem positive that they can sort that. He will need a complete rebuild of his shoulder joint at the very least. He's in surgery now but he will need a few goes under the knife it seems. It will be a few days before we know for sure.'

'Jesus.'

'It could have been a lot worse, George.'

'It shouldn't have happened at all.'

Helen made no reply.

'And what about Ed Kavski? Was he found?'

Helen shuffled from one foot to another. She still didn't reply.

'You didn't find him?'

'No.'

'Who do you have out looking for him?'

There was that shuffle again.

'Do you have anyone looking for him?'

'Listen, George, we're still trying to piece together the last few hours, we have five scenes and that's just the beginning. There are a number of actions that will be put off until we can get the right resources.'

'Actions and resources? You sound like you're writing up an investigation plan for a shoplifting incident. This man shot and killed a serving officer in front of me. Damned near blew his head off. You should have the whole world hunting for him.'

'We will deal with Ed Kavski, George. I can assure you of that.'

'And how will you deal with me? The armed officers outside my door, is that in case this Ed comes for me or in case I try and walk?'

'Both are considerations.'

'Am I under arrest?'

'No, George, you're not under arrest. We will need to talk to you in the right environment, you will understand that better than most I'm sure.'

'So I can leave? Go and see my family?'

'If you try and leave, George, you will be arrested.'

George forced a laugh. 'And what about my family? This man has already targeted my home once, what's being done to keep them safe?'

'Your family are being put in the hands of Witness Protection. They are both still here and remain under guard until your daughter's treatment is concluded.'

'So I can see them?'

Helen shrugged, 'It will be supervised.'

'And your nodding dog here, he would be from the Professional Standards Department, I presume?'

The man in the suit started to move forward. Helen put her arm out to stop him and she spoke again before he could.

'Like I said, this needs to be done right, George. You need to help us to help you, and if you do, then you have my word, that's how this plays out, with Lennokshire Police doing all we can to back you up. From what I can see this all got out of hand very quickly and that wasn't your fault. But people died, unlawfully killed and we need to be sure this is done right.'

'Ed Kavski killed at least one police officer. He will need to answer for that.'

'And if Ed Kavski answering for murder means you answering for what you did . . .'

'Then that's what happens. Put us both in court. Nothing I did was for any other reason than to defend myself. They showed the lengths they were willing to go to when they committed murder right in front of me. They would have done the same to me without a second thought.'

'It's not a competition, George. It's not *whoever is the most guilty goes to jail*. If you're guilty of something, you go to jail. That's the system.'

'Nearly twenty years unblemished service, that's got to count for something, I've given my life to this job.'

'You're highly respected George, a brilliant detective, but it's a different job these days.'

'I had the right motivation for everything I did.'

'Really? Think of what you know and how this plays out in court. You snuck out of hospital after a man tried to kill you at your own home, and badly injured your young daughter. You stole a gun from an officer and drove to where you knew this man was, and you told no one else of your intentions—'

'I told the chief constable himself!'

'So you say. He's dead, George. He's not going to be the most effective witness is he? Who else do you have? Inspector Price? Paul Bearn? The only reason you went to that location is for your revenge, you had murder on your mind and people died George — it's not a giant leap to find you responsible.'

'You don't really believe that, do you?'

'It doesn't matter what I believe. But that's not a difficult sell to a jury and all of a sudden we're in a lot of trouble. I need to keep you out of a court room, where I can influence what happens to you.'

'So you just let Ed Kavski walk? He murders a police officer, a senior officer, and he disappears?'

Helen shook her head and turned to leave. 'You need your rest, George, and you need time to think.'

'Promise me you'll do the same, ma'am.'

'We'll speak again soon. Maybe you'll come to realise that disappearing might not be such a bad idea. For both of you.'

The door slammed shut before George could reply.

* * *

Lennokshire Police Station. The Area Commander's office was flooded with the light of a new day. Graham Huntington was still, bent forward, held by the neck, he appeared to bow at a picture of his smiling wife. The handwritten note stuck to his desk read:

> *I had everything I wanted. I just*
> *couldn't stop there.*
> *I'll love you always Jannie xxx*

THE END

Thank you for reading this book. If you enjoyed it please leave feedback on Amazon, and if there is anything we missed or you have a question about then please get in touch. The author and publishing team appreciate your feedback and time reading this book.

Our email is office@joffebooks.com

www.joffebooks.com